Notes
on a
Missing
G-String

WINONA KENT

Print ISBN: 978-0-9880826-5-6
eBook ISBN: 978-0-9880826-6-3

Please visit Winona's website at www.winonakent.com
Please visit Blue Devil Books at www.bluedevilbooks.com

ACKNOWLEDGMENTS

I'd like to thank the following people, without whose assistance this novel would not have been possible:

Brian Richmond, for his continuing inspiration, wonderful story sense and clever suggestions

Brenda Woods, excellent firewalker

Deed Poll Officer Rebecca

And, of course, my mum Sheila Kent, my sister Stella Kent and my husband Jim Goddard, for their patience and understanding while I indulged in my passion and locked myself away on weekends, holidays and days off to write this novel

Apologies if I've left out anyone—it wasn't deliberate.

Thank you all!

.

CHAPTER ONE

It had been five years since I'd last seen Sal.

I was confined to a bed in the *Star Amethyst's* crew hospital after being plucked from a pitching life raft in the middle of the Gulf of Alaska. Our ship, the *Star Sapphire*—sister to the *Amethyst*—had just gone down, surrendering herself to the sea after a raging fire had spared her the indignity of a knacker's yard in India.

Sal was the captain's secretary; I was the nightly entertainment in the TopDeck Lounge—Jason Davey, performing all your vocal and instrumental favourites, eight 'til late.

When the *Amethyst* had docked in Vancouver two days later, releasing the *Sapphire's* rescued passengers and crew to a scoop-hungry media, we'd parted ways with promises to stay in touch. And we had, for a while. But Sal wasn't into Facebook or Twitter. She stayed aboard the *Amethyst* while I left the sea and went travelling. Our texts became less and less frequent until we remembered each other only on our birthdays and at Christmas.

And now, all of a sudden, here she was at the Blue Devil, five years older, her hair betraying little threads of silver, her figure still attractive but reminding me more of my mum than the love of my life—which was what Sal had been, albeit on a hopelessly platonic level, when we'd been shipmates on the Alaska run.

I have a regular gig at the club, playing guitar in a four-piece jazz combo. It was Saturday night and it was late—past 3 a.m. We'd just come offstage and were settling in to a post-show round of drinks before heading home.

1

I couldn't believe it when Sal turned up at our table.

We hugged and kissed and I introduced her to my band.

"Rudy, Ken and Dave," I said. "Sally Jones. The main reason I ran away to sea."

Rudy, Ken and Dave knew all about my maritime history, but I always suspected they doubted some of my saltier tales. Having Sal show up in person provided an instant boost to my credibility.

"Drums, sax and keyboards," Sal acknowledged, sitting down. "Hello. I enjoyed your show."

"And we absolutely enjoyed having you enjoy us," Rudy replied, ever the congenial host. "Something from the bar?"

"Thanks. A glass of Pinot Noir would be lovely."

"Some things never change," I said. "Are you still aboard the Amethyst?"

"God no. I finally came ashore. I've been the Assistant Manager at the Crestone for the past six months."

"Marble Arch?" I guessed. "Big. New. Four stars?"

"Five, Jase, if you don't mind."

Her outrage was entirely fabricated. Sal was no corporate hack and never had been, even when, as the *Sapphire's* top manager, her job had involved daily communication with StarSea Admin in Southampton.

"I always knew you'd land on your feet," I said.

"It's not a precise fit. But it's better than sitting in a stuffy office juggling entries in some lazy executive's personal calendar. I've found it difficult to...settle."

I understood. All of us who've shared a career at sea have the same affliction. We can't get used to a life that isn't in motion, to views that always look out over the same roads, the same gardens, the same never-changing lamp posts. We crave the unforeseen and thrive on the unexpected.

"Anyway," she said, "ship's captains don't need secretaries anymore. Everything's digital. They were talking about phasing my job out when I disembarked. It was one of the reasons I knew it was time to go."

Rudy returned with her wine—very generously poured—and a glass bowl filled with the last of that evening's savoury bar snacks.

"I read about your brilliant detective work tracking down Ben Quigley."

Ben was a musical legend. He'd dropped off the face of the earth a few years earlier and I'd been asked to try and find him by my son, Dom, who was studying film production at university and wanted to do a documentary about him for his course.

I'd eventually located him in northern Canada. And after I'd brought him back to London we'd both attracted a certain amount of media attention. I'd be lying if I said I hadn't enjoyed being in the spotlight.

"Thanks," I said.

"The thing is, Jase, I was wondering if you'd consider helping me with something. Actually, it's not for me. It's for someone I met aboard the Amethyst when we were doing our Mediterranean itinerary a few years ago. She was…'working'. And there was a complaint. I had to have her escorted off the ship."

"Ah," I said.

"Never a dull moment at sea," Ken remarked.

"Never a dull moment just outside our front door, mate," Dave replied, dryly.

The Blue Devil's in Soho, which used to be wicked and sleazy and forbidden. Its dodgy reputation is much diminished now, with many of its historical buildings demolished or on their way to the wrecker's ball. The area's re-inventing itself behind builders' hoardings promising vibrant new shops, chic restaurants and slick glass-walled offices. You can still catch glimpses of the past, though. Especially, as Dave said, just around the corner from our neon marquee.

"Holly Medford," Sal said. "She was quite reasonable about it. Though understandably disappointed. More, I think, because it meant she was going to miss Venice than anything to do with lost earnings."

We'd rarely been without our 'working girls' at sea, though the higher-class ones tended to avoid the *Sapphire* because she was old and creaky and decidedly unglamorous. Wealthier punters usually went for the newer and larger vessels. And ships' officers tended to turn a blind eye unless the ladies caught Security's attention. They were usually discreet, confidently self-employed, and, as far as I could tell, mostly in it for the perks: the opportunity to earn a shitload of money while they casually cruised the world.

"Rules are rules," I said, philosophically, well aware of how often the rule about Rules was routinely disregarded.

"Anyway, Jase, she remembered me. I've no idea how she found me but perhaps she spotted me in connection with the hotel. I've been doing quite a bit of PR lately so my name and face are out there. She rang me and took me into her confidence. She was in a terrible state. I couldn't refuse."

"What's her problem?"

"She's borrowed some money to pay off a debt."

"And…?" I prompted.

"She was working at Cha-Cha's."

Cha-Cha's is a lap-dancing club, around the corner and one street over from the Blue Devil. Its website advertises discretion, relaxation and fun, all-night fully-nude performers, a VIP room and private booths.

"Seems a bit of a come down after Servicing at Sea."

"Well, exactly. But I suppose the freelance market ashore wasn't everything she anticipated. So, to try and make some more money she'd decided to start working as an escort instead. She'd made arrangements to meet the man she owed the money to at Cha-Cha's. She had it stashed in her locker but when she came back after her shift, it was gone. Along with one of her G-strings."

"And you immediately thought of me," I said.

Sal laughed. So did Rudy. Ken and Dave. They knew me too well.

"I am serious, though, Jase. She's terrified. She owes this man a significant amount of cash and I have the impression he's not someone you'd ever want to cross. She's had to go into hiding."

"Why didn't she report it to the police?"

"She did. But the loan wasn't exactly above-board. And she's a sex worker. They wouldn't give her the time of day."

"What is it you want me to do?"

"I thought perhaps you'd be able to find out who took it. And get it back."

"I'm not a proper PI, Sal. And I'd have no idea how to even begin to investigate a theft."

"I know that, Jase. But I know you, and how you have a sort-of instinct for getting to the bottom of things—"

"A somewhat appropriate recommendation," I said, "given the circumstances of the theft…"

Another laugh around the table.

"I can pay you," Sal said.

"I could never accept money from you, Sal. And I honestly don't think I can actually do anything. The cash is long gone. Along with the thief."

"Sleep on it," Sal suggested. "You'd be doing me—and Holly—a great favour."

"Ships that pass in the night and all that," I said. "Like recovering alcoholics and Masons."

"Seawater's thicker than blood," she agreed, sipping her wine.

CHAPTER TWO

Early mornings don't really exist in my universe. It's 4 a.m. by the time I get home and another hour until I can properly unwind and fall asleep. And I refuse to wake up before noon.

I come from a musical background. My real last name's Figgis. My parents were the founding members of Figgis Green, that platinum-record-selling folky pop group everybody knew and loved half a century ago. My family understands late nights and lie-ins and bucking nine-to-five normality. I've never actually had to deal with the sort of job Sal was now, unenthusiastically, resigned to.

I showered and shaved, making note of a few more grey hairs in the bathroom mirror. I champion the look of an unkempt musical genius, my dark brown hair on the lengthy side and often untidy. I've got my dad's long curving nose and prominent square chin and my mum's blue eyes and her thin-lipped mouth. People say they can see more of her in me than him.

While I had my Sunday lunch (a very nice gourmet wild mushroom soup, a toasted bagel with fresh smoked salmon and cream cheese and slices of red onion; a couple of chocolates left over from a Christmas gift box; and tea) I had a look at Cha-Cha's website. They had a photo gallery: several ladies in minimal clothing sharing a sofa with a nattily-dressed gentleman in their VIP room; several other ladies wearing even less clothing wrapping themselves around the ubiquitous poles; and a third selection of ladies offering hospitality, drinks and themselves at individual tables.

I wondered if any of them were Holly.

Likely not. Cha-Cha's has been around for about a decade, and so had most of those photos.

The idea of investigating a criminal act at a gentlemen's club in Soho did entertain a certain amount of intrigue. But it was also just this side of sleazy. And it was a very dodgy minefield, politically, morally and socially. I'd always had a live-and-let-live attitude towards sex workers, a lot of whom, I knew, were in the business because they wanted to be. But for every one of those independently-minded businesswomen I also knew that just around the corner there were walk-ups and pop-ups rife with exploitation and abuse; many, many more vulnerable young women struggling with desperate circumstances; unimpeded trafficking from Asia and Eastern Europe; and a downward spiral of drugs and addictions. I'd meant what I said to Sal. I really didn't think I could do anything. And I really, honestly, didn't think I wanted to.

Still, I popped over to have a look at the escort agency website where Holly had been working—Moonlight Desires.

It was a good deal more high-class than Cha-Cha's.

All of the escorts had their own albums detailing their names (cities in the American Midwest seemed to be popular), specifics and specialities. The pictures looked professionally staged and shot and featured each lady happily posing in a boudoir, showing off a variety of extremely flattering bras, lacy thongs and stockings, followed by a good deal of saucy nakedness.

The rates started at £450 an hour for an Outcall—meaning your escort would come to the location of your choice, rather than you having to navigate your way over to where she was. I did some quick arithmetic and could easily see why Holly had decided to diversify.

I still wasn't convinced, though. I still couldn't see how I could possibly solve her theft.

I distracted myself with a phone call to my mate, Trevor Pitt.

I was chasing down a recording contract. I am aware that just verging on fifty does seem a bit late to be pursuing that sort of thing, but I'm a great believer in thumbing my nose at what's considered usual. And I'd always had that dream: it wasn't anything new.

Before Emma died, I was gigging around clubs and smaller venues with a group of like-minded colleagues. We did a little jazz but our focus was more on the kind of music you'd have heard from Mark Knopfler, Bryan Ferry and Elton John. One of my favourite songs is "Sultans of Swing"—a pub rock tune about an underappreciated jazz band.

After Emma died—after Sal had rescued me from the depths of grief and got me installed in the TopDeck Lounge (every StarSea ship has a TopDeck Lounge, built over the bridge, with panoramic windows facing forward over the bow), I became my own one-man-band, playing requests and observing the weekly turnover of passengers (sorry, "guests"). I always managed to slip a few of my own compositions in. And in doing so, I gently exposed my audience to some very accessible jazz licks and phrases.

But I'd never let go of my original plan. I really wanted to score that record deal. I'd been chasing labels for the better part of three years, sending in my demo's and waiting for their replies, which were usually a polite No Thanks and, if I was lucky, a brief apology that jazz guitar was a hard sell at the best of times and that it was no reflection on my talent and they were certain I'd soon find a home for my music. That last point largely contradicted the first point, but who am I to question a kind rejection? They could just as easily have not replied at all.

I reconfirmed Monday afternoon with Trev, who owns Collingwood Sound and who'd also composed one of the tunes we were going to demo; and then I rang Rudy, Ken and Dave to make sure it was still in their calendars.

It was.

And then I called Sal.

"Are you sure?" she said, the disappointment apparent in her voice.

"Convince me otherwise," I said. "This woman could easily earn hundreds of pounds a day at Moonlight Desires. How much does she owe?"

"She wouldn't tell me. But that's the problem, isn't it, Jase? She can't keep working and stay safe from that loan shark. He'd track her down in a minute." She paused. "Couldn't you at least meet her and talk to her?"

I really didn't want to.

But I also didn't want to let Sal down. I would always owe her, big time, for getting me the gig aboard the *Sapphire* and turning my life around.

"Where's she now?" I said.

"At the Crestone. I've comp'd her a room under my name for a couple of nights."

"Would I be able to see her this afternoon?"

"Yes, of course. Do you want me to be there as well?"

"I think it would be best."

"I'll let her know. See you in the lobby at three?"

I glanced at the time. It was ten past two.

"In the lobby at three," I confirmed.

#

The Crestone's one of those hotels that consistently rates top billing in online searches, but rarely, if ever, gets mentioned in feature stories about "the secret gems" or the "luxurious getaways" of London. It has none of the character or history of the Savoy or Claridge's and certainly isn't high on anyone's list of opulent interiors, Michelin-starred dining and royal connections.

It's new and tall and, as it gleamed over Hyde Park, it reminded me of the *Amethyst*, which has no soul and exists solely to navigate its guests through overcrowded bodies of water to overpopulated ports, offering in exchange a whiff of affluence, a hint of gourmet dining and a parade of expensive treatments at the shipboard spa.

I knew it was very poor fit for Sal, who'd loved the creaky old *Sapphire*, with her transatlantic ocean-liner history and her slightly shabby demeanour, as much as I had. But Sal had needed to keep working once she was ashore. StarSea Corporate has no pension plans for staff and crew, only for officers. And I could see how the Crestone would fill that need until Sal was at an age when she could finally retire.

I wasn't impressed with the decor. The lobby was floored with dark marble and its walls were panelled with wood that's been stained to match the floor. Everything was shiny and brown, with soft white lights recessed into the ceiling and a long reception desk stuck into an alcove and manned by three ladies and two gentlemen in matching outfits that were the same colour as the walls.

Sal was waiting for me in the Wine Bar attached to the lobby. It had dark red flocked wallpaper and red leather chairs and tiny tables that lent it the air of a bordello. She was most of the way through a large glass of Pinot Noir.

"Only twenty minutes late," she said, standing up. "You're improving."

"I'm sorry. I came by taxi. Unexpected road works."

9

She gave me a look as she rang Holly on her mobile to let her know I'd arrived.

The lifts were controlled by key cards—no admittance to floors you weren't authorized to visit. Sal had a master card which took us up to Twelve. Outside 1205 she paused and then knocked.

"It's Sal, Holly. We're here."

"Just a minute!"

There was movement on the other side of the door.

Sal's mobile rang.

"Sally Jones…Oh really? What's the problem?"

Sal looked at me as she listened. I could hear fragments of a long and involved explanation.

"Can't Louise handle it? I'm not actually on duty today…OK right."

She disconnected.

"Sorry, Jase, there's a massive cock-up at the front desk. It's urgent. Can you apologise to Holly? I have to go."

She disappeared into the lift.

The inside chain was finally released on Holly's door.

It opened.

I'm not sure what—who—I was expecting. After studying the photo gallery at Moonlight Desires, I guess I'd built up an idea of what Holly Medford was going to look like.

I reckoned she was about twenty-five, but there was something about her which made her seem older. She had long thick hair which I suspected was likely a natural brown, but she'd spent some money in an expensive salon and now it was more honey-coloured than dark and it was cut and styled in a way which suggested she had ample time to attend to its care each morning. She was wearing makeup, though not an excessive amount, and she was what Moonlight Desires would have termed "curvy" rather than "petit".

She'd put on an expensive pair of jeans and a pink cashmere pullover and she was barefoot.

She was also wearing scent—something floral and inviting that made me think of soft white petals and orange blossoms.

I suppose her room was typical of the Crestone's Superior accommodations. Again, the overall colour palette didn't stray far from brown. Dark brown wooden panelling surrounding the large picture window, which was reflecting the pale February sun. A matching headboard behind the ample bed. Walls that would have been called "light brown" anywhere else, but here, what were they? Oatmeal? Mushroom? Biscuit? Something in taupe from the Room Service menu, anyway. Two matching armchairs on either side of an impossibly tiny round table. A desk that doubled as a dresser. A flat screen TV on the wall above a horizontal plank of shiny dark brown wood that could have been a bar (the mandatory mini-fridge was underneath) or a place to put luggage or somewhere to sit if you were entertaining more guests than the number of available chairs.

"Hello Jason," she said, closing the door.

I wondered if that was how she greeted her clients, too, if or she had a series of different welcomes, each dependent on who she was expecting.

"Hello," I said. "Sal had to leave. She sends her apologies— something catastrophic at the front desk."

"Perfectly understandable," Holly replied. "I've ordered tea for us."

I saw cups and saucers, a china pot, a little jug of milk and a bowl of assorted sweeteners and a selection of petit fours, all carefully arranged on the horizontal plank.

"Shall I pour?" she asked.

She didn't strike me as someone who was terrified of a vindictive loan shark. But it takes all types. Perhaps her years employed in the sex trade had turned her into a very good actress.

"Milk and sugar?"

"Thanks," I said. "Two lumps. Shaken, not stirred."

I don't think she got my joke.

"Sit, please."

I carried my cup and saucer and three of the little icing-coated delectables across to the tiny table and sat down in one of the armchairs.

Holly joined me.

I'd brought a notebook and a propelling pencil. It's an old affectation of mine—I love the slippery ease of graphite on paper and the clever ever-sharp engineering when you click the piece of lead down to replace the bit that you've worn away. I've got a collection of them at home—because I'm always losing them—and a little utility drawer filled with packets of leads, rubber erasers, paperclips, bulldog clips and other stationery items on their way to becoming obsolete as we surrender our note-taking to keyboards and finger-swipes.

I'd also brought two phones. One was my personal mobile and the other was handy for recording things—the proceedings of meetings, voice memos, fragments of tunes.

"Do you mind?" I asked, considering that she might and that it would be best to make sure.

"Not at all," Holly replied.

Again, that airiness, no hint of fear.

I set the phone up to Record and touched the button.

"This is just a preliminary interview," I said. "I don't know what Sal's told you, but I haven't actually agreed to take on your case. I've only agreed to talk to you and after we've finished, I'll let you know my decision. And I'm not a professional PI. You do understand that?"

"Yes," Holly said. "I do understand."

"Before we begin," I said, "do you mind if I satisfy my curiosity? Is your profile on the Moonlight Desires website?"

"Why? Were you looking for me?"

"I was, actually."

"In a personal or a professional capacity?"

"Professional," I replied.

"My profile was there. But I deleted it. I thought it best. Under the circumstances."

"That was probably a wise move," I agreed.

"I'm called Saratoga," she said. "In case I reappear."

"I'll make sure I check," I said, as the orange-blossom scent drifted across the little table. I paused. "Still curious. How do you separate your personal life from your…professional life?"

Holly laughed. "You're assuming that I do."

She leaned back in her chair and crossed her legs, a little provocatively, I thought. And deliberate.

"As it happens, you're correct. When I'm working as an escort, I wear a certain uniform. Very much the same way Sally did, when she wore her uniform aboard the cruise ship. And the uniform she now wears as a hotel employee. But somewhat more attractive."

I smiled. She wouldn't have got any argument from me about the front desk clerks' gravy-coloured skirts and jackets.

"And when I'm off-duty, I take my uniform off, and I'm myself again. And, of course, it was exactly the same when I was working at the gentlemen's club. When I put on my costume, I became the dancer."

"And once you'd danced your costume off?" I inquired, a little cheekily.

"I considered my nakedness a part of my uniform," Holly answered, smoothly, "for the duration of my shift at the club."

"When did you hand in your notice at Cha-Cha's?"

"Last month. I prefer now to work exclusively as an escort."

"And what made you decide to go into the business?"

"The sex trade, you mean."

"I was trying to think of a less clinical term."

"But that is what it's called. I like showing off my body. I enjoy the reactions of men when they see it. When I danced, I enjoyed knowing I was turning them on."

"And now that you're an escort...?"

"It's very much the same thing. But far more personal. I like having sex. A lot. I always have. And I like it when my gentlemen enjoy my body. But I never have an orgasm with my clients. They've purchased my time. I'm there so that I can give them pleasure."

"What if," I said, "part of their pleasure is in seeing and hearing you have an orgasm?"

"Still personal curiosity?" Holly inquired. "Or have we arrived at the professional part of the interview?"

"A little of both," I replied.

"If they pay for the Girlfriend or Pornstar Experience then I'll make them think that is what I'm doing."

"And what's the difference between the two services?"

"The Pornstar Experience is louder and involves more moaning and groaning and rolling of the eyes," Holly said, humorously.

"That's it?"

"That's it. What more did you expect?"

"Do you have a regular boyfriend?"

"Who wants to know? Mr. Jason Davey or Mr. Private Investigator?"

"It wasn't a chat-up line."

"No, I do not have a regular boyfriend at this moment. But I have had, many times. You should know that if I'm going to be someone's girlfriend, I will be a genuine girlfriend. No uniform and no acting. I enjoy being with that person because they're not paying for my services."

"What about love?"

"I've never been in love," Holly answered, with complete

certainty.

I opened my notebook.

"Professional time," I said. "Can you tell me a little bit about your financial situation?"

"Where would you like me to start?"

"Perhaps if you were to begin with the reason why you had to borrow so much money?"

"Of course. I had been travelling…perhaps Sally told you about my adventures in the Mediterranean. I was making quite a comfortable living—so comfortable that I was able to stop travelling and live off my savings for a time. But all good things must come to an end. About six months ago I had to face the unfortunate fact that my bank account had been depleted."

"And you didn't want to go back to working aboard cruise ships?"

"I would have welcomed the opportunity…but unfortunately, the cruise ships are no longer as enthusiastic about having me aboard as they once were. Technology has become my enemy."

"They know your face at the gangway," I guessed. In the old days, the security crew had merely glanced at your cruise card as you'd boarded from shore. Nowadays your photo's taken at the check-in desk at the start of the cruise and it's sent over to a clever machine that compares you to your picture each time you disembark in port and then get on again.

"I was escorted off before I had even had a chance to occupy my cabin."

"Shame," I said.

"And so, to make ends meet, I found it necessary to take up employment as a dancer at Cha-Cha's. It was while I was there that my financial difficulties escalated."

"And the escalations were caused by…?"

"I enjoy the distractions of the casino," Holly replied. "And occasionally, those distractions get the better of me."

"Have you run into problems like this before?"

"Perhaps, once or twice."

"And what did you do in the past when that happened?"

"I've always been able to cover the costs. This time, I couldn't. So I decided to work at Moonlight Desires. The dancing at Cha-Cha's was only ever meant to be a temporary solution, to tide me over until my circumstances improved."

"So you handed in your notice."

"Yes. The escort agency takes a 30% commission. But even that is a good deal more than I was earning as a dancer, with a much better clientele and far better working conditions."

"So why did you go back to Cha-Cha's on the night your money was stolen?"

Holly thought for a moment. "A special request," she said. "A private performance in the VIP room."

"Who made the request?"

"Is it important?"

"It might be."

"If it turns out to be important then I'll provide you with a name."

"Married?" I guessed. "Or famous? Or both?"

"Or perhaps merely someone who expects—and can rely upon me to extend—a certain amount of professional discretion."

"So let's just go back to your financial problem. You borrowed some money to pay off your immediate debts."

"Correct," said Holly, stirring her tea.

"Who did you borrow the money from?"

"His name is Braskey. You've heard of him?"

I shook my head. "How do you spell it?"

Holly told me, and I wrote it in my notebook, resisting the automatic impulse to add a second "s" and a space.

"You've likely not had occasion to occupy the circles where he's well-known."

"How did you find him?"

"One of my colleagues at Cha-Cha's introduced us."

"What's her name?"

"Shaniah," Holly said, after a moment.

"Last name…?"

"I have no idea. Dancers often only know each another by their stage names."

"Why didn't you go to the bank or somewhere less risky than a loan shark?"

"I have no credit at the bank and under the circumstances I honestly wasn't thinking. I was in a panic."

"How much money did you borrow from Braskey?"

"Fifty thousand pounds."

I tried not to show my surprise. I hadn't expected it to be that much.

"And what were the terms of your loan with him?"

"The principal plus interest due in four months. The interest was 10% each week."

I did some quick arithmetic in my notebook.

"And so, four months later, the loan was due to be repaid…"

"Yes. But I didn't have the full amount."

"Why not?"

Holly smiled. "Expenses. Incidentals. A little holiday in Italy. And, of course, my unfortunate distraction. Braskey accepted what I offered, but then increased the interest on the amount which was still outstanding, and advised me that he would expect the balance in one month's time. He made it very clear that he would not tolerate further delays."

"So one month later you had the full amount."

"I had some of the full amount. I begged for two more weeks. Very surprisingly, he allowed it. But it would be the last of his generosity."

"And it was this last payment which was stolen from Cha-Cha's," I guessed.

"Correct," Holly said, again.

"How much?"

"Ten thousand pounds. Not an insignificant amount. Hence my current situation."

She'd get no arguments from me there. Again, the amount took me by surprise.

"Where was it stolen from?"

"The dressing room. I'd put it in my locker with some of my costumes at the beginning of my shift. And when I came back at the end of my shift, it was gone."

"Along with one of your G-strings," I said.

"Yes."

"Did your locker have a lock?"

"Yes, of course."

"And it was locked when you left it?"

"It was, yes."

"Was the lock broken when you came back?"

"Yes."

"And none of the other girls saw anything suspicious?"

"I don't know."

"What did you tell Braskey?"

"I didn't tell him anything. I panicked. I didn't show up for our meeting. I knew he wouldn't accept any more delays. I was afraid for my life."

"So you rang Sal…"

"It was the only thing I could think of. I was desperate. I had no money. I couldn't go back to my flat. I couldn't stay with any of my friends and my face and details were all over Moonlight Desires website. And no one could connect me to Sally. I'm safe here."

"For the time being, anyway," I said. "And then you thought of contacting me for help."

"That was Sally's idea," Holly said. "Have you reached your decision?"

"About whether or not to take on your case?"

"Yes."

"I think your money's long gone and it would be very difficult to find out who took it and to get it back."

"Then I'm sorry to have wasted your time."

"But," I said, "I don't want to let Sal—or you—down without at least asking a few questions. I'll go over to Cha-Cha's and find out if anyone might have seen something—or someone—that might give us some clues. And if there is something I can take to the police, I will. On your behalf. All right?"

"Yes," Holly said. "Thank you."

"You're very welcome," I replied.

CHAPTER THREE

Cha-Cha's is housed in an old brick building which, so far, seems to have escaped developers' attentions. It was put up around 1883 as part of a scheme to replace a collection of ramshackle houses and decaying alleys. The idea was to provide tradesmen with shops that would occupy the basements and ground floors, while the floors above would have rooms to let for those who wanted to live nearby.

The original building was four windows wide and five storeys high, including a garret at the top, three intermediate floors, and the cellar. Over the years, though, the structure's been divided vertically, so that it now appears to be two completely separate properties. But once you go inside and downstairs to the cellar, you can see where the common wall's been removed to allow the nightclub to fill the entire space below street level.

There are no garish signs and no flashing lights marking Cha-Cha's presence on the road. The entrance, on the ground floor, is painted deep burgundy and has a matching canopy. At night, the double doors are kept open and guarded by a burly-looking bouncer behind a velvet rope. During the day, the doors are locked shut and it actually looks quite forlorn.

I waited outside as I rang the club's owner, Roly Barfield, to let him know I was there. He appeared almost instantly, unlocking the door, extending his hand and greeting me with a genuine smile.

"Nice to see you again, Jason," he said. We'd been introduced once before, when he'd slipped over to the Blue Devil to catch one of my shows. He'd popped by a few times more after that—I'd spotted him in the audience. "Come inside."

Inside smelled like dirty carpets and last night's cocktails. Cha-Cha's definitely isn't on par with places like Stringfellows. It tries to be classy, but it's really a bit seedy once you get past the scuffed leather seats and the overpriced bottles lining the backlit mirror bar and the dancers who always seemed to me to be thinking about doing the washing up while they were persuading us to part with our cash.

Roly's office was a few steps away from the cashier's booth (£20 to be admitted and a good deal more once you were inside and shelling out for drinks, dances and the privacy of the VIP room or the booths), next to a newish-looking staircase that took you down to the venue in the cellar. I'm certain the stairs were never a part of the original plans for the building—they're too wide and in the wrong place (in the front, not in the back or off to the side).

"Drink?" Roly offered. He had a nice collection of bottles behind a small private bar.

"No thanks," I said. "I don't."

"Not one of 'those', are you?" His question was curious, not depreciating.

"Personal choice," I said, "though I have friends who are. I've got the Serenity Prayer on a bookmark and the Twelve Steps memorized. In three different languages."

Roly chuckled.

"I wouldn't mind a smoke, though," I said.

"If you were anybody else I'd make you stand outside. Go on then."

I got out my pack of Benson and Hedges Gold and lit up. It was my third of the day, which was an improvement. I'm cutting down gradually, not being a fan of the cold turkey school of misery and deprivation. I refuse to wear one of those patches. And if you're going to vape you might as well inhale the real thing.

Roly took a glass ashtray out of his desk drawer and slid it over to me.

"What can I do for you? You said something about a robbery...?"

I'd been a bit sparse with the details when I'd rung him.

"I'm doing a favour for a friend," I said. "Just making some inquiries. You had a dancer working here—Holly Medford."

"Chanel," Roly said.

"Sorry…?"

"Holly Medford's club name. Chanel."

"Ah," I said. Something I'd forgotten to ask her yesterday. My inexperience was showing. "You do remember her, then?"

"I remember all my girls. Mind like a steel trap, me."

"Holly—Chanel—had some money stolen from her locker when she was here last week. Did she report the theft to you?"

"She did not," Roly said. "This is the first I've heard of it."

Yet another surprise.

"Did you know she was deeply in debt?" I asked, carefully.

"I know she borrowed a substantial amount of money from a certain gentleman who is anxious to have it repaid," Roly said. "Again, my familiarity with this situation is somewhat limited. I was only made aware of it recently."

"Do you know the name of the gentleman who loaned her the money?"

"Arthur Braskey," Roly replied. "You won't be acquainted with him. You've got a respectable bank account."

I smiled. "Has he been to see you?"

"In an informal capacity only. He wanted to know if I knew where he might find her. I was unable to help."

"I've been told Holly's money was taken from the dressing room where the dancers change their clothes before and after their shifts. Do you mind if I have a look?"

"I wish she'd reported it," Roly said. "If there's a thief on the premises, word gets around. Lax security. Not good for business."

#

We went downstairs. It was half past eleven in the morning and the club wouldn't be open for another ten hours. Roly snapped on the lights and we walked through a sad-looking room that, like the burgundy doors outside, really only ought to have been seen by the kindness of nightfall.

At the front of the room was a stage featuring three poles and an abundance of red velvet curtains with flounces and valances and decorative tassels. To the side of the stage was a red wooden door.

"Down here," Roly said.

"Not locked," I observed, as he opened it. I could see a narrow staircase leading down to a sub-cellar.

"We have a security bloke," Roly said. "He stands just here. Gives him a view of the complete venue."

I turned around. It was true. From our vantage point, I could see the stage, all of the tables and chairs, the bar, a short corridor which I assumed led to the VIP room, and the row of private booths off to the side—tiny cubicles created out of the same red velvet curtains that decorated the stage. I caught myself thinking about Holly, imagining her in black stockings and high heels, a G-string and a lacy bra, performing a provocative dance around one of the poles. And then offering her services for a private performance behind the red velvet walls. And then stripping everything off to the seductive rhythm of "Birthday Sex".

"What's his name?" I asked, dragging my mind back to Roly. Holly was my client—unofficial or otherwise. Nonetheless, where my imagination was going raised some serious questions about ethics. I shouldn't have allowed myself the indulgence, however brief.

"Raj Kumar."

"Would you mind if I had a chat with him?"

Roly seemed slightly put out by my request, but remained agreeable.

"His phone number's in my office," he said. "Remind me later."

At the bottom of the narrow little staircase was an equally narrow little corridor that led to a loo—not as awful as I'd anticipated and at least the toilet was reasonably clean—and the dressing room, which had bright white fluorescent lights in the ceiling and a couple of theatrical makeup tables with unmatched wooden chairs and big mirrors along one wall, and banks of grey metal lockers against the other three.

"We're not like the Windmill," Roly said. "We don't employ someone's old mum to sit here all night and guard the girls' belongings. They lock their things up. As you can see."

Some of the lockers had combination locks on them; others had padlocks; a few had nothing at all.

"Which one was Holly's?" I asked.

"No idea. They choose their own. It's their business. I never interfere."

"Does Raj Kumar ever come down here?"

"He does not. The girls wouldn't stand for it. I had to let his predecessor go for precisely that reason."

I reminded myself what Holly had said: she'd locked her things up at the start of her shift and when she'd come back she'd found the lock broken and her money and a G-string missing.

I did a quick reconnaissance of the room. It wasn't all that big.

"How many dancers would typically be in here when you open up for the night?"

"Sixty…sixty-five."

A lot more than I'd have thought, but it made sense. There had to be enough women to work the stage, the bar, the tables and the VIP room. I guessed the club's capacity was around a hundred, with thirty tables in a variety of seating configurations and a couple of rows of comfy chairs arranged on three sides of the stage.

The few times I'd been there, the venue had seemed very crowded. This little dressing room would have been packed solid if all the dancers had arrived at the same time.

"Once the dancers are out on the floor, do they come back here at all?"

"I don't encourage it. I like my girls to be visible… available… and so do they, if I'm honest. If they're back here they're not earning."

I'd done my homework. I knew about the financial arrangements between lap-dancers and clubs.

The ladies made a commission from the sale of drinks from the bar, so it was to their advantage to ensure the tables were well supplied with vodka and champagne—sometimes costing £500 a bottle. If you invited one of the dancers to sit down with you for a drink, it was £60. If you paid by credit card, interest was charged at 20% on top of the bill.

A VIP dance in one of the tented booths was £120 for a three-minute song. But three minutes was often not enough and so the punters were encouraged to have one more…and then another…and so on.

And working at the club wasn't free. Club owners—and Roly was no different from his fellow entrepreneurs—considered the dancers freelance employees who had to pay for the privilege of using the premises. The ladies parted with a house fee of around £70 a night, which allowed them to dance. And then they were paid a percentage of whatever they'd encouraged their customers to spend.

I could see why Holly had chosen to become a high-end escort. The money was leagues better. And she only had to pay a commission to the owner of the agency. Her time—and her decisions—were her own.

"But it's not forbidden?" I said. "I mean, if one of them wanted to use the toilet or change her clothes."

"Not forbidden at all. I'm just saying, if a girl leaves a table to go to the loo, her spot's likely to be taken by one of her mates. Sharpish. Competition's fierce."

"Still," I said, "if one of the dancers knew there was a very large sum of money sitting in one of these lockers and all she needed to do was break the lock and help herself, it would rather make up for the loss of a couple of hundred quid, wouldn't it?"

Roly shrugged.

"How would I contact Arthur Braskey?" I asked.

"You don't want to go messing about with the likes of that one, Jason." The advice, I could tell, was sincere.

"Is he a client here?"

"A regular," Roly said. "But he's not the sort of bloke you just walk up to. You'd need an introduction."

"Is there a dancer here named Shaniah?"

"There was. She left last week."

"When last week?"

"I'd have to look it up," Roly said.

We walked back upstairs and through the red door to the stage.

"You have CCTV on the premises, of course," I said.

"Of course," Roly replied, indicating the telltale black Perspex half-bowls located at strategic places around the ceiling. "And outside overlooking the entrance."

"But not in the dressing room."

"That," said Roly, "would be a very bad idea. And possibly illegal."

I had to agree. It was a stupid question.

"Does the CCTV cover this red door?"

"It does," Roly confirmed.

"Mind if I have a look at your tapes?"

#

Back in Roly's office, I studied the footage from the evening in question, the dancers arriving in their street clothes, then emerging from behind the red door in their costumes. A few went back afterwards. I didn't see Holly, but there were gaps in the coverage. The technology was old; it was analogue rather than digital; the tape was fuzzy and, in some places, completely blank.

Roly was watching with me.

"Can you vouch for everyone?" I asked.

"They're all my girls, if that's what you mean. Nobody suspicious. Raj wouldn't let them downstairs if they didn't belong there."

It was very likely an inside job, then, I thought. And it could have been anyone. And because it was winter, all the dancers were arriving and leaving bundled up in their winter coats. And more than half of them were carrying bags large enough to accommodate a stash of cash as well as their costumes.

The CCTV wasn't going to be much help to me.

"Don't erase this," I said. "Just in case I need another look."

#

Before I left Roly gave me Raj Kumar's mobile number and Shaniah's resignation date. Thursday, February 23—coincidentally, the same night Holly had reported the theft. He also provided Shaniah's contact information.

I had one last question.

"I understand Holly—Chanel—handed in her notice about a month ago but then came back for that one final show last week."

"That's right."

"A bit of an unusual arrangement…"

"She was very popular, especially in the VIP room. I was sorry to lose her. One of her regulars was coming in—a rich Arab, something to do with Middle East royalty, very generous with his money, very pleasant to have on the premises. He asked for her especially. I didn't have the heart to tell him she'd packed it in."

I suspected Roly's fear of disappointing his customer had more to do with the opportunity of raking in a small fortune than any affinity he'd felt towards the well-connected prince.

"So it was this rich Arab who requested her presence and it was you who asked her to come back for a one-off performance?"

"That's right," Roly said. "And she agreed, because she knew she could make a lot of money that night—and probably even more afterwards, if she went back to his hotel in his car. Although, of course, I would never condone anything like that, and any arrangements which are made between a client and a dancer are strictly private and nothing to do with the club."

I'm sure Roly had that little clause memorized, ready to trot out verbatim should the legal occasion arise.

"Do you know if Holly went back to this guy's hotel after the show?"

"If I did, I'm sure you'd understand that I would have to be extremely careful about my choice of words."

"Are you able to confirm or deny it?"

"I am not able to deny it," Roly replied.

"Understood."

"Or to confirm it."

"Thank you," I said.

"You're very welcome, Jason. I might come and see you next week. Any chance of a decent table?"

CHAPTER FOUR

Driving round that afternoon to Collingwood Sound, which is in Kentish Town, I went over all of the questions I realized I should have asked Holly before I'd paid a visit to Cha-Cha's.

Such as, why she didn't report the theft to Roly, or at least Raj, the security guy? And what, exactly, had her reaction been when she'd discovered her locker had been broken into? And had she spoken to any of her colleagues about it?

And Holly had told me—and Sal—that she'd arranged to meet Arthur Braskey after her shift ended. And that she'd been so terrified after discovering her money was gone that she'd immediately fled and had gone into hiding.

No mention of any Arab prince and definitely no mention of going back to spend the rest of the night entertaining him in his hotel room.

I definitely needed to speak to Holly again.

And I needed a conversation with Raj, the security guard.

Not to mention a chat with Holly's colleagues at Cha-Cha's.

I pulled into the private parking area behind Trev's studio and gave Sal a call.

"Have you ever considered a second career as a private investigator?" I inquired, humorously.

"That was my second career when I was the Captain's Secretary," Sal replied. "You'd be surprised how many times I had to look into passengers' folios and help make discreet inquiries about sensitive issues. Why?"

I told her.

"And I can't very well walk into the ladies' dressing room while they're changing into their…work clothes," I added. "This requires the assistance of a female."

"I'm surprised at you, Jase. I'd have thought you'd have leaped at the opportunity."

I could tell she was smiling.

"I'm getting old," I said.

"You're still hot and sexy," Sal said. "According to Holly, anyway. And she's an expert."

"I'll bet," I said. "I need you to tell them there was a theft from one of the lockers on February 23. Nothing more. And then ask them to search their memories and try to recall if they heard or saw anything unusual—anything at all. If anyone comes forward, write down the details and tell them I'll be in touch later. Don't give them any more information than that. And ask them not to discuss the matter amongst themselves. I don't want any witness contamination."

"Even if they ask for specifics? What was stolen? Who it was stolen from?"

"Even if they ask for specifics. And watch their reactions, if you can."

"In case anyone's the actual thief?"

"Exactly," I said.

"I'll pop over there tonight," Sal said. "You'll clear it with the club's owner?"

"I will," I said.

I called Roly, who reluctantly agreed and then provided instructions to pass along to Sal. I rang Sal back and told her what to do and say when she arrived at the club's front door.

And then I collected my guitar out of the back of my car and went into the studio.

Collingwood Sound is actually Trev's house. He's kept the bit at the front as his home and turned the rest of it, around the back, into a recording studio.

He's also built an addition and renovated the lot so that now he has a completely up-to-date live room, a second space that doubles as a lounge, a control room with a digital desk and a window into the live room and an area behind it to rehearse or record if needed. There's a little kitchen and a loo with a shower and a Japanese toilet that talks to you, plays soothing music (and several other sound effects, including a continuous flush in case you're easily embarrassed), washes your nether regions and keeps your bum warm.

The main door's in the rear. It has a digital lock but Trev always provides the entry code to musicians who've booked sessions. And he changes the code regularly. The door leads into a small hallway, with the control room on the left and the kitchen and loo on the right.

I poked my head inside the control room. Ansell, Trev's technical guy, was sitting with his back to me at the console, and I could see through the window that Trev was in the live room playing something with Rudy and Ken. The soundproof connecting doors were closed so I couldn't hear what they were working on. I carried on through the kitchen to the lounge and let myself in.

It was "Linus and Lucy", the Vince Guaraldi track that everyone always mistakes for the *Peanuts* theme. One of my favourites. Trev was providing the piano lead on a gorgeous old Steinway in the corner, while Rudy was tapping the drums and Ken was improvising on his sax.

I wondered where Dave was.

"Not like him to be late," I said, conversationally, acutely aware that it was already fifteen minutes past the time we were supposed to begin and the clock was ticking on the mate's rate Trev had offered for our half-day session.

"Let's give him another five minutes," Trev said, "and if he's not here we'll carry on without him. I can sub the keyboards. No extra charge."

"Very decent of you," I said, though I knew Trev's offer was also motivated by self-interest. We were going to demo three songs, including one that I'd written and one that he'd written himself. The record deal we were after was for my group, not just me. But I was the studio lead.

I'd brought my solid body Fender, a Sunburst Strat, a copy of the one my dad used to play. The original went to the bottom of the Gulf of Alaska with the *Sapphire*.

It was Trev's idea to cut some new demo's, something that was a bit less hardcore. "You play accessible jazz," he'd reminded me. "Save the serious stuff for the passionate punters at the Blue Devil. I've seen your show. You always throw in a few tunes people would know from the radio. I've never seen anyone do 'Soul Coaxing' quite the way you do."

It was true. "Soul Coaxing" is a standard—to my mind, anyway. It was a hit written by Michel Polnareff and recorded by Raymond Lefèvre in 1967 and released in 1968, the year I was born. It was used as a theme song by Radio Luxembourg and Radio Caroline when pirate broadcasters ruled the airwaves. My mum loves it and that's probably why I do too. Most versions feature a full orchestra and a spooky soprano *ooohing* over the bridge, but my arrangement's for drums, a Hammond organ, an electric guitar and a tenor sax. According to my son Dom, it rocks. And he hates jazz.

So we were going to do "Soul Coaxing" and two other pieces. I reckoned it was my last kick at the can, since there wasn't much point going back to the labels who'd already turned me down. If they'd wanted me to send them something else, they'd have asked.

Dave hadn't rung and there was still no sign of him, so I plugged in the Strat and grabbed a chair and some headphones, while Trev moved over to the Hammond organ, Rudy tapped out the drum beats after the eight-bar intro and Ken warmed up his tenor sax.

"E or F?" Trev checked.

"E," I said, referring to the opening chords. I'd arranged it both ways.

We ran through the eight-bar intro, Ken and I handling the melody, Trev transferring the orchestral backing to the keyboards. Just as we were about to leap into the chord progressions for the next sequence, Dave let himself into the studio.

He'd definitely looked better.

"Sorry," he said. "Problems on the home front."

We weren't without sympathy. The four of us—Ken, Rudy, Dave and I—often chat about things going on in our personal lives before and after our shows at the club. I wouldn't describe us as socially friendly, but you can't work with a group of guys four nights a week and not form some kind of personal relationship with them.

Out of all of us, Dave is the least talkative and the most private. We knew he'd been married for about twenty-five years to Helen, who had been an office manager somewhere and who, during their early years together, had been the main breadwinner while Dave pursued his musical interests and played gigs that didn't usually result in any kind of steady income. But the marriage had recently ended. Helen had a new man in her life and had gone back to work. Dave was on his own and had moved into a flat nearby so he could stay close to his two younger daughters.

They had four kids. Janice was married and lived in Poole, where she was a nurse. Adam was in the Army. Tabitha and Gracie still lived at home in the house that Helen had kept as part of the divorce settlement. Tabitha was a personnel assistant somewhere. Gracie was fourteen and still in school and was turning out to be a bit of a handful.

"You all right, mate?" Rudy asked.

Rudy's closer to Dave than Ken or myself. He's about Dave's age and is married and has kids of his own.

"I'm ok," Dave said, though I wasn't completely convinced.

Neither was Ken. "You don't look it."

Ken is the youngest of the group and has a partner who's a paramedic and neither of them is particularly fond of children, even though Patrick had volunteered his sperm to a female couple who'd wished to become parents—no strings attached—and was therefore now technically the father of identical twin girls in Milton Keynes.

"Bad night," Dave said, as Trev vacated his seat at the Hammond and went through to the control room.

Dave took his place on the bench and adjusted the headphones over his ears.

"'Soul Coaxing', E," he confirmed, to us, and to Trev. "Anything I miss by way of changes, instructions, mourning women from the rejected soundtrack of Troy…?"

We laughed. Dave wasn't fond of 'Soul Coaxing'. He particularly hated the versions that featured the bridge with the *ooohing* soprano. Fortunately, my arrangement didn't.

We ran through the tune again, with Ansell recording us and Trev monitoring us behind the glass, and then we joined Trev in the control room and made notes. He keeps a mug filled with sharpened pencils on his desk and clipboards loaded with blank paper in a plastic bin on top of one of the pre-amp trolleys. We went through the charts—basically the sheet music for each individual instrument—which I'd printed off at home and brought with me, beefing up the tempo and making adjustments to the simple melody, so that each time it repeated, something new was added. We punched up Rudy's drums so they weren't just background and beat, but a driving force all their own. We added more Sounds Incorporated sax, more Alan Price organ and a playful skip-and-jump on the Strat.

We played it through and I thought it was pretty good. We did it one more time for the demo, then huddled for what I call Afterthoughts and Embellishments—tiny little melodic runs and splashes of sound, a tinkling triangle, a tambourine shake and a surprising pluck of a harp string, a fragmented bit of percussion and a clever little finger exercise on the Strat that would make it absolutely perfect. We recorded just the enhancements and then Ansell edited them into the demo.

And then Trev had the brilliant idea of putting a piano back into the mix. I'd purposely not included it in my arrangement, but Trev suggested adding a thudding keyboard that synched with Rudy's drums would be a perfect finishing touch.

It was, by then, about four in the afternoon. We'd been at it for three hours, rehearsing, playing, discussing, experimenting. I thought we were doing all right for time but Dave was beginning to look impatient.

"Can we give it a try?" Trev asked, into our headphones.

Dave glanced at the Steinway tucked into the corner behind Rudy's drum kit.

"I don't agree," he said. "It'll make it sound the same as all the other versions. Paramor, Sounds Orchestral, Lefèvre, they've all done it that way. The Ventures had the guts to break with tradition. We should too."

"The Ventures never had a pianist," Trev said, a little dryly.

"Not strictly true," Dave said. "They had keyboards. 'Walk Don't Run '64'. 'Telstar'."

"'Hawaii Five O'," I volunteered. "I've seen the video."

My humorous addition to the conversation did nothing to defuse the tension.

"Can we just try it?" Trev asked, patiently. "Jason?"

"I'm good," I said. "Rudy?"

"Sounds good to me."

"And me," Ken said.

We paused, waiting for Dave's vote—which never came. He took off his headphones, got up, collected his stuff and walked out of the room.

"Just like that," Ken said, shaking his head.

"I think he really does have some serious issues going on with Gracie," Rudy said.

"I'll do the punch-ins," Trev decided, coming back into the studio from the control room. He rolled the Hammond out of the way and manoeuvred the Steinway into place, mic'd it and did a test run on the keyboard so that Ansell could get a level.

Ansell played our master recording back and Rudy, Ken and I listened while Trev added the thuds he'd described. I had to admit, it really was brilliant.

We listened to the finished piece one more time, and then we were done. For that afternoon, anyway. We still had two more tunes to record. But we'd save those for another day.

Trev came over as I was packing up my Strat. "You know," he said, "if you'd let me mention your musical pedigree when I send off the demo, we'd have no trouble landing a contract."

"No," I said. We'd talked about that before—several times. Yes, invoking my parents' fame would have automatically opened doors. But that wasn't what I wanted to do. It never has been. There's a reason I'm billed professionally as Jason Davey. Stubborn of me, I know. And probably stupid, as some who know me have sometimes remarked. But I wanted to get there on my own. Not because I'd inherited the genetic chord charts of Tony Figgis and Mandy Green.

"See you tomorrow," Trev said. "We'll do 'Chocolate Frost'."

That was Trev's tune. He was saving mine for last.

"With or without Dave," he added, making it more of a question than a statement.

"With or without Dave," I agreed.

CHAPTER FIVE

I'm a fairly decent cook. I didn't start out that way—I grew up in the 1970s, at a time when the roles of men and women were just beginning to be questioned...mothers bravely demanding that they be allowed to return to work to resume their pre-childbirth careers...fathers (sometimes reluctantly) realizing that they might be expected to take on child-rearing and housekeeping as a shared responsibility.

My mum and dad were war babies, members of that generation who'd knocked the world on its head in the Swinging Sixties and overthrown everything that was comfortable and traditional and familiar to their parents. Yet some things never changed. When Figgis Green wasn't touring, my mum did all the cooking. When the band was on the road, my grandmother came to stay in our house to look after me and my sister, Angie. And Gran did all the cooking. I'm not even certain my dad knew how to do anything more basic than boil an egg or put the kettle on for tea.

We had a cleaner who came in to look after the hoovering and dusting and washing up, and a gardener who ensured our roses, junipers, yews and laurels were well-behaved. And it wasn't until I started going to school that I realized most kids didn't have lives like ours. Our house was in one of those posh north London suburbs the press like to refer to as "leafy" and my friends' dads were all managing directors and stockbrokers and lawyers. Their parents didn't go off on world concert tours and they didn't have to be aware that snappers and journos were often lurking nearby, hoping for a lucrative scoop.

We weren't landed gentry wandering around a slowly-decaying and hideously-expensive-to-run manor in the country. Other than the cleaner and the gardener (who both lived miles away from our polite, tree-lined neighbourhood), my parents didn't employ any domestic help. There were no nannies or cooks. Not even an au pair, which was almost mandatory in my friends' households.

When I was older, my girlfriends tried, with tentative hints and nudged practical suggestions, to get me to help with meal prep. I resisted until I met Emma, who'd grown up in a progressively-minded home with a dad who was the head chef at a trendy London restaurant. It was Em who encouraged me to learn to cook. I discovered I actually enjoyed it. And now that I'm on my own, it's something I do a lot.

I'd made myself a nice plate of four-cheese tortellini (OK, I cheated, the pasta came from a package) and a pesto sauce absolutely concocted from scratch and a Caesar salad with a dressing I'd also whipped up myself, including mashed anchovies and the traditional raw egg. I'd grated some Grana Padano over the salad, and some freshly ground pepper, and tossed in a few croutons (out of a box, with apologies to my father-in-law). I carried my dinner and a glass of Pellegrino through to my living room, where I often eat, and then looked up Raj Kumar's number on my phone and gave him a ring.

I'm not sure where he was when I reached him. It was about eight o'clock in the evening and I'd planned to catch him before he went to work. He didn't sound particularly keen to talk to me, anyway, and I wasn't sure if that was because he'd already spoken to Roly, or if he was always that generally disinterested.

"I was hoping to have a chat with you about the night of February 23," I said, after I'd told him who I was.

"Yeah?" Raj said. "Such as."

"Could I possibly meet you somewhere? It would be a bit more convenient than over the phone."

"Phone'll do," Raj said.

"OK," I said, "I'm looking into a theft. A sum of money was taken from a locker belonging to one of the dancers that night and I've been asked to investigate."

"Yeah?" Raj said. "How'd that happen, then?"

"I don't know. That's why I'm talking to people who were there at the time. People who might be witnesses and may not know it."

"Did the locker have a lock?"

"Yes."

"Did she report it to anyone?"

"Apparently not," I said.

"I didn't see anything suspicious," Raj replied. "I didn't see anyone suspicious. Can't help. Sorry."

"So nothing out of the ordinary happened during your shift."

"What's 'ordinary'?"

"Anyone who didn't belong there. Anyone acting a bit odd."

Raj laughed. "I've been on the job a month, mate. You tell me who didn't belong there. New girls every week. Here today, gone tomorrow."

"Do you remember seeing Holly Medford that night?" I tried.

"Who?"

"One of the dancers."

"What's her club name?"

"Chanel," I said.

"Don't know. What's she look like?"

I told him.

"Could be any one of them," he said. "From Eastern Europe?"

"English," I said.

"Narrows it down but no. Don't recall her. She's the one with the missing money?"

"Yes," I said.

"Tell her to be more careful next time," Raj said. "Sorry. Can't help."

There wasn't much point in continuing the conversation. One of the reasons I'd wanted a face-to-face meeting was so I could look at him. I'm a pretty good judge of character. I can usually size people up in less than a minute. If I walk into a room, I can sense the mood. My mum's the same. I don't like to label it or call it something it isn't, but I also usually know when people aren't being honest with me. And I can't do it over the phone. I need to be in that person's space.

I finished half of my tortellini and all of my salad and got myself a second glass of Pellegrino. I hadn't recorded my phone call with Raj, so I scribbled the details of our conversation into my notebook and added the date and the time.

And then I called Dave.

His landline rang seven times and then went to messaging. His mobile rang four times, with the same result. If he was there, he could see it was me—I don't hide my name or number. I left a message on both phones and then rang Rudy.

"Just trying to find out if we can expect Dave at the studio tomorrow," I said. "Have you heard anything?"

"I have, actually. I was going to give you a call. Gracie's run away. Dave and Helen have been out looking for her for most of this evening."

That explained the messages I had to leave. "I suppose they've tried all of her friends."

"All of her friends, all of the places where they know she goes."

I remembered some statistics from somewhere. Children made up the bulk of reported missing persons in the UK. Usually they were teenagers who'd decided not to come home after a night out, or were cooling off at a friend's house after an argument with mum or dad. And teen runaways were the missing person cases that were resolved the quickest, usually within one or two days.

"I'm sure she'll turn up. Has she done it before?"

"Never," Rudy said. "But she's got herself involved with an older bloke. Helen had words with her about it, as you can imagine."

"Find the older bloke," I agreed, "and you'll find Gracie."

"Easier said than done. I told Dave to call the police but he's reluctant. He's respectable. His family's respectable. This stuff happens to other peoples' kids. Not to his."

I understood. And I felt bad for Dave. When Dom was fourteen he was wise beyond his years. And equipped with street smarts that truly frightened me. It had to be a thousand times worse for a dad whose youngest daughter had grown up fairly sheltered, and who, the last time I recalled meeting her, had been Snapchatting selfies with her cat to all her schoolmates. It was difficult for me to imagine that little girl, barely out of childhood, hooking up with some guy whose age difference had caused such a rift.

"I don't think he's going to be in any shape to join us tomorrow," Rudy said.

"I don't want to cut him out."

"Let me ring Trev. Maybe we could postpone for a day?"

"Fair enough," I said. "See you Wednesday."

#

I was in the kitchen warming the leftover half of my tortellini up in the microwave when Sal called. It was about 11 p.m.

"I have news," she said. "I did as you asked…I told the girls about the theft and I asked them to try and recall anything unusual. A few of them asked which locker but I told them I wasn't at liberty to say. One of the girls approached me as I was leaving and told me she reckoned it was Chanel and that I'd got the date wrong. Who's Chanel, do you know?"

"That's Holly. It's her club name. Why did she think that?"

"She said Chanel had some things taken from her locker but it was four months ago, not February 23."

"What was taken?"

I could tell Sally was looking at her notes.

"Her bag—which apparently had about £50 in it—and some costumes she'd just bought from a woman who regularly makes the rounds of all the clubs with second-hand stuff. Apparently Chanel turned around and outright accused one of the other girls of taking her things while she was upstairs. There was some kind of feud going on between them."

"Four months ago," I said.

"Yes. And she didn't think it was reported to the club owner or the police."

"Is the other dancer still there? The one she was feuding with?"

"No. I did ask. I only got her club name. The other girl didn't know anything else about her. And no idea where she went. Do you want me to try and find out?"

"Roly will know," I said. "What's her club name?"

"Shaniah."

"You sure about that?"

"Quite sure. Why?"

"Holly told me it was Shaniah who introduced her to Arthur Braskey. And Roly told me Shaniah handed in her notice the same night Holly's money disappeared."

"Do you think Shaniah's the one who might have taken her money last week?"

"Could be," I said. "Can I have the name and details of the dancer who gave you all that information? Just for my files."

Sal gave them to me, and I jotted them down in my notebook.

"One more thing," Sal said. "The girl I was speaking with didn't seem to like Holly very much. In fact she was very surprised that Holly had come back to the club last week. She thought she'd gone for good when she left in January. I think there might have been a bit of that rivalry going on between them, as well. She mentioned a Saudi prince…no, hang on, not Saudi. He was a sheik from somewhere in the Middle East, though."

"Yes," I said. "Roly invited Holly back on February 23 to attend to him."

"And she did, according to this woman. She left with him after the club closed."

"Is she sure?"

"Yes. She saw Holly getting into his car."

"That's two confirmations," I said. "She gave you—and me—the impression she was terrified because her money was stolen and petrified about what Braskey would do to her. Something's not adding up."

"Do you want me to talk to her?"

"Wait," I said. "I want the truth out of her. I don't want to tip her off so she has time to make up another story. And I want to talk to Shaniah. Good work, Sal. Thank you."

"It's been…an interesting night."

"I'm sure it has," I said.

"You should have a proper assistant," Sal said, humorously.

"I'd get one if I was a proper PI," I replied.

"One last thing, Jase."

I waited.

"I've received a letter."

"What, a real one? In the post?"

"A real one. The kind you have to sign for."

"That sounds serious."

"It is, actually. And it's from a real private investigator. In Vancouver."

"To do with the *Sapphire*?"

Vancouver had been our home port when we were doing our Alaska itinerary. I knew there were still a lot of loose ends floating about—literally—because of the sinking, and I knew some lawsuits were continuing to drag their way through litigation. But I was still surprised.

"Actually, no," Sal said. "I want to show it to you. Can we meet tomorrow?"

"'Course we can," I said. "I'm having lunch with my sister—but after that?"

"Four o'clock? At the hotel?"

"See you then," I said.

#

It was midnight by the time I finished the last of my tortellini. But I suspected Holly was still keeping gentlemen's club hours—so I gave her a call.

It went immediately to messaging: a very professional voice— Holly identifying herself as Saratoga—promising to return the call as soon as she was free.

I let her know I wanted to speak with her again, hopefully by the end of tomorrow, and left it at that.

And then I wandered back into my kitchen to see if there was any of my favourite Cornish ice cream left in the freezer.

CHAPTER SIX

I may have followed my parents into the music business but my younger sister's creative instincts lay in another direction entirely.

When she was in school, it was a tossup whether she'd end up as an artist or a writer. I've still got two of the things she made for me in Art—a small clay slab coffin with a lid and a green moss glaze that she explained was meant to be a storage container for things like cufflinks and earrings (yes, when I was a teenager I went through that single earring phase); and a clay hot dog in a clay bun, with ketchup and mustard, everything painted perfectly to emulate the real thing (presented to me as a doorstop or a paperweight, whichever I preferred).

As for Angie's other talent, I can vouch for the fact that she was telling stories before she'd ever been taught the alphabet. Like a primitive cave dweller, she used to draw pictures on the walls of her bedroom (usually in crayon, much to mum's consternation), and then she'd invite me in for a recital of what it all meant. Mum and dad eventually persuaded her to use a blackboard and coloured chalks, and then once she'd learned to read and write she graduated to paper and pencils and there was no stopping her.

Like Beatrix Potter, she wrote amusing little stories that she illustrated herself and lent out to our neighbours to read, always requiring that they be returned in two weeks' time so that she could take her little bundles of paper to the next person on her list. When she was twelve she persuaded our parents to buy her a portable typewriter—which she taught herself to use—and upon this she created her first novel—a mystery involving the murder of an annoying newspaper reporter—the chapters of which she distributed to her classmates at school.

Angie was—and still is—a very good artist. But writing won out in the end, and if you've ever picked up a Jemima Fielding mystery at an airport bookshop, you'll have been reading my sister's current series. She writes under a pseudonym. Apparently the public's more likely to buy a novel by an author named Taylor Feldspar than one by Angie Figgis. Or, perhaps, like me, she secretly doesn't want to trade on our parents' legacy.

Angie lives with her husband Tom Leyland on Mersea Island, which can only be reached by way of an ancient Roman causeway called the Strood. The Strood is famous for being underwater twice a day for a week every month, so a journey to see my sister necessarily involves checking tide times and bringing something to read in case my calculations are off and I end up stuck on one side or the other, waiting for the water to recede.

I managed to arrive before noon, which on that Tuesday in February was a good two hours before High Tide. Angie was in full writer mode, wearing a kaftan and spectacles and two pairs of thick thermal socks because her cottage is ancient and draughty and bloody cold when the wind blows up from the sea.

"Come in," she said, greeting me at the door with a kiss and a meat cleaver.

"I'm not sure I want to," I said.

"Research," she assured me, leading me through to the sitting room, which was comfortably untidy, with cushiony sofas and armchairs, exposed wooden beams in the ceiling and an immense fireplace. "My baddie's a butcher."

"Nice," I said.

"Female," she added. "Mexican Cod."

I must have looked confused.

"Lunch," said Angie. "Tom's been experimenting."

Tom's a retired policeman who's much older than my sister. He's tall and lean and has a full head of white hair and ruddy red cheeks. I used to think it was because he was sensitive to the salt air from the sea but apparently it's rosacea, which he's suffered from all of his life.

Tom is also a man after my own culinary heart, having trained as a gourmet chef after he gave up policing. Angie's stories invariably wander down gastronomic paths. Her main character is an amateur detective—female—who solves murders which seem to occur whenever she's called on to cater a function. I'd be sorely tempted never to hire her but there are less wise people than me out there in the mystery universe, and so Jemima Fielding is never without bookings—or killings—to keep her—and my sister—on the bestseller list.

The Mexican Cod turned out to be baked with onions, mushrooms and a fiery salsa and topped with crumbled corn chips and shredded cheddar. It was delicious, and was served in the cottage's dining room, which was furnished with driftwood and bits and pieces salvaged from scrappers and shipyards, the centrepiece of which was an ancient and very battered table rumoured to have come from the cabin of an infamous pirate who'd roamed the southern English coastline in the mid-1700s.

"You mentioned something about wanting our advice?" Angie said, pouring me another glass of posh lime-flavoured fizzy water.

I told her—and Tom—about Holly—and Arthur Braskey.

"So it seems you've decided to follow Jemima Fielding into the realm of cosy mysteries," Angie said.

"I seem to have an affinity for it," I replied. "Though I don't think I'd call what I'm doing particularly cosy."

"Professional musician, amateur sleuth," Tom said. "Have Strat. Will Travel."

"I like it," I grinned.

"Bearing in mind that Jemima's a figment of my imagination," Angie said. "And you're most decidedly not. Are you quite certain you know what you're letting yourself in for?"

"I don't," I admitted. "And I do seem to be committing a few basic errors."

"If you're thinking about going legit," Tom said, "you'll need to take the course and get certified."

"If a private citizen goes nosing about in other peoples' business it can get a bit dodgy," Angie added. "And it's actually illegal to operate as a private investigator without a license."

"Jemima Fielding never seems to worry about these things," I said.

"If Jemima Fielding was on my watch I'd have had her arrested eight novels ago," Tom replied, conveniently ignoring the fact that he's been Angie's go-to person for copper-related details for decades.

"If you're after some advice, I'd tell you to examine the facts very carefully," my sister said. "Holly didn't report the theft to management and you say none of the other girls noticed anything wrong that night. Holly claims her locker was locked and when she came back to open it, she saw the lock had been broken. What kind of lock was it? How was it broken? Have you ever tried to break a lock?"

"I have actually," I said. I'd needed to in northern Alberta; my rescue of Ben Quigley had depended upon it.

"Then you'll know you need tools. Something to cut the shackle. So unless that dancer Shaniah came to work packing a bolt-cutter, the idea that it was a crime of opportunity's never going to fly. And what did Holly do with the broken lock? Did she keep it or throw it away? What happened with the first theft four months ago? Who had the tools to break the lock then?"

"I thought I might talk to Shaniah and ask her for her side of the story. And then, of course, I was going to talk to Holly. Again. And ask her to clarify, exactly, what you've just asked. Along with a few other discrepancies."

"All of the steps a good PI—cosy or otherwise—would have tackled right off the top," Tom said. "How much do you know about Arthur Braskey?"

"Crime boss. Soho. I was going to do some more homework on him tonight."

"He'll have his ear to the ground," Tom said. "If this Holly woman's seriously fearing for her life, you could turn into her biggest liability. You'd best not let it get about you're investigating that theft. Or even that you've spoken to her."

"That had occurred to me. I am being careful."

"I dealt with toms like her when I was a copper. Just saying. They're cagey. And slippery. If it was me, I'd leave it. You must know you're never going to be able to find that money. Or who took it."

"Thank you," I said.

"You won't leave it, though, will you?" my sister said, going into the kitchen to make coffee and carrying on our conversation through the open doorway. "You've always been like that. Once you've got something between your teeth, nothing's going to convince you to let go. Persistence, passion and patience. Jemima Fielding's famous 'three P's'. I modelled her after you."

"You didn't."

"Didn't I?"

Angie was smiling.

And Tom was scribbling something onto a scrap of paper.

"Ring this bloke if you run into trouble," he said. "He's with the Met. Charing Cross. I'll have a word."

I looked at the name. Detective Allan Pappas. And a phone number.

"Thank you," I said again, meaning it this time. "And I promise I'll look into getting licensed."

"The same way you promised you'd look into stop smoking programs?" Angie said, humorously, from the kitchen.

"The very same," I said, reaching for my packet of Benson and Hedges.

#

My mobile rang as I was driving back across the Strood. It was Holly, returning the message I'd left last night.

I found a place to park and called her back.

"Hello Mr. Private Investigator," she said, and for the first time I was aware of just how much her voice reminded me of dark honey. "I'm available now if you'd like a chat. What time can you be here?"

"Not for another couple of hours, I'm afraid. I'm in Essex."

"Oh," she said, sounding genuinely disappointed. "Well. I'll find something to amuse myself until you arrive. Message me when you are at the hotel."

#

It was half past three by the time I'd parked my car and found my way back to the chocolate brown lobby of the Crestone Hotel.

I rang Sal's office on my mobile. I had a previous engagement; Holly would have to wait.

"I'm here," I said.

Sal appeared from her doorway behind the Reception Desk moments later.

"Let's go in here," she suggested, taking me into the Wine Bar, where she immediately ordered a Pinot Noir for herself and a very expensive fizzy water for me.

The waiter brought both quickly, along with a little bowl of crunchy snacks that were almost on par with the ones we used to snaffle from the ship's passenger bars when we had crew parties on board the *Sapphire*.

Sal took the letter out of its envelope and unfolded it and handed it over to me and drank her wine while I read it.

Twice.

"You have a daughter," I said.

"Yes," she confirmed. "I do."

The letter said that the Peterson Spriggs Private Investigation Group had been retained by a woman named Jennifer Ann Miller, who was born on March 7, 1987 in Vancouver, Canada, and that she had been put up for adoption shortly after that.

And that Jennifer Ann Miller had hired Ted Spriggs to investigate the circumstances of that adoption with a view towards locating her birth mother.

And that Ted Spriggs had been successful on that count, and was now respecting the wishes of his client to initiate contact. But that he was required also to be mindful of the wishes of the birth mother, Sally Jacqueline Jones.

Therefore, this letter was meant to serve as an introduction only, and that Sally Jacqueline Jones should respond, in confidence, informing Ted Spriggs whether or not she wished to pursue the matter further.

If she did not wish to acknowledge and correspond with Jennifer Ann Miller, she would hear nothing further from Peterson Spriggs Private Investigation Group.

But if she did wish to acknowledge and initiate correspondence with Jennifer Ann Miller, Ted Spriggs would be pleased to continue to act as an intermediary.

I was trying to do some quick mental math.

"She's nearly thirty," Sal said, beating me to it. "And I was eighteen at the time."

"And living in Vancouver," I said.

She nodded, sipping her wine.

To say I was surprised would have been an understatement.

Sal and I had actually grown up together. We were students at one of those posh independent co-educational schools (read: private, fee-paying, thank you Wikipedia), where pupils' parents parted with outrageous yearly fees and revelled in the knowledge that their offspring would share future graduation status with "Notable Alumni" that included a prominent cross-section of politicians, sports stars, writers and artists and business people.

Sal's dad was an executive for a firm that was opening a branch office in Vancouver. He accepted the promotion, and the day after Sal's eighteenth birthday, on June 15, 1986, they officially departed the UK for the west coast of Canada.

In spite of it being the mid-1980s and the height of sexual promiscuity, Sal had been conspicuously unwilling to participate. She'd once confided in me, when we were about sixteen, that she was terrified. Teenaged boys frightened her. Sex was out of the question. She was too petrified to even go on dates. A few of my mates had tried to ask her out and had been politely declined.

"Who's the father?" I asked, curiously.

"You are," Sal said, swallowing the last of her Pinot Noir.

I looked at her. "Sorry…?"

"You don't remember. The night of my going away party. My eighteenth birthday. You were absolutely blotto."

She was right, I didn't remember. I remembered the party—the beginning of it, anyway. I was completely sober when I'd arrived, but that didn't last long. Too many glasses of wine, too many tokes of weed, too much unhappiness at the thought of one of my closest friends moving to the other side of the world. I remembered sitting beside Sal on a sofa in her parents' lounge—they'd helpfully vacated the house for the evening…and waking up with the hangover from hell on that same sofa, covered with a blanket, and no memory of anything at all from the night before.

I was stunned. "I slept with you?"

"No," Sal said, humorously. "We had sex. There was no sleeping involved. It was…" She paused to think. "Lovely."

"I was drunk."

"And high. And you still managed to make it one of the most caring, tender and affectionate moments of my entire life. I'd had no idea. You were my first. And I was always so grateful—and lucky— that it was you. Everything changed after that."

I still couldn't quite take it all in. First, that I'd actually had sex with her. Second, the result, a daughter. Third, that she'd never once mentioned it in the thirty years since.

"The morning after I wondered how much you'd remembered but it was pretty clear that you didn't recall any of it. I was actually quite embarrassed. I'd never thought of you in those terms, ever, Jase. We were the closest of friends—the only male friend I'd ever had—and the question of sex had just never entered into it. And I knew you felt the same way."

"I did," I said.

"I didn't want to spoil anything." She paused again. "Are you upset with me?"

I shook my head. "God, no. Not at all. Just a little…"

"Flabbergasted?"

"Overwhelmed," I said.

"I'm going to arrange for a DNA test to confirm everything, of course. I need to make sure I'm actually her mum."

The waiter was hovering, and Sal ordered another glass of wine and another fizzy water for me.

"I named her Gina before I gave her up. I've never stopped thinking about her, wondering who she'd become and what she'd done with her life. I don't really know what to expect, but I'm going to ask Mr. Spriggs to go ahead and put us in touch."

"What about me?"

"That was going to be my next question, Jase. Do you want me to tell her who you are?"

CHAPTER SEVEN

I was still in a state of absolute incredulousness when I rang Holly to tell her I was there at the hotel and ready to meet up. Shocked, stunned and amazed is a total cliché but it would have described me perfectly.

Sal popped into the lift and used her pass to unlock the 12th floor for me and then, with a quick kiss and a hug, she went back to work.

Holly was wearing skinny jeans and a grey t-shirt with long sleeves and silk buttoned cuffs, and shiny black patent high heels. She looked expensive. She smelled expensive, too—I caught another whiff of that perfume again as she closed the door behind me.

Her room showed signs of a recent lunch. There were plates and cutlery and silver serving containers sitting on the sideboard, awaiting collection. Two, I noted, two of everything, like before. Holly'd been entertaining.

"Would you prefer tea or coffee?" she asked, picking up the telephone.

"Tea, thanks."

"Earl Grey? I've developed a sudden taste for it."

"Earl Grey's fine."

I sat in one of the armchairs and switched on my mobile—the one I was using to record conversations—while Holly put in the request. She added a selection of *petit fours*, as she had the first time we'd met. Then she slid into the armchair on the opposite side of the impossibly small table.

"I went to see Roly Barfield," I said. "And he took me on a tour of Cha-Cha's. I had a look at the dressing room. I also had a chat with Raj Kumar, the security guard who was working the night your money was stolen. And Sal's interviewed some of the dancers."

I was watching Holly's face but she wasn't giving anything away. Her expression remained the same: a pleasant smile and inquiring eyes, as if she'd been told to pose a certain way for a photographer and hold it while the shutter clicked a hundred times.

"Roly told me that you didn't report the theft to him."

"Of course I didn't. What good would it have done?"

"With his connections…he might have been able to help."

"With his connections, word might have reached Braskey. I thought it better to keep quiet. I was in a panic. I was thinking only of myself."

"What kind of lock did you have on your locker?"

"The kind that has a key," Holly said, after a moment.

"Not a combination?"

"Not a combination," she confirmed.

"What about the first time your money was stolen, four months ago?"

Holly's expression didn't change. Perhaps a quick blink of her eyes. "Yes, that was the kind of lock you open with a key as well."

"You didn't mention that theft to me."

"It didn't seem relevant or necessary."

"Would you mind telling me about it now?"

"My bag was taken. It had £56 in it. I'd just bought some costumes from Edith—she comes around once a month or so with second-hand things. Two of those were also stolen. My bag was eventually found in the alley behind the club, but of course the money was gone. The costumes were also missing."

"Did say anything to the other dancers?"

"Of course. Because I knew very well who had done it. There were three girls from Estonia who had started working at the club a few weeks before. They acted like a gang. They were bullies. And they didn't like it that I was a favourite with some of the regular customers who had very deep pockets. So they tried to intimidate me and sabotage me. It didn't work and so they stole from me instead. And left behind a very threatening note."

"So it wasn't the dancer named Shaniah?"

"Who told you that?"

"A colleague," I said, "who interviewed some of your colleagues.

Former colleagues. At Cha-Cha's."

Holly's composure didn't change.

"Your colleague," she said, "very likely spoke to the Estonian girls. Who, of course, would have a vested interest in not implicating themselves."

"Fair enough," I conceded, writing a reminder to myself to check with Sal later.

"I still have the note," Holly added.

She got up and pulled a battered canvas-and-leather carry-all out of the bottom of the cupboard where her clothes were hanging. Odd, I thought. With her tastes, I'd have expected a set of matching Louis Vuitton or Gucci.

"Here you are," she said, coming back to the table and handing the envelope to me.

I slipped the paper out and read what had been printed in a precise hand, with a black fine-tipped felt pen.

Be careful when you go home.

Be watchful.

Someone might make you regret.

"Were you afraid?" I asked, giving the note and its envelope back to her.

Holly shrugged.

"You stopped working at the club soon after that."

"I did."

"Because of that note?"

"Not at all. I told you. I owed a lot of money to Arthur Braskey and working as an escort provided me with a means to pay off that debt far more quickly than dancing."

"What did you do with the lock?"

"It was broken. I threw it away, of course."

She stopped short of telling me what a ridiculous question she thought that was.

"And the theft that happened last week," I said. "You were there for one night only…did you use the same locker that you'd used when you worked there before?"

"No. Because it had been taken over by another girl."

"So you used a different locker and you remembered to bring a lock? Because Roly doesn't supply them…"

"Yes, I remembered to bring a lock."

"Another lock that opens with a key?"

"Yes. It opened with a key."

"I'm just curious why you'd chose a lock with a key, rather than a combination. What do you do with the key while you're dancing?

Holly smiled.

"Do you think I might hide it up *there*?" she inquired.

I smiled too. "The thought had occurred to me."

"I might sometimes like to provide my favourite customers with a little surprise while I dance for them in private. Does that answer your question?"

"It does," I replied.

We were interrupted by the arrival of our tea and *petit fours*. The young man who brought it took away the detritus of Holly's lunch, and we were alone again. Holly poured for both of us, remembering that I liked milk and two lumps of sugar.

"Shaken and not stirred," she said, amused, as she placed the little icing-covered cakes in the centre of the table, then took one for herself and bit into it, slowly and, some might say, with a hint of seductiveness.

"And so," I said, "when you came back to your locker you found the same thing had happened—the lock was broken and your money and your costumes had been stolen."

"Yes. Exactly that."

"Was the money in your bag?"

"Of course."

"But your bag wasn't taken this time. Just the money."

"Just the money, And only one piece from my costume—the G-string."

I had a thought. "Would you mind showing me the bag?"

Holly got up from the armchair a second time and went into the bathroom. She returned with just the sort of accessory I would have expected of her: brown leather, Givenchy, worth about £1,600.00.

"Your thief missed an opportunity there," I said.

"My thief had no sophistication," Holly replied, leaving the bag on her bed and sitting once again in the armchair.

"Were you planning on changing your costume that evening?" I asked. "Is that why you had extra clothes with you?"

"I always brought extra," Holly said, smoothly. "Just in case. We all did."

"Just in case of what?"

"Unforeseen circumstances," she said, delicately placing the second and last bite of her *petit fours* into her mouth, and licking her lips.

"I'm curious," I said, "how anyone would have known you had that much money in your bag."

"I have no idea. I didn't flash it about, if that's what you think."

"It's a lot of work to break a lock, Holly. Whoever took your money would have needed proper tools. Not the sort of thing a lap-dancer would normally turn up for work with. They'd have had to hide it in their own locker…and then slip downstairs when no one else was there to use it to break your lock. And that takes a considerable amount of muscle. It's not a simple snip with scissors. And that's a lot of effort for someone who had no idea what they were going to find on the other side. Are you absolutely certain no one else knew about the £10,000 you had in your bag?"

I gave her a very direct look, and for the first time I thought I detected a little flicker of uncertainty in her eyes. But only a flicker.

"No one," she replied. And then: "What makes you think it was one of the other girls?"

"You think it might have been someone from outside the club?"

"Why not? He—or she—might have had a word with one of the dancers, asked her to help. Or perhaps she came in herself and pretended to be one of us, and waited and watched to see which locker I used, then took my money as soon as the dressing room was empty."

She made it sound so easy.

"And by the way, Mr. Barfield keeps a bolt cutter in his office," she added.

"How do you know that?"

"I've seen it," Holly shrugged. "It was necessary to use it one night to open a locker that had been abandoned."

"You say that nobody knew you had £10,000 in your bag. Not even someone from outside the club. So how could anyone have known to go looking for it, if they didn't have any idea it was there? If you see the difficulty I'm having understanding all of this."

Holly smiled, and instead of answering me, sipped her tea.

She placed the china cup back in its saucer.

"The lock was not broken," she said, at last.

I waited.

"When I came back downstairs, I found that it had been unlocked. Not broken."

"So someone had the key?"

"Yes. Obviously."

"You didn't hide it up *there*, then."

"I didn't," Holly said, genuinely amused. "I put it in the bottom of one of my boots. The boots were too big to fit inside the locker and so I left them on the floor. One of the girls must have seen me do it and took advantage of my absence to see what they might be able to steal."

"Why didn't you tell me this to begin with?"

"Because I felt very foolish to admit it. And I was embarrassed to have been so stupid."

I helped myself to one of the little iced cakes. It was chocolate, with almond-flavoured icing and a fanciful dribble of something that tasted like strawberries.

"So," I said. "You don't believe it was Shaniah who took your money."

"I don't believe it was Shaniah," Holly confirmed. "She and I got along quite well. I used to do a lesbian act with her for the customers. I knew she wouldn't get up to nasty things, like the girls from Estonia. We trusted one another. Sometimes, when you work with a partner, they try to—what shall we say—push the envelope. They might try things when they perform with you that you might not be comfortable with. But you have to play along if you want the customer to buy more dances. I really don't think it could have been her."

"Roly gave me her contact info. I thought I might have a chat with her. Just to rule her out once and for all."

Another hesitation. Only a flicker. "Yes, that's a good idea. What will you ask?"

"I'm not sure. But if it seems like she might be the thief after all, I'll refer it to the police."

"You will let me know."

"Of course," I said.

I drained my teacup and stood up.

"Thank you," Holly said, also standing, allowing that white-blossom scent to waft my way once again.

"One last thing…after you finished your shift at Cha-Cha's that night, what did you do?"

"I told you. I was terrified of Braskey so I left the club without meeting him."

"Did you go home?"

Holly paused. "No. I spent the night with an acquaintance."

"Which acquaintance?"

"Since you've spoken to the owner of Cha-Cha's and your colleague has spoken to the dancers, I'm sure you know. The same acquaintance who requested my private performance in the VIP room. You'll understand, of course, if I decline to give you a name."

"I can find out."

"Then do so. You'll also, I hope, understand the terms of my agreement that night. What I might lose should those details become public. And what I gained as a result of that agreement."

"I understand," I said. "And in the morning, what did you do?"

"I contacted Sally to see if she could help me with somewhere to stay for a few days."

"Fair enough," I said. "By the way, do you have a British passport?"

"Yes, of course. Why do you ask?"

"Just curious. I've got a friend who was born in the UK but her parents emigrated to Canada when she was eighteen. She eventually took out Canadian citizenship and she has a Canadian passport. But she also kept her British passport. Dual nationality."

"I only have a British passport," Holly assured me, seeing me to the door.

As she opened it, she turned, and kissed me, on the lips. Definitely not the sort of kiss you'd get from a friend, especially one with dual nationality.

"If you think of anything else you might like to ask," she said, "please do give me a ring."

CHAPTER EIGHT

My party piece is "Bumble Boogie". Yes, I know I make a living playing jazz. Yes, I know our demo's were meant to showcase my skills with the guitar.

In truth, I'm what's referred to in the industry as a "multi-instrumentalist." My dad was a pianist before he switched to his Strat, and I'm the same. In fact, I played in a small classical orchestra for a while. But I didn't like it. Keyboards aren't really my thing. Though they often prove themselves useful when I'm composing.

I've never lost the knack, and every once in a while I trot out that tune to release tension and indulge in my passion for all-out boogie-woogie. I usually throw in some of Rimsky-Korsakov's original "Flight of the Bumble Bee"—which never fails to impress whoever happens to be there to witness my showing-off.

It was Wednesday and we were back at Collingwood Sound making up for lost time. And Dave was still AWOL.

I sat down at the Steinway and launched into my best rendition of B. Bumble and the Stingers' June 1961 chart topper.

It wasn't a surprise for Ken and Rudy, but Trev and Ansell were suitably in awe.

"Might get you on the Hammond for 'Chocolate Frost'," Trev mused.

"Don't be fooled by these nimble fingers," I said. "It's the only piece I know."

"Somehow I can't bring myself to believe that."

"Is Dave planning on showing up tonight?" I asked, as Rudy

unpacked his sticks.

I needed to know. Our gig at the Blue Devil runs Wednesdays to Saturdays, 11 p.m. until 3 a.m. We're the after-hours Late Show's main act. If Dave was going to be missing from the lineup, I had to have enough time to find a fill-in. I know a fair number of decent keyboard players. And most would have leaped at an opportunity to gig with us. But more than a couple of hours' notice would have been helpful.

"Haven't heard otherwise," Rudy said.

I tuned the guitar I'd brought with me for "Chocolate Frost": a handsome black Phoenix hollow-body, not unlike the one Brian Setzer plays.

Rudy pulled on his drumming gloves—most drummers like to go without but Rudy hates getting blistered fingers from long intense sessions.

Ken blasted a few experimental notes through his sax and Trev came through from the control room, leaving Ansell in charge, and seated himself at the Hammond organ.

We ran through "Chocolate Frost", starting with its simple melody line on my guitar, with Trev quietly following on the organ, no chords, just individual notes. Then me repeating, and Trev echoing, and then departing from the melody and playing an entirely different counterpoint. Then Ken came in and blew harmony with Trev, while I continued fingering the melody line, the three of us managing to make it sound totally improvised until we all came together and, with a massive lead-in drumbeat from Rudy and a crashing of cymbals, burst into a rollicking and completely over the top celebration of musical confectionery.

We did two more takes, but neither of them was as good at the first. Sometimes that happens. You give it everything the first time round and that's the one that works the best. I added some extra chords by way of embellishment for Ansell to edit in afterwards. Rudy smashed a couple of cymbals and overdubbed an extra beat on the floor tom, and then Ken played the whole tune through alone on his sax and Ansell put that in as well, letting him take over the lead from Trev's keyboard.

It was magnificent and I absolutely loved the final result. The only thing that was a bit of a downer was that Dave wasn't part of it.

"Tell you what," Ken said, as we listened back to Ansell's final mix over coffee and—appropriately—chocolate cake. "I honestly think Dave did us a favour. I don't think he'd have done half as good a job on the organ as Trev."

Trev didn't say anything but I could tell he agreed. And I was thinking the same thing. Trev was a keyboard genius.

#

True to Rudy's prediction, Dave was waiting in the Blue Devil's dressing room when we arrived that night. But he looked haggard and there were dark circles under his eyes. He didn't say much to any of us as we got ready to go onstage.

"Rudy told me about Gracie," I said, quietly, hanging back as the others went out to take their places. "I'm so sorry. I hope you find her quickly."

"Thanks," Dave said. "It's been very hard on Helen. We're good parents. We raised four kids. Gracie had no reason to do this to us."

I wasn't sure what to say. I often like to think I have wise answers, things that'll give comfort or encouragement or words that are filled with helpful advice. None of it sounded right in my head. I was going to add that I'd never had a daughter, but, of course, that wasn't strictly true anymore.

I'd never had a daughter who'd decided in the throes of hot-headed teenaged rebellion to run off with a much older man—at least, not that I knew of. And I had no idea of the circumstances or what had incited Gracie's behaviour.

My sister had managed to postpone her adolescent insurgency until she was an adult. At the age of twenty-one she declared her opposition to everything our parents stood for, cut off all communication with us and disappeared. She surfaced a few months later somewhere in Mexico, where—she informed me, by postcard—she was living in a shack on the beach with an artist named Emilio. A year and a half later, she came back. She had a nice tan and offered nothing by way of explanation, other than a rather dark hint that Emilio had run into a spot of trouble with a local drug gang. We made no more mention of him, Angie went round for a meal with mum and dad and that was that.

I didn't know how much her parents' divorce had affected Gracie. And I didn't know how strict Helen was with her. Parents think they're doing the right thing when they apply the rules they were brought up with. Their kids think they're out of touch and unreasonable. Somewhere there's a happy medium, and if you're lucky you can keep talking to one another and come to some arrangement that keeps both sides happy. And if not…

All I could think of was that Beatles' song, "She's Leaving Home".

"I'm always here if you want a chat," I offered, knowing how lame it sounded. If Dave was going to turn to anyone for solace and advice, it would be Rudy, not me.

"Thanks," Dave said, again. I could tell he just wanted to go out under the lights and play the sets and get the night over with.

"We're doing 'Smoke Drifts' next time at the studio…" I said.

"You'd better count me out," Dave replied. "Really sorry. I just don't think I can do it justice right now."

"No worries," I said.

We played our gig, with two intervals, to an appreciative Wednesday night audience. The second set, after the break, included all three tunes we were recording at the studio. Dave was right—he hated Trev's arrangement of "Soul Coaxing" and his heart wasn't in "Chocolate Frost" or "Smoke Drifts". I was actually glad, in the end, that Trev was going to be my keyboard guy for the final demo.

At 3 a.m. I locked up my guitars and said goodnight. Usually we stick around for a drink or two, winding ourselves down after a particularly decent show—as we had on that past Saturday, the night Sal had shown up. But Dave was impatient to be off, and Rudy and Ken had partners in bed at home. And there was somewhere else I had to be.

#

Satin & Silk is decidedly more upscale than Cha-Cha's. For one thing, it's in a new building with a multi-level cellar that has high ceilings and room for everything that's on offer: bars and performance stages and private booths on every floor, three large and very exclusive VIP rooms, three medium-sized private lounges and tables and chairs to accommodate about 300 customers. The decor is lush—gold and champagne-coloured velvets and silks and brocades, chairs that are built for ease and comfort, inviting you to stay a little bit longer, drink a few more bottles of bubbly, purchase just one more private dance.

The helpful doorman asked if I'd been there before.

"I haven't," I said.

"Right then—it's £25 entrance, then once you're inside, if you want a dance with one of the girls, it's also £25. If you want to smoke or use your mobile, you come outside here, yeah? And drinks start from £10."

"Thanks."

Inside, I asked the nicely-attired hostess about Shaniah.

"She'll be in Level 3. Downstairs."

Level 3 was a room with a long, marbled bar and a clever bartender who was putting on a performance of his own mixing outrageously decorated drinks for the punters. It was dark, but there were flashing strobes and white and pink spots beaming around the venue in time to the music, which was high-energy and pulsing. I waited for my eyes to adjust, and saw there were about a dozen tables with upholstered chairs in the middle of the floor and sections with padded benches along the far wall. At the back I spotted half a dozen private booths, each separated by tapestry walls and furnished with high-backed leather armchairs, handy footstools and tables that wouldn't have looked out of place in a French chateau.

It was past 4 a.m. and the club was still fairly full for a Wednesday night. I got a drink—London's most expensive Perrier with a twist of lime—and asked the bartender which one of the dancers was Shaniah.

"That's her!" he shouted, over the music, nodding at a gorgeous woman with dark skin and long black hair, swept back from her face and held in place by a flamboyant pink silk flower clip. She looked in her mid-twenties, and she wasn't wearing much—a pink satin bra and matching knickers and suspenders, pale pink sheer stockings and hot pink stilettos. She was pitching her act to an oily-looking guy in a salesman's suit sitting close to the bar.

I got an unoccupied table near the stage at the front (where another dancer was doing something courageously athletic with the pole) and waited. Once you have drink, you're fair game, and it wasn't long before I was approached by someone who was not Shaniah. She was dressed in slinky, cutaway white spandex and impossibly high heels. Her hair and makeup were impeccable. She got right to the point.

"May I join you, *monsieur*?"

I doubted her French accent was authentic, but gave her points for a creative sales effort.

"*Non merci, je suis en train d'enquêter sur un vol,*" I said, but I don't think she appreciated my honesty. Or understood a word of it. "No, thank you," I repeated.

Her expression unchanged and without further comment, she moved on to the next table.

I sipped my Perrier while I observed the dancer on the little round stage. She'd been wearing a skimpy white bikini and seven-inch heels when I'd arrived, but was now in the process of discarding the bikini top while hanging upside down with her legs wrapped provocatively around the pole.

The top dispensed with, she rotated upright, and, with one arm over her head and her hand grasping the pole, she tugged loose the ties that secured her bikini bottom, and it wafted gently to the floor.

I watched with a mix of basic curiosity and detached arousal. I was there to work. And I didn't have long to wait.

"Care for some company?" It was Shaniah.

I knew the routine. She'd sit with me and order expensive drinks—which I'd pay for. She'd engage in some chat to warm me up, all the while trying to sell me on the idea of a visit to one of the booths.

"Actually," I said, dispensing with the formalities and shouting to make myself heard above the constant throb of the music, "I was hoping for a private dance."

"Buy me a drink first, lover."

Business paramount: she was after her cut of the commission. "Whatever you want," I said.

"And for you, lover?"

I knew she'd be disappointed if I ordered another Perrier. The big money was in premium drinks.

"Champagne," I said to the waiter, who, with eyes like an eagle's, had promptly appeared at my table. "Bollinger."

He disappeared and returned with a bottle of Bolly and two glasses, then deftly poured a measured amount into each. I paid cash while Shaniah checked the availability of the tapestry-lined rooms.

"It's £25 a song," she said, as I put away my wallet, "or £200 for half an hour."

"Nothing in between…?" I mused.

"In between is negotiable," Shaniah said. "Come with me."

The two glasses of champagne and the bottle they'd been poured from followed us to a vacant booth in the corner. The waiter deposited them on a little gilded wood table (copied from Louis XIV, a reasonable facsimile, not at all cheap) and Shaniah drew the heavy brocade curtains closed behind us to maintain the illusion of privacy.

"Cash in advance," she reminded me.

I gave her the money, which she placed on the table beside the champagne.

"These are the rules," she said. "You must sit with your hands by your side. You mustn't touch. OK?"

The club (indeed, the law of the land) demanded compliance. A dancer might writhe all over me but I was not allowed to return the compliment. That was the official line, anyway. All the clubs had CCTV in the private booths, but I was pretty certain the dancers knew where the cameras were focused and thus could avoid their scrutiny—if they wished.

"OK," I said, arranging myself like an obedient schoolboy.

"If you touch me I'll give you a slap. As a warning."

"OK."

"If you touch me again, one more warning. Once more and you're finished. Out. OK?"

"OK," I said.

She put some music on—Billy Idol's "Cradle of Love"—and began to dance, slowly, rhythmically, snaking herself around in time to the driving beat. Her hands caressed her shoulders, her breasts, her hips and thighs; she twirled and whirled, placing her foot on the chair between my legs, bending forward to show me what was underneath the pink satin bra, and then offering me a peek behind the knickers. She reached behind and unhooked the bra and slid it off, sliding it around my neck while she offered one of her nipples to me. Dropping the bra to the floor, she caressed her breasts, then turned around and brushed my chest with her bottom, swaying her hips in time to the music.

I'd be telling a lie if I didn't admit to some serious arousal at that point. Shaniah had a gorgeous body that she obviously took care of, and she knew how to dance. Properly and with a good deal of grace and, actually, a good deal of skill.

She stood astride me and slipped off the knickers, then gradually lowered herself so that her most intimate parts were about an inch away from mine. Then grasping the arms of the chair, she balanced herself so that she was, as light as a feather, rubbing herself against me.

"You like that, lover?" she said, stroking my cheeks with her nipples.

"I do. Very much."

She slid away and turned around, gliding her hands over her bottom, sitting on my lap again, pumping and gyrating, then twisted herself away, caressing her arms, her legs, her breasts, between her legs.

As the song ended, she touched my lips with her fingers, quickly, deftly, then slid away to the floor and posed for me, so that I could see her beautiful naked body in its entirety.

"Want some more, lover?"

That was how she made her money…one 4:38 minute song at a time. Or, more likely, 3:00 minutes. Those 85 extra Billy Idol seconds were a clever enticement.

"You mentioned something about negotiable," I said, as she put her bra and knickers back on.

"What did you have in mind, lover?"

"I'd like to meet you after your shift's over," I said.

I caught the look on her face. Not allowed. Breaking the rules.

"Just coffee," I said. "I'm not after a date. I'm investigating a possible crime. I'd like to ask you some questions. I'll pay for your time."

"You a copper?" she asked, suspiciously.

"No. But I've been asked to look into a reported theft. At Cha-Cha's."

"Whatever got taken, I had nothing to do with it."

Her demeanour was changing, rapidly. Suddenly, she wasn't so much a hot and sexy seductress as she was a defensive and slightly annoyed young woman, half-dressed in a bra, knickers and stockings.

"I didn't say you did. I'm asking because you might have some information that could help me."

"Doubt it," she said, not looking at me. "We're finished here, yeah?"

"I'll pay you. Cash. Two hundred pounds for half an hour. More if we talk longer."

That got her attention. The offer of £200 for nothing more than a chat was appealing. And if she'd just stolen £10,000 from Holly's locker I doubted she'd have been anywhere nearly as interested.

"And I'll buy you breakfast," I added. "Full English."

That made her laugh. "Sausages and all?"

"Sausages, eggs, bacon, tomatoes, toast, the lot."

"OK," she said, relenting at last. "I'm off work at six. Meet me outside the front door."

"Thank you."

I took another £25 out of my wallet, and left it beside the cash and the drinks on the faux Louis XIV table.

"See you at six," I said.

CHAPTER NINE

It was about 5 a.m. and it was beginning to rain. I walked round to a 24-hour cafe in Frith Street and stood under the awning while I had a smoke. Then I went inside and ordered their Full English Breakfast for myself and made it last for an hour.

Just before six I went back to Satin & Silk, half-expecting Shaniah wouldn't show. But I was wrong. She appeared in jeans and a sweatshirt and an anorak, still wearing all of her makeup but minus the brightly coloured hibiscus in her hair.

I took her back to the cafe. I had a coffee, and, keeping my promise, bought her a Full English, to which she added a glass of milk.

"If I have coffee or tea I'll never get to sleep," she said. "And I've got a class at two."

"A class?" I asked, thinking she was honing her dancing skills or perhaps indulging in a spot of yoga.

"I'm doing my Master's in Medieval and Renaissance Studies at UCL."

That did surprise me.

"Lots of girls strip to pay for their studies. Shall I entertain you with some Middle English? *But wel I woot expres, withoute lye, God bad us for to wexe and multiplye: That gentil text can I wel understonde.*"

I set my spare phone to Record and placed it in the middle of the table. "I've no idea what you just told me, but could you say it all again?"

"Chaucer," she said. "The Wyf of Bathe. *The Canterbury Tales.*

She's waxing lyrical about the joys of sex."

"Astounding," I said. "Who knew?"

"Well, clearly, I did," she said, amused, "even if you didn't." She glanced a little apprehensively at my phone.

"You OK with that?" I asked.

Shaniah thought for a moment, then nodded. "So what got stolen at Cha-Cha's?"

"Ten thousand pounds," I said.

"What, from the bar?"

"From a locker," I said. "In the dancers' dressing room."

Shaniah gave me a look. "Whoever's locker it was, she must have had a bloody good night."

I smiled. "The locker belonged to a woman who called herself Chanel. I've been told you know her."

"Oh yeah?" Shaniah said, cutting up a sausage. "Who told you that?"

"She did, actually. You used to do private dances together."

"Yeah," Shaniah said. "We did."

"She gave me the impression you were pals."

"Did she," Shaniah said, clearly unimpressed.

"However my colleague interviewed some of the other dancers and they suggested you and she might have been involved in some kind of feud."

"I'd take the word of the other dancers if I were you."

"Chanel also told me you'd provided her with an introduction to Arthur Braskey."

"I don't remember that. And why would I, anyway?"

"But you know who Arthur Braskey is?"

"'Course I do. He's a regular at Cha-Cha's. Very fond of private dances. If he takes a liking to you, you're more or less guaranteed an exclusive evening every time he comes in."

"So Chanel wouldn't have needed an introduction."

"No," she said. "She could talk to him anytime she liked. Why? Is it to do with the stolen money?"

"Tell me more about Chanel," I said.

"She wasn't popular with the other girls," Shaniah said, with a little snigger. "If you popped away from a table to use the loo or if it was your turn up on the stage, she'd move in and steal your customer. And she was rude. If she didn't like you, you soon knew it. Me, I like to get along with everyone. Not a nasty bone in my body. But Chanel." She shook her head.

"What about the lesbian act you did with her in the private rooms?"

"I never trusted her," Shaniah said, with her mouth full of egg. "She was nasty. She'd push the envelope, you know?"

I didn't say anything.

"She knew what you weren't comfortable doing. She knew your limits. And she'd do it anyway because it meant more money from the punters."

"And that was why you were feuding with her?"

"I wouldn't really call it a feud. More an all-out general dislike. But you do what you need to do to make extra cash. And we did look good together. It's all about appearances in this business."

"How much do you actually know about her?"

"Not a fuck of a lot. I can tell you she's not what she claims though. For one thing, she's not bloody English."

"I noticed that too," I said. "I've got a good ear. She has an accent. She covers it well, but it's slightly…what? Eastern European?"

"Could be. A lot of the girls are."

"She has a British passport."

"Have you had a look at it?"

I shook my head.

"You should. It would tell you where she was born, wouldn't it?"

A competent investigator would have asked to have seen Holly's passport at the door. But she'd distracted me with that kiss. Clever girl.

"Do you know anything about the money that went missing from Chanel's locker last week?" I asked, carefully.

"Told you," Shaniah said. "No."

"So that night—the last night you worked there—she didn't say anything about it, or mention it to anyone?"

"She didn't say a word. And we were all in the room together changing after the club closed."

"Is it usual for dancers to keep their keys in their boots?"

Shaniah laughed. "Is that what she told you?"

"It is, actually."

"No, it's not usual. You don't trust anyone. You don't bring anything valuable to work and you certainly don't put your key where everyone can see it." She drank her milk. "I have a combination lock, in case you were going to ask. Easy to memorize the number. No messing about with keys."

"What do you keep in your locker?" I asked.

"Not much. Outside clothes. Jacket. Bag. Makeup. Hair stuff. Couple of costume changes. Nothing worth stealing unless you're desperate."

"Would anyone notice if one of the girls opened a locker that didn't belong to them?"

"Have you seen the size of the dressing room at Cha-Cha's?"

"I have. But it wasn't occupied when I was there."

"Imagine it with about seventy of us coming and going. Some might notice, most wouldn't."

"Did you know Chanel was deeply in debt?"

"I know she liked going to the casinos. But no. She kept to herself. Some girls like to share everything, every bloody detail of their lives. Not her. And if she owed so much, why did she have £10 thousand in her locker? Seems bloody stupid to me. She knew how dodgy it was. She'd had money stolen before."

"You know about that?"

"Yeah, last November. Fifty-six pounds. She let us know all about that one. Screamed the bloody place down and blamed it on the Tallinn girls. Three of them, from Estonia."

"I understand they operated a bit like a gang. They didn't like her."

"They didn't," Shaniah agreed, wiping off her plate with a slice of toast.

"I understand they sent her a threatening letter, trying to intimidate her."

"No idea. Doesn't surprise me, though. Shit happens."

She'd finished her breakfast. I could tell she was impatient to leave and get some sleep before her afternoon class at the university.

I took £400 out of my wallet and slipped it across the table. "As promised."

"You only promised me £200."

"For half an hour. We've been talking for an hour."

"You must have very deep pockets," she said, with a grin, counting out £200 and giving me back the rest. "I'm not greedy. Buy yourself another private dance."

"I won't be going back," I said. "I was only there to have a chat with you."

"Have I helped?"

"Very much. Thank you." I paused. "What's your real name? Just curious."

"Cathy," she said. "What's yours?"

"Jason."

"Nice to meet you, Jason. See you again some time."

I watched her as she walked away. It was a bit peculiar remembering that a few hours earlier she'd been brushing her nipples against my lips and writhing naked on the floor at my feet. Somehow all of that had disappeared from my mind as I was talking to her.

Still, an evening spent in a lap-dancing club was not without its after-effects. I switched off the mobile and popped it into my pocket, then went outside.

It was past 7 a.m. Katey would be awake and getting ready for work. I dialled her number from my regular phone.

We'd met on the same cruise which had brought about the end of the *Sapphire*. Katey Shawcross was with a group of British travel agents. We'd discovered one another in the middle of an Alaskan rainstorm, seeking shelter by the coffee machine on aft Lido. I'd ended up saving her life.

We'd caught up with one another again after I came back from my travels. I would call our relationship independently faithful. Thoughts of marriage have never been entertained.

"Do you absolutely have to go into the office today?" I asked, lighting up a post-breakfast smoke.

"Well," she said, thinking. "I've got a cruise to arrange down the Rhine for the top fifty salespeople from a chain of furniture stores you wouldn't be caught dead in. And a thatched beach hut in a lagoon in the Maldives for a randy exec who fancies a romantic fuck with his bit on the side. What did you have in mind?"

"I wouldn't mind a romantic fuck in a thatched beach hut," I said. "But since we're stuck in London, a morning of passionate love-making in a dusty Georgian conversion will have to suffice."

"You've convinced me," Katey said. "See you in an hour?"

#

I don't drive in Central London if I can help it. Aside from the Congestion Charge, it costs a fortune to park anywhere within walking distance of the club. And after a long night onstage I'd really rather just pay a taxi driver to whisk me home.

Soho was stumbling out of bed as I made my way towards Shaftesbury Avenue, where I knew I'd have a better chance of finding a cab at that hour.

As I trudged down Frith Street I became aware that I was being followed. Not by a person—by a car. It was motoring along quietly behind me, keeping up with my pace, deliberately not pulling ahead.

Just before Shaftesbury Avenue the driver suddenly shot past me and came to a dead stop. The back passenger door opened, blocking my way on the pavement. I'd seen that sort of thing in films. It was never a good thing.

"Mr. Figgis."

The voice was coming from inside the car—it was a Mercedes E-type. Lunar Blue. Very new.

I bent down and met the gaze of a fellow who looked about seventy, with thinning grey hair combed gracefully back from his forehead, carefully-tended eyebrows and a dimple in his chin that somehow managed to lessen the severity of his thin-lipped scowl. He was wearing an expensive camel overcoat and he was sitting in the back seat.

"Please join me, Mr. Figgis."

I thought it best to accept the offer.

"Shut the door."

I did. The driver immediately pulled away from the curb and turned north onto Shaftesbury Avenue.

"My name is Arthur Braskey, Mr. Figgis. I understand you've been asking after me."

"Word travels fast."

"It does in Soho."

"There are actually one or two questions I would like to ask you," I said.

"I don't normally accommodate private investigators but since you're not a professional, I'll allow you to humour me. I'm hosting a charity event on Friday evening at 7 p.m. I'd like you to attend."

"I'm afraid I have to work Friday night."

"Tsk tsk," said Arthur Braskey. "Incorrect answer. Shall we try it again? I'm hosting a charity event on Friday evening at 7 p.m. It would be in your best interests to attend."

He waited for my response. We were speeding towards

Bloomsbury.

"OK," I said.

"Excellent. I guarantee we'll be finished in time for you to take to the stage at eleven."

The Mercedes slid to a smooth stop at Russell Street.

"Open the door, Mr. Figgis."

I did as I was told.

"I'll send you the details. I have your email address. And the address of your flat. My driver will pick you up at five. You may exit the car, Mr. Figgis."

I climbed out.

"See you on Friday, Mr. Figgis. Shut the door."

I closed it with care and the Mercedes glided away.

There was a taxi idling about ten feet ahead of me. I got in.

"I'll give you an extra twenty if you can get me home in the next ten minutes," I said. "Because I really fucking need to use the loo."

CHAPTER TEN

I was rattled.

I don't have anything to do with London's underworld. I'm a decent guy. There's nothing remotely dodgy in my background and I've never had any kind of reason to seek out one of Soho's most infamous crime figures. I may have chatted with one or two of them at the club, but that's it. They were there to be entertained and I was there to oblige.

Arthur Braskey was different. I had knowledge of something—someone—and he was concerned about it.

My flat's on the first floor of a Georgian-era conversion near Angel tube station on Pentonville Road. I've looked up the building's history. The family who lived there when it was first built occupied all four floors: kitchen in the cellar, servants in the attic, 18th century family discourse conducted everywhere in between.

My lounge and kitchen were created out of what used to be the main drawing room at the front of the house. And my bedroom at the back takes up most of what was once a second drawing room.

The former ante-room between the two is now a very compact but functional loo. Which was where I headed as soon as I got in.

And then, while I waited for Katey to arrive, I made myself a strong cup of coffee and downloaded the chat with Shaniah off my phone and onto my computer for safe-keeping.

I'd also made notes. I reviewed them quickly, just to make sure I hadn't missed anything, then I wrote the date on the last page and tucked the notebook into a box on a shelf in the lounge where I keep all my important stuff—tax receipts, investment notices, scraps of paper where I've scribbled ideas for songs.

And then I checked my emails.

A message from Arthur Braskey was waiting in my Inbox, with the subject line *Invitation: Little Brickford Charity Firewalk*.

I could literally feel my heart dropping into my stomach.

Braskey really didn't think…oh fuck, oh yes he did.

I read the message with that cold feeling you get where you can literally taste the dread in your mouth.

Dear Mr. Figgis,

You have been invited to walk on fire!

Firewalking is the practice of walking barefoot on hot embers. The Braskey Foundation is offering you the opportunity to prove what you're made of in Little Brickford this Friday night.

No previous experience is required. Experts have been retained to train you in a special session prior to the event.

Ask your family, friends and colleagues to sponsor you to take on this highly motivational challenge. And then ask them to come along to watch you and the other participants and cheer you on while you battle the burning embers and raise money for a worthwhile cause.

Live music and food will be provided, and there will be a bar with drinks for the spectators.

Your registration fee has been waived by Mr. Braskey, as has the need to register at the event beforehand. Your fundraising target is £100.

Training at 6pm, firewalk at 7pm.

Important: you will not be allowed to take part without full training beforehand.

Please read the attached Frequently Asked Questions.

Please read the attached need-to-know document.

Mr. Braskey's car will call for you at your flat at 5pm this Friday.

Best wishes,

The Braskey Foundation

Fucking hell. I'd heard of firewalks. Big companies used them to motivate their workers and build confidence and foster teamwork under the umbrella of "employee engagement". Firewalks also featured big in charity fund-raising events. I'd never been to one. And I'd never ever entertained thoughts of taking part in one.

"It'll be a doddle," Katey assured me, when she finally arrived, bearing artisan chocolates, a bottle of posh-smelling massage stuff and a new little toy with six speeds and freshly-inserted batteries.

"Have you ever done one?" I countered, sceptically.

"No, but I know people who have. The training they give you beforehand is part instruction and part motivation. There's nothing mystical or magic about it. It's pure physics. "

"I don't suppose you could educate me in the physics part," I said.

"I would if I could remember exactly how it worked," Katey replied. "I'd have to look it up. And anyway, we're not here to discuss your feet—although if we got naked quickly…" She kissed me. "…I might think about including them in a fully-inclusive tour around your very attractive body, "

"I love it when you go all travel-agenty on me," I said.

"I'll skip the cheesy flight attendant euphemisms," she said, switching on her new buzzy toy and skimming it lightly over my chest, teasing me, leading me to my bed. "Assume the position…and prepare to be oiled."

#

Afterwards, basking in exquisite contentedness at opposite ends of the bath—it's large enough for two and has taps in the middle—Katey kissed my toes and said:

"You're in for a bit of a surprise on Friday."

"You're not making me feel any better about it."

"I promise I'll be standing by to assist with any tender ministrations that might be required afterwards."

"Even worse," I said.

"And I'll sponsor you for twenty quid. Will that help?"

"I still need another £80."

"Says the guy who inherited a lifetime of royalties from "Roving Minstrel" and, like Hugh Grant in *About a Boy*, doesn't actually need to work in order to pay his bills."

"Doesn't need to," I said. "But wants to. Obviously."

It's been an ongoing conversation with us. I would gladly assist with Katey's financial well-being. She won't let me. We seem to enjoy the friction that arises from this arrangement. It certainly keeps things interesting.

"So," Katey said, changing the subject. "This newfound

obsession of yours…private investigating. Is it going to be a thing?"

"It might be," I said.

"Have you always wanted to solve intriguing mysteries or has your *Inspector Morse* passion finally got the better of you?"

I laughed. "I don't think I meet the criteria of a police procedural."

"No," said Katey, "you don't."

"Perhaps a cosy…?"

"Like the stuff your sister writes? Not enough sex. And the protagonist is usually a female. I think you very definitely fall into the category of unlicensed amateur sleuth."

She slid up in the water so that she could kiss me.

"Shall we go back to the thatched beach hut or stay here in our personal lagoon to continue our discussion about private investigations?"

\#

"I like doing it," I said.

"What," said Katey, as she pulled on her knickers, "making love to me?"

"Yes. But aside from that."

She reached for her bra, which had ended up slung over the back of a chair in the bedroom. She has nice breasts. Perfect nipples. Much prettier than Shaniah's.

"I enjoy solving things," I said. "And I seem to be good at it."

Katey pulled on her blouse without comment and began a hunt for her trousers.

"Under the bed," I said.

"Thanks."

She found her boots.

"You know the money's long gone," she said, at last. "If it was ever there in the first place. You suspect—no, you know—this Holly woman's lying through her teeth. And now you've stumbled into London's criminal underworld and if you don't show up for Arthur Braskey's firewalk tomorrow, you and any number of the digits you require to play your guitar may end up regretting it. Why on earth are you bothering?"

It was a fair question.

"I just wanted to return a favour for Sal," I said.

"And now?"

"I want to know what Holly's really up to."

"You have a need to distinguish yourself," Katey corrected. "Which stems from the rather annoying certainty that you will never, ever, be able to escape from the musical legacy that was Figgis Green. In which case I think you should take your brother-in-law's advice and do it properly and get yourself licensed."

"It involves a course."

"Then do the course," Katey said, putting on her coat.

"I haven't done courses since I left school."

"Oh please. Now you're just making excuses. Look at me. Lifelong learner. I had to get proper certification to work as a travel agent. And I have to do workshops to stay current. Plus I did that thing last year in Greek and Roman Mythology through the Open Uni…" She wrapped her scarf around her neck and leaned over to kiss me goodbye. "Not because I had to, but because I wanted to. Proper assignments and an end-of-module essay. Ask me anything about the *Fall of Icarus* or Ovid's *Metamorphoses*."

"What years did they represent Britain at Eurovision and are they available on Spotify?"

"Clever clogs," Katey said, opening my front door. "I'm going to work. Have fun at the studio. And don't worry too much about the firewalk. They can do amazing things with skin grafts these days. See you tomorrow."

And with one more farewell kiss, she was gone.

I didn't have time to faff about. I was due at Collingwood and it was my song we were doing this time. I didn't dare show up late.

I got dressed and collected my guitar and sheet music and carried it down to my car, which was parked around the back of the building in a paved-over space that had once probably been a small private garden.

I've got an old silver Volvo V70. It's fast, reliable and tough, and has room for all my gear in the back if I'm playing a gig somewhere that isn't the Blue Devil. I bought it second-hand from the police after a tip from Angie's husband.

I was stowing my guitar when I realized I'd left my mobile sitting on the kitchen table.

I ran back inside and up the stairs and grabbed my phone and went out again, just in time to see an opportunistic scumbag helping himself to my Strat.

"Oy!" I shouted, racing off after him as he bolted.

He didn't get very far. Solid bodies weigh a fair bit—don't let that devil-may-care onstage attitude of rock gods fool you. When you see a wide strap over a musician's shoulder instead of a trendy slim one, it's there for a reason. Muscle strain's just one of the side-effects of slinging six-strings. And my guitar was in its hard travel case, too.

This guy quickly decided it was him or the Strat and correctly sussed that I'd much rather have my guitar back than beat him to within an inch of his life for taking it. He ditched it and disappeared around the corner.

I wasn't winded in the least—but he was. I made a mental note of his description as I picked the case up off the ground. He'd looked about thirty. Not scruffy. Needed a shave but he'd had a decent haircut recently and his clothes definitely didn't look as if he'd been sleeping rough in them. I'd remember him if I saw him again.

I put my guitar into the back of the Volvo, and then I drove to Collingwood Sound.

#

It was my turn to shine. We were doing "Smoke Drifts", which I think falls somewhere between easy swing and highly accessible jazz, and which I hoped was going to be the ticket that finally got us through the door of a major label in London.

I'd written it so we could play it at the club. But after listening to the rough demo I'd done on my computer, with me playing lead guitar and the rest of the instruments dubbed in digitally, Trev had made an executive decision and had hired a few extra musicians. The live room at Collingwood now contained—in addition to the Hammond organ, the wonderful old Steinway, Ken's tenor sax and Rudy's full drum kit—an upright bass, two trombones, a couple of trumpets and an extra sax. And all of the ladies and gentlemen whose job it was to play them.

It was a tight fit once we'd all taken our places. But I had a feeling it was going to sound magnificent.

Since my main melody line was largely going to be echoed by the Hammond organ with support from the Steinway—and since Trev's skills were needed behind the desk for what was going to be a fairly complex production—he'd hired two excellent keyboard players: Mary Clarke, who I knew from many, many gigs around London, and Joss Wilson, who'd provided the piano on dozens of British chart toppers in the 1960s and 1970s and had not been out of work since. In fact, the entire band was Trev's UK version of the Wrecking Crew.

I plugged myself in, perched on my high stool and tuned up. The nice thing about my Strat is that, although it's a copy of my dad's old original, it's a newer issue, so it's got a five-way pickup selector switch instead of the three my dad had to jiggle to get the sound he wanted. I set the switch for Middle and Neck and I was ready to go.

We rehearsed "Smoke Drifts" three times. timing it at three minutes, ten seconds. The musicians were so excellent that by the third time through, it was perfect. Trev recorded each run-through in case one of them proved to be better than the final take, but when we went live for the demo, I knew we had a winner.

It was six o'clock by the time we were done and people were hungry. There was an Indian restaurant near the studio that had a private room for a group as large as ours.

"Not coming, Jason?" Rudy asked. "I've never known you to turn down a celebratory Chicken Biryani."

"There's someone I need to speak to," I said. In truth I'd have chosen a Ruby over Holly any day, but Katey's questions had hit home and I hadn't been making it up: I really did want answers.

"See you at the club, then.

I had a thought.

"I've been signed up to do a charity firewalk tomorrow," I said. "Would you like to sponsor me?"

Rudy laughed. "Walking on hot coals? You? After what you went through on the *Sapphire*? You're a glutton for punishment, you are."

It was true. The ship had caught fire before she sank—the fire was actually the main reason why she'd gone to the bottom—and I'd been caught in the middle of it. It was the main reason I'd ended up in the hospital.

"Come along and cheer me on," I said. "I'll text you the details."

"Why not," said Rudy. "And put me down for twenty quid. All for an excellent cause, I suppose."

I didn't tell him that the excellent cause was my continued wellbeing. And I realized, as I was walking back to my car, that I hadn't thought about the *Sapphire* at all when I'd been reviewing the details about the firewalk. But I'd nonetheless been overcome by a terrible feeling of apprehension… and now I knew why. Your subconscious never lets you forget.

I checked the time. Six forty-five. Sitting in my car, I rang Holly. She took her time answering.

"Hello Mr. Private Investigator," she said, as, obviously, my name had flashed up on her screen. "What can I do for you?"

"The last time we met, you told me if I thought of anything else I might like to ask, I should give you a call."

"I did," she mused. "Didn't I."

"I've got a couple of hours before I'm due at work. Could I come round?"

She paused. "Actually, it's not convenient. Not at the moment."

I wondered briefly what might make a visit from me inconvenient when she owed Arthur Braskey £10,000, had no means to repay the debt and was counting on my services to locate the missing cash. And, just as briefly, I'd sussed the answer. I wondered if Sal had any inkling.

"How about a quick five-minute chat over the phone, then?" I said, surmising that whoever she was expecting wouldn't be there 'til seven. Billing would begin at the top of the hour. Much tidier that way.

"Yes. All right."

"I've had a little talk with Shaniah. And she contradicted a few of the details that you'd shared with me."

"Well, she would, wouldn't she? I ought to have warned you that she is not to be trusted. She didn't mention, I suppose, that she was—still is—one of Braskey's 'favourites'."

"She did say that if Arthur Braskey took a liking to a dancer, he would ask for her each time he came into the club, and that he paid well."

"There are other…shall we say…advantages."

"So she's still in touch with Braskey?"

"Of course. You must exercise great caution. You are on precarious ground."

As much as I didn't want to believe her, what she was saying might have been the truth. After Shaniah had left me, there'd been a short lag of time while I chatted with Katey and then walked back through Soho. Had it been enough time for Shaniah to contact Braskey, and enough time for him to get up, get dressed, summon his driver and, from wherever he happened to be in London, locate me and follow me down Frith Street?

It seemed unlikely, but for all I knew he'd been sitting in his car around the corner and had been five minutes away the entire time.

"Perhaps," Holly said, "it would be best—for you—if we simply abandoned the investigation."

"What about for you? What about the money you owe Braskey?"

"Use your imagination, Jason. How do you think I might be able to solve that dilemma? I'll manage."

"Before he discovers where you're hiding?"

"I've moved. I'm no longer at the Crestone Hotel."

That was a surprise. I was pretty certain she hadn't told Sal.

"Would you care to share the details of where you're staying?"

"I don't believe that would be in my best interests."

"Fair enough. One more question—where were you born?"

There was silence at Holly's end. Then: "Enfield. Why do you ask?"

"Because you have a slight accent and I can't quite pinpoint it."

"My parents are from Kazakhstan. I was born here but they spoke Kazakh in our home and so it was the first language I learned. I didn't speak English until I started school."

"All right," I said. "When were you born?

"April 12, 1990."

"And Medford isn't really your last name."

"Correct. My father changed our surname when I was a child. He thought it would help him find work. He was a structural engineer in Kazakhstan. He anglicized all of our first names, too. He was Marat—and he became Matthew. My mother was Dinara...Diana."

"And you?"

"Halila."

"Of course. And did it help?"

"Did it help my father find work? Not really. His CV got him noticed, but once they heard him speak, even though both of my parents took lessons to improve their English, he was never able to master the interviews."

"What was your last name before your father changed it?"

"Medenov," Holly said. "Couldn't you guess?"

"Not being overly familiar with Kazakh naming conventions...no."

Holly laughed. It was genuine, and not at all mocking.

"I must go," she said. "It was lovely to speak with you again. Please consider what I've told you about Braskey."

And she disconnected.

I'd been taking notes while we talked, scribbling fragments of words and sentences onto the back of a sheet of paper that had the Hammond organ chords from "Smoke Drifts" on the other side. I transferred everything into my notebook before the details faded from my memory.

And then I rang Sal.

CHAPTER ELEVEN

"I didn't know she'd moved," Sal said, sounding truly taken aback. "But it's just as well—I'm in trouble for comping her a room for more than a week and I was going to have to ask her to leave anyway. I was just ringing around to other hotels to see if I could call in any favours. Where's she staying?"

"She wouldn't say. I did ask."

"Hang on, Jase…"

There was a muffled conversation as Sal put her hand over her mobile, and then she was back with me.

"Sorry…I'm still at work. One of our clerks has been skimming guests' credit cards. I'm having to deal with the fallout."

"I thought your video surveillance took care of that sort of thing."

"It does. But the front desk camera's been down for a week. We're waiting for repairs."

"How fortunate for your clerk," I said. "Will you have her arrested?"

"Him. Of course, if the police can find him. He quit yesterday before he could be sussed."

"What's his name?"

"Stanislav Turcan."

"From Eastern Europe."

"Moldova," Sal confirmed. "Why?"

"Just a thought. Probably nothing. While I have you on the line, did you send a reply to that PI in Vancouver?"

"I did, actually. I emailed him and told him I wanted very much to be put in touch with Gina. Jennifer. And I got an answer straightaway. The thing is, Jase…she's here. She's in London now."

I didn't say anything. I'd expected an update. Some back and forth conversations and deliberations and some well-thought-out decisions. Some breathing room.

This was happening far too quickly. I was still getting used to the revelation that I'd had sex with Sal. I hadn't even begun to process the fact that I had a daughter who was nearly thirty and that Dom had an older sister—half-sister—and that my mum and my own sister and Katey were going to be dumbfounded.

Or worse.

"And we've been in touch," Sal said.

"You and Jennifer?"

"Yes. We've spoken. Over the phone."

Again. I didn't know what to say. I felt like someone had punched me in the stomach and paralysed my lungs. I was literally struggling to breathe.

"She's lovely, Jase. I was so worried about what she'd think…why I'd given her up…how I could have done it. But she hasn't got any anger in her at all. She understands why. She grew up in a wonderful family. She always knew she was adopted…they told her as soon as she was old enough to understand. She loves her parents. They're both teachers. She has a brother and a sister…also adopted."

"It all sounds perfect," I said. It was a useless thing to say. But I was, at that moment, incapable of anything more profound.

"It is perfect. I'm so relieved. And happy. We're having dinner. Tomorrow."

I still couldn't breathe.

"I've got a DNA kit from Boots. She's absolutely fine about doing the test. If it's positive we'll arrange for the proper legal one, just so everything's done the right way."

I'd never heard Sal sound so animated.

"She doesn't want anything…does she?" Wrong thing to ask. Wrong tone of voice. Totally wrong timing.

"How do you mean, Jase?"

"Sorry, Sal. Just my sense of caution. Maybe I've been unduly influenced by this whole Holly thing. I don't want you to be hurt. You don't know anything about her…only what she's told you. She might have…other motives."

"Such as money?"

"Or she might be in a bad way, she's lost her job or her flat and she needs somewhere to live…"

"I think that's extremely ungenerous of you."

I deserved that. And there was an edge in her voice I'd never heard before.

"Anyway, your fortune is safe. I haven't mentioned anything about you."

"Thank you," I said. "And I didn't mean it to come out that way. I'm sorry."

"I know what you meant, Jase. But I think it was uncalled-for. I appreciate your concern. I'll be careful."

#

Suitably chastised—I'd deserved it—I rang Angie and she promised to part with £20, as did Tom. For good measure I asked my mum, who was both bemused and concerned at the thought of me walking on hot coals.

"Does it involve some sort of voodoo or exotic mumbo jumbo?" she inquired. "Ought I to come along and wave a silver cross or something to ward off pagan fire demons?"

"A £20 sponsorship would accomplish much the same thing," I said.

"Then I shall, dear. Can you at least wear thick wool socks?"

"Unfortunately not," I said. "I'll be barefoot."

"I'll say a little prayer for you. I'm just trying to remember…there must be a patron saint of feet."

I waited.

"Ah," she said, after a moment. "Google is our friend. Saint Servatius. I shall send him an extra special invocation."

"Thank you," I said. My mum's religious leanings have got more pronounced as she ages. I suspect she's hedging her bets for the afterlife, just in case. She's seventy-six, but I expect her to be around 'til at least her mid-nineties. Her side of the family is exceptionally long-lived.

I was overcome by an odd sense of relief. I'd done it. Arthur Braskey wasn't going to be able to render me into a block of concrete for not meeting my £100 minimum.

I had a few more hours 'til I was due at the club, so I drove home and went online to seriously look into what I needed to do if I wanted to become a licensed PI. To be honest, it was all a bit daunting. There were a lot of places offering introductions to the industry and "tasters" of what you needed to know. Suggestions for those who were thinking of a career in investigations (*Seek training in legal matters as well as business, prepare a stellar CV, offer your freelance services to credit reference agencies, charities and banks, and above all, don't expect adventure, excitement and romance!*). And, of course, the Institute of Professional Investigators, who had a course—*the* course, which came with an IQ Level 3 Examination—that I would be required to complete before the UK government would even begin to consider granting me a license.

My academic CV was dismal. No college—I'm from the generation that went straight out to work at sixteen after graduating from the local Comprehensive, when university wasn't the mandatory qualification it is now. I have three GCSE's—English, Maths and Music. My passport says I'm a musician. That's all I've ever been. Not a very good recommendation for someone wanting to embark upon a midlife career in professional sleuthing.

I tried to distract myself with the notes Arthur Braskey had provided with his invitation to the firewalk. One was a FAQ, the other a need-to-know document, and neither of them was particularly useful. I wanted to find out what to expect. Instead, I was advised to attend the training session beforehand, where all of my urgent questions would be answered in due course.

I googled firewalking and found some great photos and glowing reports...but nothing that actually explained how I ought to prepare, mentally and physically. You'd have thought I was trying to find out how the world's most infamous magic tricks were performed...everywhere I looked had cagey references to the mysterious pre-event orientation, but offered up nothing by way of what actual knowledge was imparted to the participants in the process.

I eventually had to abandon my search.

It was time to go to work.

#

The red brick building that houses the Blue Devil is three storeys high. The club occupies the basement and the main floor and the top two floors are offices. It was built around 1838 and the club's been occupying the premises, in one form or another, since about 1930.

The public side of the venue's been upgraded and renovated a couple of times, but the dressing rooms are still tiny and old and windowless and a bit on the shabby side. I imagine, in 1838, they were probably used for storage. At least they have private loo's, which were thoughtfully added when the club first moved in.

The dressing room walls are bare brick, painted white, and they're lined with rows of framed photos of famous guest artists who've played at the club over the years. We have large mirrors and some good lights and the usual counter space, a sofa and some chairs, a small fridge (a nice addition—I keep a couple of bars of my favourite chocolate, Green & Black's Organic Ginger, in there) and a rack for hanging jackets and other clothes, if required—though we usually show up in what we're going to wear onstage.

At that particular moment, all four of us were having a conversation with our reflections.

"It was, as Ruby's go, one of the best in recent memory."

Rudy was letting me know what I'd missed earlier at our post-recording-session dinner.

"New chef?" I guessed.

"And a new and improved menu."

"With new and improved prices," Ken added, giving his hair a quick comb in the mirror. "Trev reckons we have a winner with those demo's. They're going out first thing in the morning."

"Excellent news," I agreed, glancing at Dave.

He looked terrible. There were deep shadows under his eyes and I knew he hadn't been sleeping. Or eating properly. If it was possible for a man to appear truly haunted, he definitely met the criteria.

"Nothing new about Gracie…?" I asked, as carefully as I could.

Dave shook his head. "Honestly, Jason, I don't know what else we can do. We've looked in all the places where we thought she'd go—where we know she always meet her mates, or goes shopping, or stops for something to eat."

"Have you talked to the police?"

He'd been reluctant, the last I recalled. This time, he surprised me.

"Helen rang them. They had her check with all of her friends—

nothing. They suggested we look at her emails, Facebook and Snapchat, all those things. Tabby knows her passwords but nothing's been updated since she disappeared. And she hasn't sent any messages. To anyone."

"Well," I said, "she may well have set up an email account that only a few of her closest friends know about."

If it had been me investigating her disappearance, I'd have gone back to those friends and grilled them about that. But Dave hadn't asked me—and I hadn't offered.

"What about the guy you think she ran off with?"

Dave gave me a look. He was surprised—perhaps ashamed—that I knew about that.

"Helen doesn't even know his name, Jason."

"But Helen had words with her about him. How did she find out Gracie was seeing him?"

"She overheard her talking to him on the phone. She demanded to know what was going on. She has the right to know. Gracie's fourteen. She has no business messing about with a bloke who's nearly thirty. Helen took away her mobile but of course she'd already erased his number."

"And her mates don't know his name either?"

"They claim they didn't even know she was seeing someone. She's never had any boyfriends."

I didn't say anything. I doubted Gracie was as innocent as her dad believed.

"Kids can be loyal to one another for all the wrong reasons," I said.

"The police suggested we go out and physically look for her. Which we've already been doing, night and day. But once you've eliminated the obvious…what then?"

"I could offer some suggestions," I said. "You won't like them."

Dave gave me another look. He was desperate.

"Chances are," I said, carefully, "this guy she's been seeing is in it for the money."

"She hasn't got any money. We're not all blessed with your kind of musical pedigree."

"Dave," I said. "That's not what I meant." There was no other way to say it. "He may have her working for sex. He may be pimping her out."

I knew he didn't want to think about that. And it was a hell of a thing to suggest just as we were about to go onstage.

But Dave surprised me again.

"Helen told me the same thing. I think she must have been talking to Gracie's brother. You learn a lot about the other side of life in the army."

"That should be your next step, then," I said. "There used to be a lot of activity along Edgware Road and around King's Cross, but that's all disappeared now. It's all gone online and into private brothels and massage places." I paused and nodded vaguely in the direction of Roly Barfield's club. "You should probably start here. In Soho."

There was a brief light in Dave's eyes—very brief—and then it was replaced by that gaunt look again.

"Thanks, mate," he said. "Next steps."

Before we went out to play, I tackled Ken to see if he wanted to sponsor my firewalk. It didn't feel right asking Dave. And after Ken had stopped laughing, he pledged £50—"For the sheer pleasure of witnessing you trying to hot-foot it over a bed of burning embers."

CHAPTER TWELVE

I tried to sleep after the taxi dropped me off at home after the show, but I wasn't remotely tired. I spent a good hour lying in bed, thinking about what was going to happen that evening. Actually it was more than thinking—my thoughts had turned into pure, unadulterated fear.

I had no idea why I was so terrified. Hundreds, thousands, of people had done charity firewalks and none of them had ended up in hospital with third degree burns. None that I'd ever heard about, anyway.

But they weren't involved with Arthur Braskey.

And they hadn't nearly been killed in a fire aboard a cruise ship and they hadn't lost their life partner to arson before that.

I'd gone for counselling. I'd needed it after the *Sapphire* sank, and chatting with a professional who understood what I'd gone through went a long way towards helping me come to terms with that and with losing Em five years earlier. I'd resolved the anger, the sense of helplessness, the nightmares about drowning and burning. I thought I'd been mended.

Why, then, was this one brief evening playing such havoc with my confidence?

I remembered what my wonderful psychologist had asked during our very first meeting.

"How do you usually deal with things which have upset you or caused you unhappiness or undue stress?"

It was an easy answer—something I'd always done automatically, without even thinking.

"I play my guitar," I said.

I rolled out of bed and woke up my computer and put on Pat Metheny. *Still Life (Talking)* from 1987. It won a Grammy for Best Jazz Fusion. It's got everything—jazz, folk, pop—and it's one of his most accessible albums. And that's what makes him my hero.

I got out my hollow-body Phoenix and plugged it in to a little amp I keep under my computer desk and played along to "Last Train Home", which I've always loved. It's so familiar—it's been everywhere: a Christmas commercial, a film, TV and radio theme, even an ad for bedding.

It was this last iteration which I hoped would work its magic on my restless imagination. And it did…eventually. I finally got to sleep around dawn, and stayed asleep until two in the afternoon.

I got up and had something to eat. I can't even remember what it was—scrambled eggs with cheese, probably, smothered in HP Sauce. And then, at precisely 5 p.m., as promised, Arthur Braskey's blue Mercedes pulled into my road and the driver rang me on my mobile to let me know he was waiting downstairs.

I thought Braskey had been cutting it close sending his driver around with just an hour to spare before I was due to attend the orientation. Little Brickford was in Hertfordshire, to the north of London, inside the Green Belt, but just far enough away that any delays enroute would absolutely guarantee I'd be late.

"Mind if I smoke?" I asked.

"Not at all, Mr. Figgis." The driver was silver-haired, respectable-looking. Someone's grandfather. The same guy who'd been behind the wheel earlier when Braskey'd followed me down Frith Street.

I lit up, and wondered if Little Brickford was actually where Grandad's boss lived. To distract myself as we slid through Islington, I tried to imagine his house: something hideously ultra-modern hidden away behind a high wall of hedges, probably built on the grave of an ancient character cottage he'd had bulldozed when he'd bought the property. An indoor pool. A huge kitchen with every conceivable convenience. Did he have a wife? A partner? A friend with benefits? Perhaps he employed a cook. Absolutely a gardener. And, of course, someone to look after the pool. And a housekeeper to keep the eight bedrooms—and their ensuite loos— presentable.

I checked my watch. I still wear one—a lovely old Rolex Explorer my dad gave me when I was in my twenties—though many people I know have abandoned them and rely on their phones to tell them the time. You need a watch when you're performing. When you chat, or make jokes, or meander off into impromptu musical explorations, you need to know when your gig time is up and you need to get offstage.

Holloway and then Highgate, negotiating heavy rush hour traffic. I was on my third ciggie. I know people who are OCD about being late. They'll arrive an hour before they're due somewhere because the idea of being delayed, even for two minutes, terrifies them. I'm not one of those. But why couldn't Braskey have sent his driver to collect me half an hour earlier?

Relax, I tried to tell myself. This is beyond your control. You're with his driver, for fuck's sake. If anyone's going to get a finger chopped off as punishment, it'll be him, not you.

It was twenty minutes to six and we were somewhere near Elstree on a tiny tree-lined lane, barely wide enough for a single car, when Grandad glided to a silent stop and turned around to apologise.

"Sorry, Mr. Figgis. Hopefully only a small delay."

It was my worst nightmare come true.

I opened the window and poked my head out. The lane was blocked by an accident. A car had hit a tree and crashed back onto the road, landing on its roof. A rescue crew was trying to extricate the driver while paramedics were tending to the passenger, who had been thrown clear but was in a very bad way. Lights were flashing. The police were in attendance, and ambulances.

"Can you turn around?" I asked, desperately.

"Not enough room," Grandad said. "And three cars behind me."

They must have come out of nowhere. Our road, 'til then, had been deserted.

I got out of the car, treading out my cigarette with the sole of my trainer.

"Could you possibly reverse down the lane?" I asked each of the drivers, in turn. "I'm in a bit of a dire situation and I need to be in Little Brickford in…" I checked my watch. "Fifteen minutes."

They were agreeable.

The last driver—a young woman with a sullen-looking boy in the passenger seat—put her Range Rover in reverse and pressed the accelerator and drove for about ten feet—then stalled.

"Fuck," she said, quite audibly, echoing exactly what I was thinking.

She tried again. The motor turned over but wouldn't catch.

She kept at it. I was afraid she was going to drain the battery. Nothing.

"Sorry," she said, with a hapless shrug. "I'll have to ring AA for a tow."

The Mercedes was boxed in. I briefly considered recruiting the other drivers to push the bloody Range Rover all the way back to the closest driveway, which I reckoned was about a quarter of a mile. But now there wasn't time.

I ran up to where the accident was. The police car was on the other side of it. I collared one of the constables.

"I'm sorry," I said, "but I need to get to Little Brickford. Quickly."

He gave me a withered look. "Not a lot I can do, son. As you can see."

"Could you possibly give me a lift?"

"In a word, no."

"It's a matter of life and death," I said, desperately.

"And this isn't?"

It was true. And I was stupid for even thinking it. The driver of the accident car was still trapped and was bleeding from a head wound. I didn't even know if he was conscious. His female passenger was being loaded into one of the ambulances—which was also on the other side, with the police cars.

I thought of pleading with the ambulance guys for a lift but realized in almost the same moment that they'd be speeding towards the A&E at the nearest big hospital and detours through tiny market towns to drop off demented musicians were not an option.

There were no other cars on the other side of the accident. The little lane was deserted.

I pulled out my phone and consulted Google Maps and saw that I was still a good 3 km away from Little Brickford. I could just about manage it, if I ran.

"I'm going on foot," I said, to Grandad. "Can you let Mr. Braskey know I'll be there as soon as I can?"

"Certainly, Mr. Figgis. I'll explain the circumstances. I'm sure he'll understand. Perhaps he can find someone willing to come out and collect you."

"That would be extremely helpful," I said.

I've never been a runner. I was on my school football team when

I was a kid, but that was forty years ago. Jogging's never appealed to me, and if I do any exercise it's usually just a long leisurely walk. I love walking. I don't love running.

My body reminded me of that after about two minutes. I was wearing trainers, which helped, but my lungs and my legs could only function on adrenalin for a limited amount of time before they surrendered to advancing middle age and stopped cooperating. I slowed to a brisk walk—I knew I could manage that—and began to rehearse in my mind the words I would use to plead with Arthur Braskey to spare my livelihood, if not my life.

Based on what Grandad had promised I half-expected to be met by a bemused vicar on a Moped or a minder with a scar on his face in an old black Rover…but neither of them materialized. Par for the course. It was half past six by the time I got to the outskirts of Little Brickford and found my way to the venue, which was a very large garden attached to a very ancient pub, The Cock and Maggot. It was pitch black outside and although a forecasted rain had held off, the night air felt decidedly damp.

Good, I thought, looking for Arthur Braskey. The more humidity the better. Perhaps they won't be able to light the fire.

Locating my host turned out to be more difficult than I'd supposed. Nobody seemed to know where he was. I found someone who was attached to the firewalk's organizers, who informed me that I'd missed the orientation but if I looked to my left I'd be able to see all of the participants coming out and if I wanted to join the well-wishers I was welcome to line up behind the rope and cheer them on.

Which I would gladly have done, but for a tap on my shoulder. I turned around. It was Arthur Braskey.

"You've arrived then," he said, rather more jovially than I would have thought the situation warranted.

"Yes. I'm sorry. There was an accident…"

"Not to worry, Mr. Figgis. Mr. Edwards explained all. My apologies for not sending someone along to collect you. I was unable to locate anyone under the legal drink limit for driving."

I halfway believed him. The assembled onlookers—about 100 of them—did seem rather well-lubricated.

"It seems because I've missed the warm-up chat I won't be allowed to participate…"

"Nonsense," Arthur Braskey pronounced, clapping his hand

over my shoulder and dragging me across to the organizer. "A late addition. He's walking."

A moment of doubt flashed across the guy's face. "But we have strict rules, Mr. Braskey…"

"I know the rules. I'll assume the responsibility should he come to harm."

I wasn't filled with any great sense of relief. I was most definitely going to come to harm. Having Arthur Braskey step in to accept the blame for it wasn't going to soothe the scalding burns on the soles of my feet!

"But—"

"I'd advise you to agree, Mr. Grundig. Unless you consider your daytime employment a less-than-necessary fixture in your life."

Mr. Grundig opened his mouth, and then closed it again, obviously thinking the better of what he was tempted to say.

"Come with me," he said instead, taking my arm.

"Excellent," said Mr. Braskey. "Good luck, Mr. Figgis. I'll be waiting to chat with you afterwards."

Great, I thought. Not only will I be writhing in pain with medium-rare feet—he's going to prolong my agony by making me sit through a lecture.

At that moment, I truly and honestly wished I had never heard of Holly Medford. Or her fucking G-string.

#

A lot of people had promised they were going to be there to cheer me on. I didn't see any of them. Not even Katey. I looked for her as I accompanied the less-than-happy Mr. Grundig to the assembly area where the other walkers were waiting.

"Just watch the others," Mr. Grundig advised. "Do what they do. Don't think about it—try to think past it, to the end. Walk quickly but don't run. Don't stop for anything. Remember the Leidenfrost Effect."

He was going to leave me there. Abandon me to the fire. He was going to walk away.

"Wait!" I shouted. "What's the Leidenfrost Effect?"

A woman who was standing last in line turned to me and said, "Goodness, weren't you paying attention earlier? When the embers are at 700 degrees Fahrenheit, the water on the soles of our feet will produce a protective cushion that stops the skin from burning."

"And that's proven, is it?" I asked, sceptically.

"Of course it is. Stop being silly. You'll frighten the others."

I couldn't see how any of the others could possibly be more terrified than me. To make matters worse, Arthur Braskey was standing front and centre behind the ropes, grinning at me like a bloody Cheshire Cat.

The reason I could see him in the dark was because there were four tubs filled with blazing logs, one at each corner of the fire pit, which I judged was about ten feet long and three feet wide. It was shimmering orange and red and looked extremely hot. It felt extremely hot too. The warmth was radiating out, cloaking us as we stood in the lineup waiting to prove our mettle. Or have it melted.

"Are we ready, ladies and gentlemen?"

It wasn't Mr. Grundig—it was one of his colleagues, a flashy showman sort of guy, a natural with a mic. I found out later his name was Pete Barnum. I'm not joking. He checked the fire pit with a thermometer on the end of a long wand, then, satisfied it was at just the right temperature for a perfectly seared top sirloin, made the announcement:

"Shoes and socks off, if you please!"

Most of the walkers were already in flip-flops. A few, like me, were in trainers. I couldn't sit down on the grass as it was soaking wet and I really wasn't keen to make my jeans look as if I'd shit myself. I got my trainers and socks off balancing on one foot at a time, and I was actually rather pleased to be standing on sopping grass because I reckoned that meant I'd be giving the famous Leidenfrost Effect a fighting chance.

"Ladies and gentlemen, boys and girls and to borrow my favourite line from *Kinky Boots*—those who are yet to make up your minds—I give you your Firemaster, Braden!"

Braden was as flashy as Pete Barnum and was dressed in a spangly white jumpsuit, the sort of thing Elvis would have worn while he belted out "Viva Las Vegas". I had to hand it to Braskey—he knew how to deliver a show. Braden quickly rolled up his trouser legs and made sure they were going to stay up by applying a pair of diamond-studded bicycle clips just below his knees.

"Our brave Braden is going to be the very first to go, just to prove there's nothing to fear. Braden—if you please!"

Braden bowed to us, then trod onto the burning embers and

walked quickly and efficiently all the way to the end, where he stepped off, planted his feet on the wet grass, and took another bow to enthusiastic applause.

"Next in line is—" Pete paused to ask the woman her name.

"Alma!" she shouted, raising her hands over her head while her friends and family cheered from the sidelines.

"Are you ready, Alma?"

"I'm ready!"

"Off you go then!"

With an enormous grin on her face, Alma purposefully walked from one end to the other. She landed on the wet grass, shuffled her feet as if she was cleaning them off, then scooted around to where I was standing and re-joined the line.

"I'm going again!" she shouted, high on her success.

I was no longer the last participant.

Braskey was determined to make sure I went through with it— and that I knew he was watching me. He stayed for the entire performance, impaling me with his piercing gaze. I tried to ignore him, focusing instead on everyone else as they took their turns, trying to concentrate on what they were doing, how quickly they were walking, how honest they were at the end when they jubilantly claimed there was nothing to it and, with adrenalin-fuelled exhilaration, cheered their fellow walkers on.

But all I could think about were those desperate minutes when I'd run into my burning house to try and save Emma…and the utter defeat and helplessness I'd felt when the thick, choking smoke had forced me onto my knees on the floor, nearly killing me as well. And then, five years after that, the utter terror I'd felt as I'd crawled blindly along the smoke-filled and suffocatingly hot corridor on the *Sapphire*, one watertight compartment to the next, leading Katey and another passenger to safety in the old hold, and then leaping for our lives into the freezing water, while the raging fire blew out the ship's portholes and eventually sent my beautiful liner to her watery grave.

I suffered burns both times. I know what it feels like. I still have the scars, though you can't see them unless I take off my clothes.

There were twelve people ahead of me…and then eight…and then two. The assembled guests had been cheering non-stop and at the end of each walk they'd erupted into appreciative whoops and claps.

It was my turn.

"You ready, mate? What's your name?"

"Jason," I said.

"Ready to go, Jason?"

I wanted to say no. I wanted to turn around and run as far away from the fire as I could get. I could feel the grass wet and cold under my feet as I forced myself to ignore my galloping heart and pay attention instead to the science.

"Hang on, Jason. We need to rake the fire."

Fuck.

No.

I closed my eyes. I couldn't wait. It was now or never.

Balling my fists, I opened my eyes and started to walk, just as Braden finished redistributing the hot embers.

"And it's Jason's turn—let's hear it for Jason!"

My heart was racing. I barely heard the cheering. I could feel the heat on either side of me where the burning wood had been stacked higher. Science, I thought. Water. Feet. Focus!

I was halfway there. I could feel a tingling on my soles but it wasn't burning…it was like walking on the hot sand at Seven Mile Beach in Grand Cayman. Fuck you, Arthur Braskey, I thought, pumping my arms the way I'd seen the others do it. Fuck you, fire. This time you won't have your way.

I was breathing deeply by the time I stepped off the burning path and onto the soothing wet grass. The onlookers on the other side of the rope had been encouraging me the whole way but it was only at the end when I actually heard them—and recognized Katey's voice shouting my name and sending me congratulatory cheers.

Exhilarated, heart pumping, I turned to Arthur Braskey and gave him my best Fuck You Too look before I strode off the grass and away from the fire pit to join my special lady.

CHAPTER THIRTEEN

I was gasping for a cigarette.

The Cock and Maggot wasn't having any of it, not even in the garden, so I took myself off to the designated smoking area, which had two very sorry lights and looked like the sort of place where you'd either go to arrange a drug deal or collapse into a desperate pee. Smelled like it, too.

I lit a ciggie and smoked it furiously, and then I smoked a second one. And then I walked back to the pub and got myself a celebratory orange-flavoured fizzy water and went out to the garden find Katey, who was munching crisps and drinking shandy at a wooden table with a view of the now-extinguished fire pit.

I barely had time to sit down when Arthur Braskey, who had obviously mistaken my fuck-off look for one of intense admiration, appeared from nowhere and ambled across the lawn to join us. He introduced himself to Katey and took her hand as she supplied her name.

"Can we buy you a drink?" Katey inquired. She knew exactly who he was. She was humouring me.

"Thank you, Miss Shawcross." Not one for modern titles. I knew that would especially rankle her, since she was adamant about being addressed as Ms in her professional life. "I have some business to discuss with Mr. Figgis."

He waited.

Annoyed, I collected my glass and stood up. "Back soon," I promised.

#

"I'm impressed," Braskey said, taking me back inside the pub and seating me at a table which had a plastic RESERVED sign propped on it.

"With my firewalking skills or my companion?"

Braskey laughed. He took off his leather gloves and slipped out of his camel overcoat.

"Both, in fact. You have excellent taste in women. And you rose to the firewalk challenge, in spite of missing the training session. I like that."

I glanced at the bar. One of the men chatting with the guy who looked like the owner looked curiously familiar. I'd have sworn it was the police constable from the traffic accident earlier who'd refused me a ride. Off-duty already?

And the woman beside him. The passenger who'd been thrown clear of the car, who I'd clearly seen being loaded into the ambulance with life-threatening injuries.

"I do like to see if you have backbone," Braskey said.

I turned around to face him again.

"You engineered my delay."

"Of course I did."

"They were all actors."

"Members of my staff," Braskey suggested, as the bartender brought over a tall glass of tomato juice garnished with a stick of celery. "I don't drink. You and I have that in common. That also impresses me."

Words cannot express the anger that overcame me at that moment. It generally takes a lot to make me upset. He'd deliberately delayed me and then he'd enjoyed watching me squirm, like a sadist child torturing a small animal. And then he'd judged me on my "performance". I'd been his source of amusement, beginning to end.

"Are we finished?" I said.

"Not at all, Mr. Figgis. I promised I would entertain questions from you after you'd contributed to my charity. You've done your part. And now I'll uphold my end of the agreement. Ask away."

"Halila Medenov," I said. "Sound familiar?"

"Not at all, I'm afraid. Should it?"

I couldn't work out if he was telling me the truth or if he was exceptionally good at concealing it.

"The owner of that name claims she's from Kazakhstan. Or her family is, anyway. She was born in Enfield."

Braskey was giving me a blank look.

"Holly Medford," I said.

"I believe you must be mistaken, Mr. Figgis. Tsk. Not an auspicious beginning for what you hope will turn into an illustrious second career."

"What's her real name, then?" I said, glaring at him.

"I've no idea. Does she have another name? I've only ever known her as Miss Medford."

I seriously doubted that. He'd gone to the trouble of looking up my real name. He had to know what Holly's was.

"How much does she actually owe you?"

Braskey smiled. His thin lips reminded me of two stretched rubber bands.

"A good deal more than she's likely told you and exponentially more than she claims was stolen from her locker at the club."

"Why would she lie?"

"I don't know, Mr. Figgis. What's your hypothesis?"

"I haven't got a hypothesis," I said.

He tutted again. It was an annoying gesture and it was having its desired effect on me.

"A good private investigator always has a hypothesis. Which, after careful consideration of all of the collected evidence, may be accepted, modified, or rejected. I'm surprised by your admission—especially after interviewing as many people as you have, and asking as many questions."

"I have theories," I said. "And suspicions."

"Good for you. An open and curious mind is an asset. Might you care to share them with me?"

"I've been told you're known to have favourites at Cha-Cha's."

Braskey gestured his head in a way that indicated I wasn't wrong.

"Was Holly one of your favourites?"

"At one time, yes. A long time ago. However, my patronage is fluid. Circumstances change."

"How long ago is 'a long time'?"

"More than three years."

"And not since…?"

That gesture again.

"I've been told that Holly could talk to you anytime she liked. Are you usually that accessible to the dancers?"

"I make myself accessible," Braskey replied, "if required."

"And it was required with Holly?"

"I prefer to keep the lines of communication open where business transactions are involved."

"Was Shaniah also one of your favourites?"

A slight furrowing of the forehead. He honestly had to think.

"Describe her," he suggested.

I did.

"I recall seeing her at Cha-Cha's on a number of occasions. But I found her unremarkable."

To each his own. I actually believed him.

"Holly's financial problems began about six months ago when she ran up a gambling debt at a casino. Is that your understanding?"

"It is my understanding, yes."

"She'd had similar debts before but she'd always been able to cover them."

"Indeed."

"This time, for whatever reason, it got out of hand. So she approached you for a loan. For £50,000, with the principal plus interest due in four months. The interest you were charging was 10% a week."

Braskey was silent.

"And you say the amount she owed you was more than that?"

"A good deal more, yes," he replied.

"She managed to repay you some of that amount—"

"She did not."

I digested this. Another of Holly's lies.

"She says you accepted the partial payment, but then you increased the interest on the balance, and told her you'd expect full payment in one month's time."

I waited. So did Braskey.

"One month later, Holly said she still didn't have the total of what she owed you and asked you for an additional two weeks. Which you again allowed. She was then able to get the money, and took it to work with her because she was expecting to meet you afterwards to hand it over."

"She was expecting to meet me afterwards. That part is correct."

"Were you anticipating that, at this meeting, she'd bring along the full amount of what she owed you?"

"I believed I might retrieve what she owed me, yes. But I held no unrealistic expectations. I was well aware of her circumstances."

"Regardless of how much money she says was actually taken from her locker...she was terrified of the consequences of not being able to repay you, and because of that she was a no-show for your meeting."

"So terrified, it seems, that she departed the club in the company of a prominent member of a royal family from the Middle East."

I ought to have anticipated Braskey would know about that, too.

"Perhaps she considered the gentleman a potential solution to her financial dilemma."

"Perhaps," Braskey conceded. "Although I doubt he would have been willing to part with that much money. In spite of Miss Medford's considerable talents. And now I have a question for you."

It was my turn to wait.

"Where is she?"

"No idea," I replied, truthfully. "And with all of the resources at your disposal, I'm surprised you have to ask."

That rubber band smile again.

"Miss Medford has proved to be exceptionally clever at concealing her whereabouts. And in limiting her contacts. I'm well acquainted with the website which featured her services once she'd decided to abandon Cha-Cha's to become a gentlemen's escort. But she guards her identity and her profession well. Her clients are exclusive and troublesome to identify. She's since removed her profile from Moonlight Desires but I will, of course, eventually find her."

I didn't say anything.

"I'm quite certain you do have an idea where she is, Mr. Figgis. I commend your chivalry. No doubt she's convinced you I want her killed."

"And you dispute that...?"

"If I were to arrange to have her killed, Mr. Figgis, it would of course send a message to others who might consider crossing me. But it wouldn't bring back what she owes me, would it? Likewise if she somehow came to harm...if, for instance, someone was to throw acid in her face, causing a disfigurement, or some body part or other became...detached...what would be the point in making her unable to continue to earn a living and become a burden to society? It would only benefit me if I arrived at the conclusion that what she owes me is irretrievable and I was never going to see it again. If you understand my point."

Again, I said nothing. He was right. I was chivalrous.

"If you do happen to see her," Braskey continued, "perhaps you might convey to her what I've just told you. Perhaps she might make certain that she returns what she owes me by…say…next Sunday?"

"I doubt I'll be seeing her," I said.

"I genuinely like you, Mr. Figgis. But I don't believe you."

I had a thought. A spark of a thought. Something that hadn't occurred to me before, but now it was dancing in front of me, like Shaniah had, enticing and dangerous.

"How would you describe your relationship with Holly Medford?" I asked, levelling my gaze at him.

Arthur Braskey removed the celery from his tomato juice and drank from the glass, then put the glass back on the coaster on the table and placed the stick of celery beside it.

"Inconvenient," he replied. "And vexatious."

"Nothing more?"

"Be careful where you tread as you negotiate the glowing embers, Mr. Figgis."

He reached inside his jacket pocket and handed me a small brown envelope.

"What's this?" I said.

"Open it."

Inside was a photo. A printout of a photo, anyway, of a string of perfectly round, translucent green beads.

"A necklace?"

"How much would you say it's worth?"

I shrugged. "My grandmother had a dressing table drawer filled with beads like that."

"Don't disappoint me, Mr. Figgis. I'd have thought your curiosity would encourage a more acquisitive supposition."

"I'm all out of ideas," I said, handing the photo and the envelope back to him.

Braskey refused to take them.

"I printed the picture for you."

"Why?"

"You aspire to be a private investigator, Mr. Figgis. Put your analytical mind to work and see what you can come up with."

I slipped the piece of paper back inside its envelope.

"Any more questions?" he said.

"I'll let you know."

"Excellent. You may return to your companion."

I was being dismissed.

I went.

#

"Give us a peek, then," Katey said, after I'd told her what Braskey had said and done.

She studied the printout.

"Definitely not your nana's plastic popper beads," she concluded. "They look like jade to me. Remember all the jewellery shops in Alaska when we were aboard the *Sapphire*?"

I did. The ports—Ketchikan, Juneau, Skagway—were dotted with them. And they all sold precious stones and minerals, both domestic and imported. Tanzanite was a perennial favourite. And jade—the state's official gemstone.

"Have you got a hypothesis as to why Braskey's given you this picture?" Katey inquired. I love her sense of humour.

"Not yet. Obviously it has something to do with Holly. He likes playing games. He could have come right out and told me. But no, he wants me to investigate."

"He's buying time."

"Why?"

"He's trying to find out where she is. Perhaps he thinks if he'd told you, you'd warn her, and she'd move again."

"What's to stop me ringing her up anyway and asking her what this picture means?"

"That's what he wants you to do," Katey said, cleverly. "He's probably tracking your phone calls."

Katey's a big fan of spy stories. The kind where the hero just has to snap his fingers and all sorts of illegal things are carried out under the guise of national security.

"He can't," I said. "Not without a warrant."

"Haha. What if he's got connections at the telecommunications firm that supplies your mobile signal? What if it's one of his exes? What if he's promised her a little holiday in the Canary Islands if she agrees to throw the switch that lets people listen in on private conversations?"

"Are you happy being a travel agent? Because you'd make a great PI."

"Perfectly happy, thank you. But I bet he's got people on standby, on foot and on motorbikes and in cars. And if you manage to see Holly again, they'll be right behind you."

"You've convinced me," I said. "I'm not going to take the bait."

"I know you better than that. I think you should ring her up and ask her what the jade beads mean. Using a disposable mobile, of course."

"I doubt she'd tell me. The last time we spoke, she gave me the distinct impression she'd rather I just dropped the case altogether. And she wouldn't be honest with me anyway. She hasn't been from the start."

"You're too nice," Katey said. "Why are you being so honest with her? You need to level the playing field. Get tough."

"What are you suggesting? That I do something unethical?"

"You're not a professional," Katey shrugged. "You're not bound by a license or a code of conduct. You can say and do whatever you like."

CHAPTER FOURTEEN

True to his word, Braskey made sure I was back in London in time for my Friday night show.

His driver guaranteed it.

And this time there were no unfortunate delays along the deserted country lanes.

Grandad waited outside my flat while I ran inside for a change of clothes. And then he drove me over to the club, depositing me at the front entrance and holding the rear passenger door open for me as I climbed out, feeling for all the world like one of the VIPs who paid premiums for exclusive seats at the main show downstairs.

In our dressing room, I collected my pledges from Ken and Rudy. I showed off the bottoms of my feet—not a red mark or a blister to be seen.

I bounded out on stage with an energy I didn't recall owning since our early days at the club, when we were fresh and new and chomping at the bit to prove ourselves to the critical fans of jazztime Soho.

After we finished, I stayed for two post-show drinks, and then I took a cab home, arriving just as my neighbours were getting up for their middle-of-the-night pee and then staggering back to their rumpled Saturday morning beds.

I woke up around eleven and got myself some breakfast, though by the time I'd assembled everything on my plate it was more like lunch. Chinese pickles (I have no idea what they are—everything's written in Cantonese on the packet—but they're very spicy and their primary ingredient seems to be something that grows in a swamp); some excellent slices of Colston Bassett Stilton (La Fromagerie could pay their monthly rent in Marylebone with what I regularly spend in their shop); and eggs. Of course, eggs—this time scrambled with some chopped white onion and cubed Canadian cheddar and finished with a splurt of Frank's Red Hot Wings sauce (I take their slogan literally—*I put that shit on everything*.)

I rang Sal while I waited for my kettle to boil.

"I wanted to apologise," I said. "Again. I was…distracted the last time we talked."

"I know," Sal said. "No need. I was distracted as well."

"How was your dinner with Jennifer?"

"It was actually really lovely, Jase. She's a professional photographer. Freelance. Her photos have been published in all sorts of places. She's sold some to agencies for a small fortune. She does celebs, but she's not one of those annoying paparazzi types. She's making quite a good living. She was a little apprehensive about meeting me, because she wasn't certain what my reaction would be. She wasn't actually sure what her own reaction would be. It was so…"

"Overwhelming?" I guessed.

"Flabbergasting," Sal replied, and I could tell she was smiling. "I was flooded with so many emotions, Jase. And I could tell she was, too."

She paused.

"She has your eyes."

There it was again. That unbelievable pang. The knowledge that someone else besides Dom was the recipient of my genetic bits and pieces. Once upon a time I'd been absolutely certain about their singular dissemination.

Once upon a time was no longer the case.

"Did she ask about me?"

"Not you, specifically. But about who her dad was. I told her a few things in very general terms. That we were schoolfriends…that we'd never really lost touch. That you're a musician. Her eyes lit up when I said that but I didn't go into details. I know she's very curious."

"Are you seeing her again?"

It was a ridiculous question. But Sal knew what I really meant.

"Tomorrow," she said. "The hotel has themed high tea every

Sunday afternoon in the winter…something our PR people dreamed up to draw in the crowds during the off-season. We've got a special room adjacent to the Wine Bar all done up like a magical enchanted forest…fairies and toadstools and twigs and mossy things. We're meeting there at three."

She paused again.

"Would you like to come along?"

I wanted to say yes. But I wasn't ready.

Not yet.

"I suppose if I just showed up and you introduced me as your friend it would be a bit obvious, wouldn't it?"

"A bit," Sal said. "Though I don't have to tell her you're coming. You could change your mind at any point prior to actually sitting down at the table with us and she wouldn't know."

"You mean that?" I said. "Honestly?"

"It's a huge step, Jase, and I completely mean it. It has to be right with you."

"Thank you."

"See you tomorrow, then. Maybe."

"Maybe," I said.

#

And then I took Katey's advice and set about being unethical.

The first step was to buy a couple of new pay-as-you-go smartphones that couldn't be tracked. I was serious about that. Katey had made a very good point. Braskey obviously wanted to know what had happened to his jade necklace. And he obviously believed Holly knew something about it. And I was the person he believed he could use to get that information.

Not if I could help it.

I took the two new mobiles back to my flat and then I went online and did a crash course in How to Secretly Follow People. If you know how to do it yourself, you stand a fighting chance of being able to avoid others doing it to you. That was my theory, anyway. The trouble with human bloodhounds, of course, is that if they're really good at their job, you won't know they're there. The best you can hope for is that your evasive tactics will outsmart them.

I went downstairs and rang Holly from the park across the road. Because it also occurred to me that Braskey might have managed to mic my flat—either from inside, or by aiming something outside at my windows or my plumbing. Have you ever seen that film *The Conversation*? Gene Hackman's character drives himself to the point of distraction trying to uncover how the baddies have been listening to him. He demolishes his flat. And he never does find out.

Holly answered my call right away.

"Oh hello Mr. Private Investigator," she said, betraying nothing once I'd identified myself. "I didn't think I'd be hearing from you again."

"I'd pretty much come to the same conclusion," I replied. "But then I had second thoughts."

"And as I told you, Jason, I honestly think it would be best if you just dropped the investigation. There's nothing to be gained."

"Who said anything about the investigation?"

"Isn't that why you've called?"

"As a matter of fact," I said, "no."

"What then?"

"The last time we met, as I was leaving, you made it clear you had other things on your mind."

I waited while she processed what I was suggesting.

Then: "My fee is £500 an hour. Cash only, of course."

"Of course," I said.

"And if a gentleman should require additional hours or special personal services…there is a fee for those as well."

My mind went into overdrive imagining what this was going to cost me. But if you're going to be unethical, you might as well take the plunge. Forget about paddling on the shore.

"I would like to meet you for one hour," I said, "at your hotel. I'm particularly interested in your special personal services."

"You surprise me, Mr. Private Investigator. But I'm happy to oblige. Shall we say, at two o'clock, then?"

I checked the time.

"Perfect. Where are you staying?"

"I will meet you outside the Marble Arch tube station," Holly replied, "and once I've ensured you are alone, we will go to my hotel."

"Excellent," I said. "See you at two."

#

I showered with my favourite lemon-and-lime scented foaming gel (irresistibly sexy, according to Katey, who gave it to me for Christmas). I had no idea what Holly's typical punters wore to impress her—not that she needed impressing when she was pocketing £50 an hour more than the minimum posted rate on the Midnight Desires website to accommodate them. I decided on a new pair of Levi's and a white linen shirt from Gant. I put on my best winter jacket and walked to Angel and then took the Northern Line one stop west to King's Cross.

Whenever I go through King's Cross, I'm reminded of the devastating fire that destroyed the ticket hall under the road in 1987. I was nineteen years old when that happened, and I always remember the date—18 November—because it's my sister's birthday.

I also remember it clearly because I was there. Not at the exact moment the flashover happened and the flames and superheated air shot up the Piccadilly Line escalator and incinerated the walls, the ticket machines, and thirty-one people who were trying to get out of the way.

I was there fifteen minutes before that, at about half past seven in the evening.

I'd been shopping in London for Angie's birthday gift. I was going home to Totteridge, where we lived at the time. Angie was still in school. She had a celebratory dinner at a posh restaurant planned with us for Friday and a party with her friends for Saturday. It was just going to be a normal Wednesday night at home.

I was late. Mobile phones existed in 1987 but back then they were prohibitively expensive and the size of a small brick. I'd rung Mum from a callbox to apologise and she'd promised to keep my dinner warm.

I was near Euston Road and King's Cross was the closest tube station. It was the end of the evening rush hour. I went in and bought my ticket from a machine and stepped onto the escalator.

In those days at King's Cross, in order to get to Totteridge, you had to go down to the Piccadilly platforms and then take another short escalator to the Northern Line, which ran underneath the Piccadilly.

As I stood on the Piccadilly escalator, I passed the place on the up side where a tiny wisp of smoke was drifting out from underneath the slatted wooden steps. The escalator was packed with people and it was hardly noticed—a small fire in the machinery, some grease that had been set alight by what turned out to be someone's discarded match. Smoking wasn't allowed on the trains—it had been banned three years earlier—and it wasn't supposed to be allowed in the stations, either, but people routinely ignored the rule and used to light up as they rode to the surface.

I remember the slight haze in the air and a faintly acrid smell and the looks on the faces of the passengers: they were curious and concerned but not to the point of alarm. I read later that small fires were common under the machinery and the flames usually extinguished themselves.

Someone reported the fire to station staff at about the same time that I arrived at the northbound Northern Line platform for my train home. Someone else pressed the emergency button that stopped the escalator from moving, and that allowed the fire to catch hold of the wooden steps and start to burn through from below.

I'd just missed a train and had to wait for the next one, which came along at about 7.42 p.m. I remember seeing about fifty people get off, presumably to either change to a different line or go upstairs to exit the station. I didn't know it at the time, but a minute or two earlier all of the Victoria and Piccadilly Line trains had been ordered not to stop at King's Cross because of the fire. But the trains were still coming out of the tunnels, and they were disembarking passengers who were then being redirected up to the concourse by way of the nearby Victoria Line escalators. And passengers who'd been waiting on the platforms were being evacuated that way as well. And down where I was, on the Northern Line, the trains were all still running as if nothing was wrong.

I got aboard and sat down. The flashover happened three minutes after we left the station. By the time I got home, about forty minutes after that, the fire was all over the news and my parents were frantic with worry. I'd had no idea.

"That could have been you," my mum kept saying, as the footage of victims on stretchers, under blankets, played out on TV.

It might very well have been me, but for the grace of fifteen minutes, and the fact that I'd decided to carry on straight home instead of stopping to get a coffee on my way into King's Cross.

When you're nineteen you feel invincible. When you're nineteen, you don't think about your life suddenly ending. It was a sobering thought, one that's stayed with me. Just like fire itself…which seems to follow me around like a malevolent spirit.

King's Cross Underground Station has all been rebuilt now, with two more ticket halls and a direct escalator down to the Northern Line. But the original ticket hall and Piccadilly Line escalators are still in the same place.

I got off my train and rode the new escalator up to the Northern Ticket Hall. And then, I purposely walked into King's Cross Mainline Station. I knew it would be busy. And there were lots of shops where I could duck inside and wait. Or not wait, as the situation might require.

King's Cross is a beautiful old terminus with its original facades preserved, along with a super-surreal new roof that looks like some kind of intergalactic space vortex.

It has a Harry Potter Shop and a grocery and about a dozen other places where you can kill time. And a bank of ATM's, where I withdrew the cash I would require for my appointment with Holly. Then I walked over to the WH Smith on the main concourse opposite the ticket office. You can stand and browse there as well as keep a watchful eye on who might be tailing you.

I picked up a Tom Clancy paperback and did my best Michael-Caine-as-Harry-Palmer impersonation, but really, it was an amateur attempt at best. I realized I'd neglected to notice who'd got off the train with me, and without that first point of reference, everything else was just guesswork.

In any case, the only thing I could realistically do was conduct a slow, sly recon of the bookshop, and then a similar assessment of everyone who was in the general vicinity outside. Nobody stood out, but then, logically, they wouldn't. The best trackers were the ones who blended in with their surroundings and followed you without being noticed.

I left the WH Smith and walked through the station and outside to Euston Road, now extra-conscious of everyone who was around me. According to my crash course in Surveillance, one of the best ways to track someone is to have two or three spotters spelling each other off: one behind, another in front, a third waiting a little bit further ahead of where they anticipate you might go next.

On Euston Road, I ignored all the helpful—and predictable—signs directing me back onto the Piccadilly Line via the way I'd just come and instead went into the Underground through the old original concourse—the one which had caught fire in 1987.

As I said, it's all been rebuilt and everything's now bright and white and gleaming. But there's a memorial on one wall, with a clock, which is dedicated to everyone who lost their lives, and there's another memorial in the tunnel under Euston Road, which names all thirty-one of the victims. I stopped to acknowledge both—I always do, with a moment of reflection and something like kinship, because I might have crossed paths with some of them as they'd got off the train that I got onto. I might have taken the seat of someone who'd gone upstairs and not survived.

As I was standing in front of the memorial with the clock, I took the opportunity to check to see whether I recognized anyone from the mainline station. But, again, nobody looked familiar.

Still sufficiently cautious, I walked down the Piccadilly escalator and waited on the platform. A train was just arriving. I allowed it to leave, and then casually observed who was still standing on the platform around me.

Nobody.

But the platform filled quickly with new passengers.

I got aboard the next train at the last minute—just as the doors were closing. I'd seen that in a film.

It was two stops to Holborn. I stood the entire way, making a note of all of the faces of all of the passengers in my carriage. At Holborn, I got off and went up to the Central Line, and after practising the same sequence of observations, caught a train going west.

Marble Arch was four stops after Holborn. I deliberately overshot the station and stayed on the train until Lancaster Gate. Then I walked over to the eastbound platform and rode back to my original destination.

By the time I got up to the surface at Oxford Street I was congratulating myself on my subterfuge, utterly convinced that nobody could possibly have followed me without my knowledge.

CHAPTER FIFTEEN

I looked for Holly as I stood outside the station entrance on Oxford Street. I couldn't see her, which didn't surprise me. She was obviously determined to stay out of sight until she was absolutely certain I was alone.

When she finally did appear, it was from the doorway of a nearby souvenir shop. She was wearing a very stylish winter coat and a fox fur hat, high-heeled leather boots and sunglasses—in spite of the grey mid-afternoon overcast.

"Hello Mr. Private Investigator," she said, very quietly. "Walk beside me, engage me in a conversation, we are really just old friends meeting up for a cup of tea."

"English Breakfast, I hope," I said.

"Whatever you wish."

The Asher Hotel was two blocks west of Marble Arch and was a good deal more posh than the Crestone. At least, at street level.

Holly's room was on the fifth floor, with a window that overlooked another window and the brick wall belonging to the building next door. I could tell that although she'd booked herself into what could probably be called a Deluxe Double, it was very likely the least expensive accommodation on the premises.

The primary colours were olive green and a sort of burnished gold—curtains, duvet, chairs. There was a gold-accented antique-looking desk on one side of the bed and a matching table on the other, a generous flat screen TV on the wall at the foot of the bed, and a formidable loo that was nearly as big as the sleeping area and offered—according to the stand-up amenities menu on the bedside table—the same luxury toiletries that I remembered you could buy in the spa on board the *Sapphire* for what a week's worth of groceries would have cost on shore.

Holly removed her hat and placed it on the bedside table, and hung her coat in a sliding-door wardrobe against the wall opposite the window. She collected my winter coat and hung it beside hers.

"Do you approve?" she inquired, standing before me in her leather boots, a short black skirt and a cream-coloured silk blouse.

"Very much so," I said.

"Would you like me to take off my clothes for you? Or do you like to undress the ladies yourself?"

"I would like you to take off your clothes," I said. "Very slowly."

"A small matter of the reimbursement first," she hinted. "In advance, as we discussed."

"Yes," I said. "Of course."

I went back to the wardrobe and took out the wad of cash. It was a bit uncouth of me not to have put it in an envelope first, but I didn't usually engage the services of an escort and my experience to that point had been limited to watching episodes of Billie Piper in *Secret Diary of a Call Girl*. Holly quickly counted the money, then placed it on the bedside table beside her hat.

And then she kissed me. A long, lingering kiss involving a very aggressive tongue.

At the end of it, she said: "You prefer to be in charge? You like your lady to be submissive, not so forward? Tell me your pleasure."

"Take off your clothes," I suggested. "I'd like you to be my private dancer…strip for me."

She did…beginning with the cream-coloured silk blouse, which she unbuttoned slowly and seductively, revealing a lacy white bra which cupped her breasts exquisitely. She slipped out of the blouse and then stepped out of the tiny black skirt. She was wearing a lacy white thong that matched the bra, and white stockings with suspenders.

She unzipped her boots and removed them, and stood before me, nearly naked.

"Nice?"

"Very nice," I said. She did have an amazing body—tanned and toned and perfectly proportioned. She reminded me of a model from Victoria's Secret.

"Will you join me on the bed?"

She lifted up the corner of the duvet and pulled it back in one smooth motion. And then she slipped off her bra.

And kissed me again, pressing her nipples against my chest and her lower body against mine. "Would you like me to undress you, Mr. Private Investigator?" she whispered. "I can tell you're becoming very…interested."

"I would like," I said.

I took off my shoes and socks and laid back on the bed and allowed her to strip off my shirt, my jeans and my pants. I was completely naked.

"You are impressed," she observed, teasing my impressed body part with her fingers. "I didn't suspect we would end up engaged in these activities when we first met. Did you?"

"I didn't," I admitted. It was going to be a bit of a challenge to bring my mind back to the task at hand. "Do you mind if we talk?"

Holly paused. "You prefer a conversation first?"

"Yes please. If you don't mind."

"I don't mind, my love. Whatever you want. You've paid for an hour of my time. It isn't always about having sex. Sometimes the foreplay is talking about the things which arouse you. Tell me what will make you excited."

"Perhaps we should put our clothes back on," I said.

"Whatever you wish," she said, surprised.

I could tell she'd been looking forward to showing me all of her body. And fucking me. I was almost sorry to disappoint her.

I watched her replace her bra, and then her skirt and her blouse. Each motion was calculated, careful, a striptease in reverse. A well-rehearsed show.

Instead of her boots, she slipped on a pair of high-heeled, strappy sandals.

I put on my own clothes while she was arranging two chairs in front of the window so that they were facing one another.

"Is this what you'd like?" she inquired.

"Perfect," I said.

"Please join me."

I sat in one of the chairs. She also sat, crossing one leg over the other, assuming the role of a sexy, sympathetic listener.

"Would you like to ask me some questions? Or perhaps there are some things you would like me to ask about you? I think you are very attractive, Mr. Private Investigator. With or without your clothes. More so, in fact, without…"

"I would like," I said, "to know how you're managing to make connections with your clients when you don't have your own website and you're clearly not using the agency anymore."

Holly stared at me. It took a moment for the penny to drop.

"I think you should go."

"I've paid for an hour of your time. We've still got forty minutes."

She was uncomfortable. She didn't like being caught off-guard. She was used to being the one in control.

"I can have you thrown out. I won't hesitate to call the hotel's security."

"I don't doubt it," I said. "But I've been to see Arthur Braskey. He very much wants to know where you are. The minute you call Security I'll be on the phone to him."

I pulled my little disposable mobile out of my jeans pocket to make my point.

"You're bluffing," she said.

"Am I? He held a charity firewalk last night in Little Brickford. I'm pretty certain he lives there. He invited me to take part…and I couldn't really refuse. We had a chat afterwards in the pub. The Cock and Maggot."

"I don't believe you."

"He's missing the top part of his middle finger, from the third knuckle on. I saw it when he took his gloves off."

"You could have read that anywhere."

"I don't believe I could. I did a lot of research about him online and that particular detail's not mentioned. But you obviously knew about it."

Holly didn't say anything.

And then: "What did he tell you about me?"

"Not a lot, really. But he did mention that what you owed him was quite a bit more than what you originally claimed. And that, contrary to what you told me, you hadn't repaid any of it. Oh, and he's never heard of anyone named Halila Medenov."

Again, silence.

"You must have run up a huge debt at the gambling clubs," I said.

"I suppose I did."

"Which you'd always been able to handle…but then, for some

reason, you suddenly weren't able to pay off those debts."

I had an idea what that "some reason" was, but I wasn't quite ready to play that hand. I wanted to be absolutely certain about my facts.

I got up and went to the wardrobe and got the photo of the green beads out of my coat pocket. I took it back to Holly.

"Do you know what that is?" I asked.

She looked at the printout, then shook her head. "Should I?"

"Braskey seemed very keen that I investigate it. He seems to want me to believe it has something to do with you."

"I'm very sorry, but I have no idea."

She was so exceptionally good at not telling the truth.

"How are you connecting with your clients?" I asked, again.

"I have a friend."

"A pimp."

"A friend," she repeated. "It was always my intention to work on a freelance basis. Why pay the agency a commission when I can keep all of the money for myself?"

"Other than what you pay your friend."

"I've built up a small list of clients. Regulars. I rely on discretion and word of mouth. I will eventually have my own website, once I've dealt with Braskey. And then I will be able to advertise."

She looked at me.

"You won't tell him you've met with me…"

"I won't," I said. "I do have some scruples. Who's your friend?"

Holly smiled. "I don't believe you need to know that."

"Stanislav Turcan," I guessed. "The front desk clerk at the Crestone. Ex-front desk clerk."

I knew I was right, in spite of her silence.

"Have you got all of the answers to all of your questions?" she asked, instead.

"Not all. But I can wait. I am curious though…if you're so frightened of Braskey, why didn't you leave London? As soon as you had the money from your after-work liaison that night, why didn't you fly off somewhere else? It would have been so much easier to hide from Braskey in another country."

"You underestimate his reach, Mr. Private Investigator. I would not be safe regardless of where I went. Might as well stay where I have a steady source of income and I don't have to begin over. I'm sure you understand."

I did. I stood up. "Mind if I use the loo?"

"Be my guest."

I really did have to pee. But I also took advantage of human nature: people keep things in their bathrooms that reveal amazing details about their personal lives. Brand of toothpaste, toothbrush. Deodorant or antiperspirant. What they use to wash with, women especially: cleansers and exfoliants and makeup remover. The makeup itself. Creams and serums and magical potions.

And scent.

There it was. That wonderful wafting fusion of gardenia and jasmine and orange blossoms and three or four other flowers that she wrapped around herself like a chiffon sheet. It was in a small glass bottle with a rather functional glass top, nothing elaborate. The bottle had a label which looked almost handmade. *Nemilos*. And the name of the shop. Coleridge and Wordsworth, Purveyors of Fine Perfume.

I took photos of it, front and back, then used the toilet and flushed it and went back out to Holly. I'd promised Braskey I'd tell her about his deadline of next Sunday for the repayment of his loan. She stared at me, impassively, as I dutifully conveyed the required information, along with Braskey's veiled threats of disfigurement or worse.

"Have you finished?" she said.

"I'm done," I confirmed.

"Then I really do believe you should leave now."

I honoured her request, removing my overcoat from the cupboard.

"Goodbye," I said, pleasantly, at the door.

"Goodbye," she replied. No lingering kiss this time. I'd refused to be manipulated and she hated me for it.

I let the door close softly behind me and left, smiling at a waiter who was wheeling a room service cart to the other end of the hallway. I took out my Benson and Hedges and as I walked out of the hotel, lit up my first cigarette of the day.

CHAPTER SIXTEEN

I stood outside the Asher Hotel until I'd finished my cigarette, then stubbed it out in a clever upright tube the management had helpfully installed far enough away from the main entrance that guests wouldn't be bothered, even if they had recognized it for what it was.

I went back inside to the lobby, where there was a cluster of sofas and armchairs set up in two geometrical squares in front of a trendy coffee shop. I settled myself there while I looked up Coleridge and Wordsworth on one of my new smartphones. It took a moment for Google to realize I wasn't asking about England's most famous Romantic poets.

Coleridge and Wordsworth (not the poets) turned out to be a bespoke perfumery located at the quiet end of Oxford Street with St. Giles on its north side and Soho to the south. According to their website they sold unusual brand name perfumes, but they were best-known for concocting one-of-a-kind fragrances for their discerning customers. A glance at their prices confirmed those customers would have to be extremely discerning.

I googled *Nemilos*.

It wasn't the name of a branded perfume. So Holly had to be on Coleridge and Wordsworth's books as one of their exclusive customers.

Nemilos itself turned out to be a Romanian word meaning compassionless, ruthless, merciless.

That made me pause. She'd obviously chosen the name deliberately. But Romanian…?

Curiously, I looked up countries where Romanian was spoken. If you're interested, it's the official language of Romania, but also of the Republic of Moldova and the European Union, and it's a recognized minority language in Bulgaria, Hungary, Serbia and Ukraine. But not, as it happens, Kazakhstan. Where Holly claimed her parents were from.

The official languages of Kazakhstan are Russian and Kazakh.

I typed "ruthless" into Google Translate and asked for the Kazakh translation. I got аяусыз, which is Cyrillic. I asked how someone might say it.

Google said: *Ajalsız*.

I used my other new smart phone to ring Holly back. She picked up my call immediately.

"You know," I said, "for someone who's terrified of being discovered by Braskey, you're not very good at keeping yourself hidden. What if it had been him calling and not me?"

She didn't say anything.

"I was just wondering if you could tell me what *ajalsız* means."

There was another moment of silence, and then she disconnected.

Snap.

Holly's boyfriend Stanislav Turcan—the front desk clerk—was from Moldova. He could have been the one who bought her perfume as a gift. Or he could have been its inspiration. Somehow, I doubted either was the case.

\#

Coleridge and Wordsworth was on the ground floor of a narrow little building squeezed in between two larger ones at the quiet end of Oxford Street.

I was intrigued enough to google the address, which informed me that in a previous century, it had been a pub.

I sometimes wish I'd been an architect, so I'd have the vocabulary to describe, in technical terms, what the various features of a preserved building like that are called. All I can tell you is that it was four storeys high and, like so many other places in London, it was constructed of red brick and stone, and that an additional search came up with the helpful note that it was "floridly detailed and crowned with a gable."

On the outside, the top floors were more or less untouched. But the bottom floor, where the pub had once stood, had been completely made over to house the shiny modern glass-and-chrome entrance to the perfumery.

Inside it was much the same, but scented: a heady mix of everything you'd imagine going into about a hundred different perfumed concoctions—violets and roses, sandalwood and cinnamon, balsam and patchouli and lavender.

There were glass counters topped with clear and coloured bottles in all shapes and sizes; glass cabinets on the brick walls, similarly equipped; open shelves stocked with boxes and more bottles; fresh flowers in glass vases; and all of it lit from below with bright white LED's.

A young woman in totteringly high heels stepped forward to greet me. She was wearing a nametag: Rosemary. "Good afternoon. How can I help you?"

"Hello," I said. "My sister has a friend who buys her scent here and I was wondering if I could get a bottle of it for my wife. A surprise for her birthday."

"How lovely," Rosemary replied. "Do you know what it's called?"

"*Nemilos*," I said, showing her the photo I'd taken on my phone.

"It's not one of the brand names we stock…but I do believe that could be one of our bespoke labels. Let me check."

A quick search on a handy tablet confirmed it.

"I'll take you upstairs to speak with our perfumer."

I followed Rosemary up a flight of impossibly steep steps at the back of the shop. Her five-inch heels terrified me; I was prepared for a backwards topple and made up my mind that if she fell, I'd have to step aside or risk breaking my neck with well-intentioned but misguided valiance if I tried to catch her on the way down.

The room at the top of the stairs looked very much like the one at the bottom: more glass countertops, cabinets, shelves. But now there were droppers and collections of brown bottles and glass measuring tubes. Dipsticks with which to sniff and sample. Comfy swivel stools to accommodate the sniffers and samplers as they devised and formulated.

The purpose of my visit was quickly explained to another young woman in another pair of frightening heels and a white lab coat. Her nametag identified her as Jasmine. I wondered if it was a pre-req for employment at Coleridge and Wordsworth to be named after their ingredients.

"And may I ask the name of your sister's friend?" Jasmine inquired, as Rosemary abandoned me and tottered back downstairs.

I told her. She looked it up on her tablet.

"Hmm," she said, her face showing genuine consternation. "I don't seem to be able to find that name. You're certain she shops here?"

"Absolutely positive," I replied, showing her the photo of Holly's perfume bottle.

"That is one of ours," Jasmine confirmed. "But it's not Holly Medford…it's Tatiana Melnic."

"Of course," I said. "I'm so sorry. Her pen name's Holly Medford. She writes mystery novels and her agent didn't think Tatiana Melnic would look appealing on book covers."

That got Jasmine's attention. "She's never mentioned that to me!"

"She's not very well-known. Yet. But she's quite good. She has an amazing imagination and knows how to weave a good yarn. Look her up on Amazon."

"I will! I'd never have guessed. I wouldn't have thought she had time to write novels with all the other things she's got on her plate. All that charity work. And of course, looking after her husband's business. He's so wealthy, she certainly doesn't need the extra money."

"I think it's more about getting satisfaction from making up stories," I said, lending a deliberate tone of inside confidentiality to my voice. "They say all writers are liars, don't they?"

"Of course," Jasmine replied, though I didn't think she'd ever read anything by Neil Gaiman, least of all the novel that contained the quote I'd just misappropriated.

"Although not all writers dress as well as Tatiana," I added. "She has an excellent sense of fashion."

"Oh yes," Jasmine agreed (because now I was her new best friend and we were discussing something she was more familiar with). "I'm so jealous. She's always so well-dressed. And that gorgeous green necklace—"

"The one made out of jade?"

"That's the one. Her husband gave it to her as a wedding present. Worth a small fortune. She always wears it when she comes in to collect her perfume and I always make a point of noticing it when she does. She always arrives in a car with a driver."

"I know the car," I said. "A blue Mercedes E-type, isn't it? And the driver's about six feet tall with grey hair."

"That's him. And the car. I always look out for her here—"

She walked across to the window in question, which had a straight-down view of Oxford Street.

"When was the last time she came in to collect her perfume?"

"It must have been about six months ago, when she told me about her marriage being over. Such a shame."

"I was gutted," I said. "I thought they were such a wonderful couple. And you haven't seen her since?"

"No, alas. She collected her five bottles and she hasn't come back."

"Five bottles! Isn't that unusual?"

"Not at all. She buys five bottles each time she comes in. We all think she must be pouring them into her bathwater!"

The bottle I'd taken a picture of was three-quarters empty. If Holly hadn't been back in six months she must have drastically rationed her supply. Or switched to showers.

"I'd love to have a bottle of Tatiana's scent for my wife. It's her birthday on Monday. Is it possible?"

"I'm so sorry, no," said Jasmine, her face falling. "It's proprietary—it's Tatiana's—and we've guaranteed exclusivity. It's in our Terms and Conditions and it's one of the things that makes us so special to our clients."

Seeing my disappointment, she had an idea.

"If you'd like to ring her and ask her permission to share…I'm sure we could accommodate your request."

"OK," I shrugged.

I dialled my own number and let it ring until my voicemail cut in, identifying me as me and telling the caller that if I wasn't asleep I was probably at work and I'd get back to whoever it was as soon as I could and in the meantime perhaps they'd enjoy listening to me play about a minute and a half of Pat Metheny's "It's for You" on my guitar and at the end of it, they could leave a message or hang up and ring back later.

"Not there," I said, disconnecting. "Damn."

"What a shame. But perhaps I could make up a bottle of something else for your wife? Something very similar…? So similar…you might never be able to tell the difference unless you had a complete list of the fragrances and the exact amounts used…?"

#

An hour later, I left Coleridge and Wordsworth with a silver and pink gift bag that contained a glass bottle identical to Holly's, but with a label that said *Dolcemente*.

The nearest tube station was Tottenham Court Road. I changed at Euston and was home in twenty minutes.

Sitting at my kitchen table, I went online and paid for one of those websites that gives you full access to recent voter lists and details about who occupies what house and how long they've lived there.

Arthur Braskey. Little Brickford. There he was. Electoral roll going back to 2002. Other occupants. Tatiana Melnic. From 2014 until now.

I'd guessed as much. I just hadn't had the proof. But between Jasmine at the perfumery and findoutanythingaboutanyone.com, now I had it in black and white.

I found another website where I could pay another fee and access marriage records for the UK.

But there was no match.

All four of Arthur Braskey's previous marriages and divorces were there. But nothing more recent.

I tried using both names—Holly Medford and Tatiana Melnic. Nothing.

On the off-chance Holly had been telling the truth for once, I keyed in Halila Medenov.

Still nothing.

They'd either never been formally hitched…or they'd exchanged their vows in another country.

I tried to look up when Holly had changed her name and, indeed, if it was ever done legally, or if she'd just assumed a new identity without going through official channels. But because of the processes involved, it was next to impossible to find the answers.

"Yes, it's me again," I said, ringing Sal. "I still haven't made up my mind about tomorrow…but I was hoping you could tell me something about Holly. When you were arranging her disembarkation from the *Amethyst* all those years ago, did you ever see her passport?"

"I didn't," Sal said. "Why?"

"Just trying to figure out what name she was using."

"Whatever was on her passport would have had to match the passenger manifest. And I did have access to that. She was Holly Medford."

"So she couldn't have come aboard using different name?"

"Not possible," Sal said. "Not even back then. Why?"

"I'm trying to find out when she gave up being Tatiana Melnic and started calling herself Holly Medford. I'm also trying to sort out if she was ever legally married to Arthur Braskey."

"You're joking. How did you manage to unearth that tasty little morsel?"

"Unethically," I replied.

Sal laughed.

"Not only that," I said. "Your front desk bloke, Stanislav Turcan, was probably working with Holly when he was stealing your guests' credit card numbers. She didn't deny knowing him when I put it to her. It looks like she was telling porkies to you and me both."

"I'm so sorry for involving you, Jase. I was only trying to help her out."

"I know," I said. "And you're a good person for doing that. But I'm dropping the case. I think I've gone as far as I can with it. Let's write it off to lessons learned and get on with our lives. What time are you meeting Jennifer tomorrow?"

CHAPTER SEVENTEEN

Saturday nights at the Blue Devil are prime time for me and my band. We're sometimes sold out during the week, especially if there's a big name onstage just before us or headlining downstairs in the main lounge. But we're guaranteed a full house on Saturdays and our audience is always enthusiastic and genuinely stoked.

I arrived in our dressing room to find Ken and Rudy in the middle of a conversation about our demo.

"Who did Trev send it to?" I asked, taking off my coat.

"Blue Boy Records," Ken said. "HyFy. And Knave."

"I've already tried Blue Boy and HyFy," I said. I must have sounded discouraged. I tried to recall who the rep was at Knave. They'd never indicated any interest in jazz, which was why I hadn't pitched my stuff to them before.

"You're not Trev and you don't have his connections. Have faith."

"I have had Faith," I said. "And Hope. Although Charity turned me down on Tinder."

Ken chuckled.

"I wouldn't mind a nice fat record deal," Rudy mused, allowing himself to indulge in the kind of fantasy I knew we were all secretly entertaining. "Comfy retirement. Cosy cottage in Henley-on-Thames adjacent to Friar Park."

"Accountants embezzling our royalties and jazz groupies making plaster casts out of our tonic minors," Ken said.

"I'd miss living next door to the bloke who's one half of that

126

Simon and Garfunkel tribute act."

"I've heard they do Peter and Gordon, too," Ken said. "And Chad and Jeremy. And the Kalin Twins."

"They're very versatile," said Rudy. "'When Will You Be Mine?'."

"Steady on," said Ken. "What about Patrick?"

"Nobody's ever managed to come up with a Figgis Green tribute band, have they?" Dave said, to me, from the sofa, where he was studying Google Maps on his iPad.

"No," I said. "And I think it would be really weird watching people pretending to be my mum and dad."

"They could call themselves The Greenish Figs," Rudy said, cleverly.

"Or the Roving Minstrels," Ken replied. "Which would make far more sense from a touring and marketing point of view. I'm sure there's a serious fan base. You should look into that, Jason."

"No thanks," I said, meaning it.

We were interrupted by a knock on the dressing room door. It was Jeremy, the intern from the front office. One of his jobs was to let us know when there were VIP's in the audience.

"Arthur Braskey," he said. "I've never heard of him."

"You're young," I said. "There's time."

"What's he famous for?"

"Criminal undertakings." The knowledge that Braskey would be sitting at a table in front of us, watching me play, made me distinctly uneasy. I'd really thought he wouldn't bother me anymore. I was obviously wrong and Katey was right: there was a reason he'd given me that picture. And he wasn't going to let me forget about it.

"He asked me to give his regards to you, Jason."

"Of course he did. Thanks."

"Rubbing elbows with the Krays now," Rudy said, after Jeremy had left. "There's a turnup for the squeaky-clean Figs legacy."

"You wouldn't say that if you knew Rick Redding like I knew Rick Redding," I replied.

Rick Redding had played rhythm guitar—briefly—in my parents' band. His career had ricocheted off the rails after he slugged my dad backstage after a concert and my dad had him arrested for ABH. That was just one of the fascinating details about Figgis Green that their excellent highly-paid publicists had managed to keep out of the papers. They wouldn't have been as successful nowadays, social media being what it is. Back then my dad grew a beard to hide the scar on his chin and a press release was put out informing the public that Rick Redding had decided to leave the group to pursue a solo career. The Rick Redding episode was only one of about two dozen inconvenient events that were decidedly not in keeping with Figgis Green's cheerfully polished public image.

"You should publish a tell-all book," Ken said. "Serialize it in the *Mirror*. You'd make a fortune."

"*Keith Richards Raid Shocker*," I said. "*Previously unreleased documents reveal how police found Mandy Green and Tony Figgis frolicking naked under a fur rug with Marianne Faithfull.*"

"Throw in a Mars Bar," Ken said, as we went out to play, "and you'll be on the *New York Times* bestseller list for years."

#

I tried to see Braskey from the stage but the overhead spots were shining straight at us and it was impossible. I finally caught sight of him when we had our first break, sipping his signature tomato juice with its stick of celery.

He'd also, from the looks of the empty plates, just enjoyed a substantial midnight snack.

He acknowledged me but he didn't get up from his table and he didn't invite me to join him.

I got myself a soda with a twist of lime from the bar and went back to the dressing room battling, unsuccessfully, an overwhelming sense of intimidation.

Dave had been very quiet while we were onstage. Usually we engage in banter, some chat in between the tunes, a little give-and-take with the audience which is always appreciated.

Dave's reluctance to relax was understandable, and now he wanted to tell me why.

"I know where Gracie is," he said. "We took your advice and went looking for her. Helen came here—Soho—and she spotted her late last night, walking along the road. She tried to talk to her but Gracie ran away. Helen tried to follow her but she was scared off by a bloke. We think it might be the guy Gracie's been seeing. He looks a rough lot, Jason. God knows why she's fallen in with him. We keep asking ourselves what we did wrong. What didn't we give her? When did we not listen to her? When did she start to think it would be better living like this?"

"Impossible questions," I said. "With impossible answers. It's good to know that you at least found her. And that she's all right."

"She's not all right," Dave said. "Helen says she looks ill and she's too thin and she's not dressed properly for this weather. She looks uncared for."

"I'm so sorry, Dave," I said.

"I was going to ask a favour."

"Anything."

"She knows you, Jason. She trusts you. She doesn't seem to want to talk to Helen or me. But she might listen to you. If I told you where Helen saw her, do you think you might go out tonight, after the gig, and just have a quick wander round the manor to see if you can spot her?"

"Of course," I said, readily. "Where did Helen see her?"

"Brewer Street. Up near Walker's Court."

Not the greatest of areas. At least there would be a lot of people about—Soho never sleeps these days, even in the dead of winter.

As we went back onstage I checked again for Braskey, but his table was empty, everything cleared away and fresh settings in place for the next customer. He'd accomplished what he came for.

#

It was about 8°C outside, not uncommon for three in the morning in Central London in early March. I put on my winter jacket and wound my scarf around my neck and set out for Brewer Street where it meets Walker's Court, a five-minute walk west of the club.

I know what you're thinking about Soho. It has a history and a reputation.

In fact, its early origins were fairly aristocratic, but by the 1800s its well-heeled inhabitants had moved away to greener fields and their properties were taken over by theatres, music halls and the inevitable ladies of the night.

In the first half of the 20th century, Soho was somewhere exciting and multicultural and slightly forbidding. You could venture into its dark little alleys for a quick Italian or Greek meal before catching a show in the West End. And my mum and dad often visited Denmark Street, which was packed with recording studios and guitar shops, songwriters and session players and places where you could rub shoulders with all of them over a couple of pints.

There were music clubs and coffee bars and the area had a slightly risqué, rebellious air to it.

By the time I was a kid in the 1970s, it had all become much dodgier. The sex industry flourished, although prostitution itself was off the streets and indoors and usually up a flight of stairs.

There were narrow little roads with neon signs advertising *Girls! Girls! Girls!*, and there were dubious bookstores with sunbleached magazines in their windows, offering kinks I'd never even heard of. There were tiny clubs with narrow doorways and even narrower steps leading down into dark mysterious cellars, and there were shoebox-sized cinemas with sticky floors. There were massage parlours offering negotiable services and peep-shows promising forbidden thrills in exponential numbers. And there were cards in shop windows, signs tacked to dark little doorways and pasted to the insides of phone boxes, advertising euphemistic services ranging from French Polishers to Strict German Governesses.

Nowadays the tatty sex shops have been driven out of business by the friendly respectability of Prowler and Harmony, and the internet offers far more satisfactory enticements than the neon-flash promise of *All-Nude Revue!* next door to a boarded-up shop that used to sell porn on DVD and VHS.

Soho has become gentrified and respectable again.

I was right about the streets being busy. A few people seemed like the sort you'd want to give a wide berth to, and were likely doing a drug deal or looking for a chance to negotiate one. But others were window-shopping or hunting for something to eat or just wandering through on their way home.

It wasn't impossible that Gracie was staying somewhere nearby. I spotted the dozen or so walk-ups that were the last holdouts of the infamous "red-light" district—open doorways with handwritten signs instructing customers to come inside and go up to the top of the stairs. I debated doing that, just to ask about Gracie, but decided not to as it would likely have been more harmful to her than helpful.

I walked past a couple of adult bookshops, a massage place, a handful of restaurants and a pub undergoing renovations on the corner at Great Windmill Street. There's a huge 24-hour car park at Lexington—and it was still reasonably busy at that hour. Gracie might have been there, but I wasn't going to venture inside on my own to look. I turned up Lexington, which is narrow and not very friendly and decidedly less-populated than the much wider road I'd just left. At least it had streetlights. But, for the first time, I felt not-very-safe. Anything could have happened to me as I walked north, and it didn't help that I was still slightly freaked out by Arthur Braskey's appearance earlier at the club.

I tucked my chin down into my scarf and jammed my hands into my coat pockets as I caught sight of a young woman, walking alone, who could have been Gracie from the back. She was terribly underdressed for the cold, with bare legs and a short skirt and a long woolly sweater. I trailed behind her, following her into a short pedestrian path that led to another small road that turned south and eventually put me on Peter Street, which has flats and a red brick college and a lot of reconstruction going on. The young woman seemed to be on her way to somewhere definite.

I overtook her so that I could turn around quickly and see her face.

It wasn't Gracie.

She disappeared into a nondescript doorway.

I carried on to Wardour Street and turned south again and walked past Brewer Street to another little pedestrian alley called Tisbury Court.

And that's where I spotted her.

She was wearing white satin shorts and high leather boots and a skimpy fake fur jacket that ended at her waist.

She was walking up Tisbury Court towards me, her eyes focused on the pavement.

"Gracie," I said.

She raised her head and stopped.

"Jason." A genuine smile. Quickly replaced by a scowl. And hunching shoulders. "What do you want?"

"Your mum and dad are really worried about you, Gracie. They just need to know you're all right."

"I'm OK. You can tell them that. Both of them."

"I think they'd much rather hear it from you."

When Dom was fourteen he had more sense than Gracie. I tried to imagine what I would have said, and done, if he'd bolted from everything that was secure and safe and comfortable to live like this. I couldn't quite get there. Nothing in my experience came close to giving me any sort of wisdom.

Gracie wasn't saying anything. But she hadn't turned around and walked away from me, either. She was struggling. She had to be. She knew I was right but her pride, still halfway mired in childhood, wasn't going to give in easily.

"If you come back with me now…" I said. "If you *want* to come back with me…I'll stay with you while you talk to your mum and dad. I'll make sure they listen to what you have to say."

Grace shook her head. The words came tumbling out, quickly, defiantly. "They don't understand. They'll never understand. It's not just mum's stupid rules and her stupid boyfriend and treating me like I'm ten."

"I understand," I said.

"You don't. You've never had a daughter. And I bet your parents didn't get divorced, did they?"

"They didn't," I said. "And if I did have a daughter, and if she was your age and she was in your situation…I'd be out looking for her, just like your mum and dad are. Not because they're angry or trying to make you come back and live with your mum's rules. Because they love you and they don't want you to be hurt…or worse. Because they're frightened for you. Even if they're not married to each other anymore. They still care about you."

The struggle inside was making its way onto her face. She was trying not to let it show.

"If you did have a daughter," she said, "she'd be happy and popular and she'd have a boyfriend."

"Perhaps," I conceded. "But I raised a son, and I know Dom was quite shy when he was your age. It took a lot for him to get up the courage to ask a girl out."

I remembered something else.

"Dom was a little bit younger than you when Em—his mum—died. He was ten. And he had a really difficult time dealing with that. I know it's not the same as your mum and dad getting divorced, but it's still the end of something, a huge change that everyone expects you to get used to, and it's not that easy, is it?"

She shook her head and I knew from the look on her face—in her eyes—that I was getting through to her.

"Did Dom's mates all have girlfriends?"

"I suppose they did."

"I bet none of them would have bothered with me. I'm—I was—such a loser. Sister Mary Grace. The Holy Virgin. That's what they call me behind my back at school. Even my mates—my so-called mates. All of them laughing at me."

"You're just taking a bit longer to grow up, Gracie. And you have a lot to deal with right now."

"Yeah. And now I have grown up, haven't I. And I've got a boyfriend who loves me. And buys me nice things. And he's six times more mature than the losers all those girls hang around with. So who's laughing now."

"I know he's probably promised you things…"

"We're going to travel and have the most amazing adventures and see the most amazing countries. Not like two weeks stuck in bloody Majorca with mum and stupid Barry."

I smiled, remembering the defiant conversations I'd had with Dom as he'd struggled through adolescence. "What's your boyfriend's name?"

"Radu. Rad. He likes it when I call him Rad."

"What's his last name?"

"He says it's Medford but it isn't really. That's just for business. It's Melnic."

I went cold. Literally.

My heart plummeted.

Was he Holly's brother?

"Where are you staying, Gracie?"

"Rad has a flat…it's very posh. Brand new. Near here."

"Just you and him?"

Gracie nodded. "There were three other girls before. But it's just us now."

"Young…like you?"

She nodded again. "They were there last week and then they left. One of them's Rad's cousin from Moldova and the other two are her mates. They're visiting England for the first time and he thought it would be better, after I showed up, if they went to stay at his other flat. In Battersea. It's even nicer than this one in Soho."

"Gracie," I said. "Does Rad make you have sex with other men?"

"He doesn't make me. It's my choice. I do it because I love him."

"Gracie…"

"He's got loads of overheads. He owes money to people. Because of his two flats. And other things. And he needs to repay his debts. I'm just helping him pay back what he owes."

"I'm sure he didn't mention any of that before you decided to move in with him."

She shook her head. "It's only temporary. I'll stop when he's paid back all the money he owes."

"Gracie…" I felt helpless. How could she believe all that rubbish? "Does he frighten you, Gracie?"

"He has a temper."

Was that a tiny crack in the wall of defiance? I tried a different tack.

"Are you scared about what'll happen if you try to leave?"

Struggling. Again.

"I have to go," she said, quickly. "He's expecting me back. I only popped out to buy something to eat."

"Do you need money, Gracie?"

"He loaned me a couple of pounds. There's a place around the corner that's open all night. I can get a Coke and some chips."

Even in the murky light thrown down by the overhead street lamp, I could see that something wasn't right. And that rapid rush of words. "Does Rad make you take things?" I asked. "Drugs?"

"Nothing bad. Just something to help me stay awake."

I had to say it. "You know, Gracie, if he really truly loved you, he wouldn't make you work like this. You know that."

She shook her head again, stubbornly.

"He'll get you addicted to whatever you're taking now. He'll put you onto more drugs—harder stuff, heroin, crack—and you'll be in debt to him and you'll never be able to pay him off. You'll end up working like this permanently."

Silence. She had to know I was right.

"Please come back with me," I said. "Your mum and dad won't blame you. I'll make sure they know none of this is your fault. And we'll keep you safe. He won't be able to come after you. Promise."

I took out my wallet and gave her £20.

"Think about it. You know you can call me. Anytime. And at least get something decent to eat. On me."

She hesitated, then took the money.

"Thanks."

I felt a pair of hands grab my arms. "She's a minor, mate, and you are very definitely nicked."

Gracie's face crumpled as handcuffs snapped around my wrists and the plain clothes guy who'd obviously been following me and watching from a safe distance issued me the standard caution and radioed for support.

"No!" Gracie shouted. "He was just trying to help me!"

"That's what they all say, love. A female officer's on her way to look after you. And as for you, mate." He gave me a shove in the direction of Wardour Street. "I hope you have a good explanation ready for your missus because you are very definitely spending the rest of tonight in custody."

CHAPTER EIGHTEEN

I'd never been arrested before.

Ever.

I knew people who had, though. And I was angry. Not only because I'd been wrongfully taken into custody—but because I didn't know what was going to happen to Gracie. I had no control over what the police were going to tell Dave and Helen and worse, how Dave and Helen were going to react. At least with me there I could have tried to mitigate the damage and show Gracie I was on her side.

I stayed angry, which did me no favours at the police station where an officer wrote my details onto a form and listed the reasons for my arrest.

"I was not paying for the sexual services of a child under the Sexual Offences Act of 2003, Section 47," I countered.

"What were you doing, then, laughing boy?"

"Giving her money for a proper meal."

"I've heard that one before as well. Step over there."

I was searched and my personal details were entered into a computer, and then they took my photo and fingerprinted me and made me give them a DNA sample and checked me against the National Database in case I was a rabid child molester who made a habit of seeking out vulnerable fourteen-year-olds to satisfy his carnal urges.

"You want to look up Radu Melnic in that thing," I said. "He's the villain in this piece."

"Empty your pockets."

They took away everything I had on me, including my watch, my mobiles, my coat and scarf, my belt and my shoes.

"You have the right to obtain free legal advice, to tell someone where you are, to have medical help if you're feeling ill, and to see the police Codes of Practice. You have the right to see this in writing."

The custody officer showed me a laminated piece of paper that repeated everything he'd just told me and included some extra stuff about regular breaks for food and using the toilet.

"Do you require an interpreter to explain this to you in another language?"

I looked at him.

He repeated it.

"No," I said.

"You have the right to have a lawyer present when we question you. You have the right to free legal advice. If you turn either of these down you can change your mind later."

"Just get on with it," I said.

"Do you wish to call anyone to let them know you're in custody?"

I glanced at the clock on the wall. "Not at half past four in the morning," I said. "Mind if I delay that decision 'til they're actually awake?"

"Your choice."

Then they put me into a holding cell, which is easily the most depressing place I've ever had to spend any time in. It had white shiny tiled walls and a window which was more like those opaque bricks you see in public loo's. They let the light in but you can't see out. It had glaringly bright overhead fluorescents and a CCTV in the ceiling and a vent for heating and an intercom screwed into the wall. Down at my level there was a bench topped with a padded mat like the thing you see in gyms, and another smaller mat for a pillow, and a blanket. There was a one-piece toilet and a tiny sink recessed into the wall. And there was a solid door with a hatch.

After the door was locked behind me and the hatch slammed shut, I stood for a moment in the cell, taking stock of my situation, trying to work out what I was going to do next. My brain was exhausted but I had too much adrenaline working its way through my body to lie down and try to sleep. I didn't think I'd be able to sleep anyway, because the noise from other detainees in the holding cells around me was constant and fairly alarming. Some of it involved swearing. Most of it involved rage which I could readily sympathise with. A few of the comments convinced me that summoning an on-call mental health advocate might have been a good idea.

I ended up pacing, trying to wear off the fury and the frustrating, pounding need to do something, anything, to try to sort out the mess I'd created.

In the end I sat down on the bench, and then I laid down, and I must have dozed off because the next thing I recall is the door opening and a police officer bringing me breakfast. This consisted of tea in a polystyrene cup and a little cardboard microwave tray filled with beans in sauce and two sausages. And a plastic spoon to eat it with.

"What's the time?" I asked, sitting up.

"Half past seven."

"Can I make my phone call now?"

"I'll let the Duty Officer know."

#

I rang Allan Pappas, the Met detective my sister's husband had told me about. Tom had promised to have a word with him. I really hoped he had.

The number Tom had given me was for Allan's personal mobile.

"Who?" he said, after I'd told him my name. Not an auspicious start.

"Jason Figgis," I said, again. "My sister's Angie Figgis. Married to Tom Leyland."

"Ah," Allan said. "Right. Yes." There was a pause. "What can I do for you?"

I told him what had happened and where I was.

"Hold tight," he said. "I'll make a couple of calls and I'll be there as soon as I can."

I had no idea where he lived but it obviously wasn't nearby. "As soon as I can" turned out to be another two hours by my reckoning, though without my watch it was only an estimate. But his intercession must have worked. The other detainees—all men except for one very loud hoarse-voiced woman with an Irish accent—were released from their cells one by one and taken away. A couple of newcomers were locked up, with predictable vocal protests. But I was left alone.

And then a police officer opened my door. A middle-aged guy was with him, mid-forties I'd say, with a lot of curly black hair and a friendly Mediterranean face.

"Allan Pappas," he said. "You're being released, no charges."

"Thank you," I said. I don't need to tell you my sense of relief was exponential.

I got my shoes and watch back, my jacket and scarf and gloves, my wallet and mobiles and keys and about £4 in loose change and a tube of lip balm from my jeans pockets. The clock on the wall over the counter outside said half past nine. My sense of timing was spot on.

"Let's have a decent breakfast," Allan said. "The stuff they give you in here's vomit-inducing."

"You won't get any arguments from me," I replied.

#

He took me to another one of those places that does a Full English all day long. He was obviously well-acquainted with it—the staff knew him on sight and gave us a table by one of its large windows overlooking the road. Our waitress was also very Mediterranean-looking, under twenty I guessed, with a headful of unruly black hair she'd attempted to tidy back with a sparkly gold headband.

"Your usual?" she inquired, delivering a carafe of freshly-brewed coffee, a jug of cream and a bowl filled with packets of sugar and sugar-substitutes.

"My usual," Allan replied.

"I'll have his usual too," I said.

"Excellent choice," the waitress said. "Tea, or is the coffee OK?"

"I'd love a cup of tea," I said. "Please."

She went away to fetch it, and returned with a large white mug filled with a strong morning builder's brew.

"My daughter," Allan said. "Marnie. She's at uni. This is her weekend job."

"Nice," I said. "My son's at college too. Studying Film. Dominic. Dom. He's eighteen."

"Marnie's doing something called Digital Culture. They should meet."

"They should," I mused. "How do you know Tom Leyland?"

"My dad was a copper. They were on the force together. I followed him into the business."

"Much like me and my dad," I said.

"I remember Figgis Green. Folky pop. 'Roving Minstrel'."

"Their anthem," I acknowledged.

"And they had a sort-of colour thing going…a really distinctive shade of green. Your dad had that velvet vest he used to wear…"

"And my mum had a floppy hat," I said.

"That's it." I could tell he was enjoying the reminiscence. "Sorry…we're getting way off-track."

"Not a problem," I said. It made a change from the obsessives in the online chat groups who got into arguments about which accidental notes my dad played in the third bar of the fourth song on their sixth album.

"I'm sorry you had to spend the night in the lockup. The guy who arrested you takes his job very seriously."

"Understood."

"He's involved in a bigger operation…they're investigating Radu Melnic. You triggered all sorts of alarm bells when you mentioned his name at the desk."

"I'm glad," I said. "They needed to be triggered. Good to know London's finest are on the case. The girl I was talking to's the daughter of my keyboard guy. Melnic's groomed her and got her working. I was trying to get her to see some sense and go home."

"It's not that easy, mate."

"I know." I drank my tea. God, that was good. "Did Tom tell you about the case I'm investigating?"

Allan gave a little gesture of his head: yes and no. "You're doing a favour for a friend."

"True," I said.

"Any plans to go legit?"

"Possibly."

"I suggest you do. If you want to stay on the good side of people like me."

"The theft I'm investigating involves a woman named Holly Medford. Her real name's Tatiana Melnic."

I knew I'd hit paydirt.

"Brother and sister," Allan confirmed. "She's well known to us. Changed her name by deed poll. And she's got her hooks into Arthur

Braskey. You know who he is?"

I nodded.

"The best advice I can give you about that lot is to steer clear. You should walk away. Quickly."

"Thank you," I said. "What can you tell me about Radu?"

"Nothing, if you're planning on poking your nose in."

"I'm not," I said. "Promise. Just curious."

"Guys like Melnic recruit vulnerable women and girls—usually but not exclusively from Eastern Europe—and move them around brothels in various countries—including the UK. This guy specializes in girls who look young. He pimps them out to punters who'll pay top price for that sort of thing. Some of them are legally adults but most of them really are underage. Runaways. Like the girl you were trying to help."

"Gracie comes from a good home," I said. "She's just very...naive."

"Not so naive anymore, unfortunately," Allan said.

"What happened to her after I was arrested?"

"She was released into the custody of her mother but Social Services will be following up. I hope she's smart enough to realize you probably saved her life."

Our breakfast arrived—two huge plates of toast, bacon, sausages, eggs, tomatoes, mushrooms and beans.

"Thanks, love," Allan said, to Marnie. "Your mum wants to know if you'll be home in time for dinner tonight. She's making something foreign-sounding off that cookery program..."

CHAPTER NINETEEN

I went home frustrated. Quite possibly I was also suffering from delayed shock.

I'd been so focused on Gracie that I'd neglected to ask Allan more about Holly. I'd made a tick in my mind—like a shopping list—the moment he'd mentioned she was well-known to him and that she'd got her hooks into Braskey. I'd meant to ask him for details, but it didn't happen.

After I'd unlocked my door and sunk into my favourite armchair and closed my eyes and thanked whatever gods were looking down upon me that I'd curried their favour, I rang Dave. The person I really needed to speak with was Helen but I didn't have her number. I wanted to ask about Gracie. But nobody was picking up.

"Just making sure everything's ok there," I said, to the recording. "And that Gracie's all right. I don't know how much they told you about last night. Can you ring me back when you have a moment? Thanks."

I got my pencil and my notebook and wrote down all the questions I wanted to ask Allan about Holly.

Then I rang him on the same number I'd called earlier. But he wasn't answering now either.

"Me again," I said. "Jason. Just want to thank you once more for your help. I have a few things I'd like to discuss with you. Some questions. About Holly Medford. If you could call me back when you're free?"

And then I fell asleep. In the armchair. For two hours. When I woke up it was past one in the afternoon and there weren't any messages from Dave or Allan.

Sleep hadn't made my anger go away, but now it was directed very squarely at Holly for wasting my time and using me for whatever scheme she had going to try and screw Braskey. I was angry about her sleazebag brother. And I was angry at myself for being stupid enough to fall into her tangle of lies.

I opened a tin of tomato soup and poured it into a bowl and warmed it up in the microwave. I popped a slice of bread into the toaster and buttered it and wolfed everything down with a cup of coffee. I showered away the memory of the holding cell. I put on some clean jeans and a new lilac-coloured shirt. I felt like burning the clothes I'd come home in.

And then I got a cab into Central London and told the driver to take me to the hotel where I'd met Holly on Saturday. I didn't bother calling her in advance. I wanted to confront her face-to-face.

The Asher was new enough and posh enough that it had the same kind of security as the Crestone: you could only get up to your floor if you used your room card to let the lift know you were a legitimate guest.

Since I wasn't a legitimate guest I went up to the roof, where there was a nightclub, a restaurant and a bar. And then I went down again to the lobby. Three people got in, but none of them had rooms on Holly's floor. Up again and down again. Nobody waiting in the lobby this time. I stepped out and went hunting for the loo. There's always a toilet near a hotel's reception desk. The trick is to look like you belong there and have a desperate need to use it.

Two minutes later I was back at the lifts. This time there were ten guests waiting. Four of them got off on the third floor. Another four on the fourth floor. And the last two...on the fifth floor.

I followed them out.

I hadn't rehearsed what I was going to say to her. I knew what my thoughts were, though, and I trusted myself to organize them properly and state exactly what I was thinking. It would not be pleasant. But at least I'd feel better, and by then, that was all I wanted.

There was a Room Service cart outside 5012 with remnants of breakfast for two on white china plates and a half-empty teapot. An all-nighter. £1500, according to the menu on the Moonlight Desires website. Nice work if you can get it.

I hammered on the door and waited.

Silence.

Of course.

She was in there. I could hear someone moving around on the other side.

I banged again. "Room Service!"

The door opened. It was a bloke in a blue silk dressing gown. I tried to see past him but he was blocking my view.

"We didn't order any more bloody room service," he said. He had an Australian accent. "Our breakfast things are there." He nodded at the cart.

A few more seconds and he was going to realize I wasn't wearing a white waiter jacket and I wasn't really bloody Room Service.

"Holly Medford, Room 5012," I said, quickly.

"As you can bloody well see, mate, I'm not Holly Medford. You must have got your orders wrong."

"What's the matter, darling?"

A female voice. And then a female. In a matching blue silk dressing gown.

"I'm sorry," I said. "I'm looking for Holly Medford."

"Call the front desk," the bloke said to the woman, who was decidedly not Holly. And then, to me: "There's no bloody Holly Medford here. We checked in this morning after a very long flight from Sydney. And I'd advise you to fuck off now before I get Security onto you."

I left. Expeditiously.

A man and a woman in the lift were coming down from the roof restaurant and getting off at the third floor. I followed them off in case Security was waiting for me in the lobby. I found the fire exit and ran the rest of the way down the stairs.

I was right. There they were, two guys in suits. They didn't see me as I slipped out behind them and made my way back to Oxford Street.

I crossed over and walked into Mayfair and made a beeline for the Crestone. It was nearly three o'clock.

I went in and looked for a sign that might direct me to the fairies, toadstools, twigs and mossy things. There it was. A smallish room along the hallway near the Wine Bar with a little podium outside, behind which stood a host sporting a whimsically embroidered vest that reminded me of the one my dad used to wear when he was fronting Figgis Green.

"Enchanted Tea?" I checked.

"Have you a reservation, sir?"

"I'm with Sally Jones," I said. "She's expecting me."

"Ah yes, of course."

He didn't bother looking me up on his screen. He took me inside.

The room had a low ceiling that was painted black and the walls were covered with well-stocked bookshelves. The carpet was a kind of deep forest green. The shelves were decorated with twists of ivy and fern fronds and hanging mosses, along with some gnomes that looked like they'd escaped from that old Travelocity ad on the telly. Each of the tables was spread with a black cloth and more strands of ivy and moss, and upon the tables were cross-sectioned cuts of tree trunks covered with tiny scones, sandwiches, tarts and cakes, all prepared to resemble a whimsical log, a spotted toadstool, a pine cone, a fairy ring.

I could see Sal sitting in the corner, facing me. All I could see of Jennifer was the back of her head: long brown hair, hanging loose. The rest of her was obscured by her chair.

Sal spotted me but gave nothing away.

"Thank you," I said, before the vested host could take me any further. "I'll just wait here, if that's all right. I'd planned this as a bit of a surprise for her guest."

"Certainly, sir."

He left me and returned to his podium.

I stood beside a pillar, wrestling with my emotions.

The tea room was absolutely packed with families, some of the little girls wearing fairy dresses with gauzy wings, some of the boys sporting elf hats.

Sal glanced at me again, then went back to the conversation she was having with Jennifer. True to her word, she was leaving it up to me.

I closed my eyes. So many thoughts were tumbling in front of me. This was something new. This was something I'd never had to deal with before. This was something...

...I truly honestly wanted to do.

I opened my eyes and walked purposefully towards the table in the corner.

"Hi," I said.

"Hi," Sal said, giving me the most amazing smile.

"I'm Jason," I said, to the young woman sitting opposite Sal.

Her face seemed so familiar to me. She was mine. It was the same when I met Dom for the first time, after I'd coached Em through his birth and watched him being delivered. He was wrinkled and red and squashed and incredibly cross about being forced out of his warm dark comfy hideaway. But after he'd been tidied up and we'd got a proper look at him, we could so clearly see the bits and pieces of ourselves that had gone into creating the features of his tiny face.

It was something like that seeing Jennifer for the first time, except that Jennifer was all grown up. It was the oddest sensation.

Sal obviously hadn't told her what her father's name was.

"Hi," she said, her eyes questioning. She was working it out. "Jenn Miller." She had a lovely Canadian accent. I suppose I was expecting something English but, of course, she'd grown up in Vancouver.

"Are you joining us for tea?" Sal inquired.

"I am," I confirmed, sitting down.

"Do you have a last name, Jason?"

"I have two last names. When I worked with Sal aboard the *Sapphire* I called myself Jason Davey. It's sort of stuck with me over the years. It's the name I still use when I play. Perform." I was incredibly nervous. The words were tumbling out.

"What do you perform?"

"Music. I'm a musician. My real last name's Figgis. I play guitar. I have a band. We're the feature act at the Blue Devil. Jazz club in Soho."

I felt like an idiot. I sounded like one, too. I couldn't believe I was actually stammering.

Jenn was looking at Sal, her eyes still questioning.

"His parents had a band too," Sal said. "In the '60s and '70s. Figgis Green. They were quite famous over here."

"The name sounds familiar."

She wasn't going to admit she'd never heard of them. She was born too late and in the wrong country. Figgis Green had some overseas success but the majority of their hits were in the UK and Europe and, oddly, Australia and New Zealand. But they never really charted in North America. And they were never big in Japan.

"Would you like some tea?" Sal asked.

"Yes please."

She poured it into a china cup decorated with swirly gold and green filigrees and added cream and sugar.

"There you are. English Breakfast."

I tried not to gulp it down.

"Fairy ring tartlet? Profiterole pine cone?"

"Are you my dad?" Jenn asked.

I looked at Sal, but Sal wasn't going to throw me any Enchanted Forest life rafts.

It had to be my decision, all the way.

"I believe I am," I replied, putting down my teacup. "And you'll have to help me out here, Jenn, because I truly and honestly don't know what to say or do next."

CHAPTER TWENTY

What we said next would fill two of my little interview notebooks, and that would only just about touch upon the next three hours of intense, focused and utterly amazing conversation.

The Enchanted Tea had two sittings. We stayed at our table through both of them; I'm certain if Sal had been anyone else, we'd have been politely asked to leave to make way for the next set of parents and their gauzy-winged fairytots.

More pots of tea were procured, and another three-tiered tree trunk tray filled with red-and-white spotted scone toadstools and wild mushroom tartlets and smoked salmon and cream cheese mossy logs.

I had no doubt Jenn was my daughter. She looked like me. She had my long, untidy dark brown hair, to which she'd introduced subtle, occasional streaks that were just a shade or two lighter than the silver filaments that were infiltrating mine. She had a fringe. And yes, my eyes. Sal's nose and her smile. My chin.

Jenn repeated what she'd already told Sal...that she had no ulterior motives other than to try and connect with her birth parents. That she was a successful photographer...and that she had a comfortable income...

"I'm thrilled beyond words to meet you, Jason...and to find out who you are...to finally know where I came from."

"It's all come as a bit of a shock to me," I confessed.

"A bit," Sal said, with a smile. "You had no idea."

"None," I admitted.

We told Jenn the truth about the night she was conceived.

"Wow," she said, shaking her head in amazement.

"Very similar to my reaction," I said.

"I'm so happy you're both such good friends. If you'd lost touch with each other that would make it so much more complicated, wouldn't it? I know Sally's never married but what about you, Jason?"

"I was married. To a makeup artist…Emma…she worked in film and TV. She died in a fire eight years ago. We have a son, Dominic. I'd love it if you could meet him…but he's a bit of a lone ranger and I'm not sure how he's going to react to the news that he has an older sister. I'll have a carefully thought-out chat with him first."

"No chance, I guess, that you and Sally might end up together…?"

Sal smiled, a little wistfully, I thought. "No chance," she said.

"What about you?" I asked Jenn.

"I was married," she said. "A very long time ago. We were way too young and way too impetuous. Of course, it didn't last. No kids."

"That'll make you feel better, Jase," Sal said. "You're not a grandfather. Yet."

"I've had a few serious relationships since then," Jenn said, "but it's not really something I want to do again. I don't need a husband to define who I am."

She looked at me.

"I love your face. You've got the most amazing features. I want to photograph you. I work mostly in black and white and your skin tone and your dark hair and those amazing eyes would make such an interesting portrait. Could I?"

"Of course," I said.

"How about Tuesday? And I don't want you to shave."

"Nothing unusual there, then," Sal said, pouring herself another cup of tea.

"It'll be a wonderful opportunity for you and me to get to know one another better," Jenn added. "I have so many things I want to ask you."

"Likewise," I said. The Enchanted Forest was a lovely venue, but it felt all wrong for the kind of conversation I really wanted to have with her. And, to be honest, though I'd initially thought it would be better to have Sal present, I was now finding myself craving something more private and personal. I was still getting used to the idea that I had a daughter. It wasn't something that was going to settle easily.

"Perfect," Jenn said. "Tuesday it is. Text me your address and phone number."

She paused to help herself to an Elfin Flower (described in the tabletop menu as quince chutney, smoked pork rillette, pickled pearl onion and teardrop chilli).

"To think that you were both working on a ship that docked in Vancouver every Saturday, and I was living there all that time…really close to the pier, in fact—I love watching the ships sail in and out in the summer…I love walking from my apartment along the seawall to the Convention Centre and Canada Place…I might even have seen you!"

"I thought you looked familiar," I said. "Starbucks. At the Pan Pacific. Venti Latte Macchiato with Almond Milk…"

Jenn looked at me.

And then grinned.

"You joker," she said. "I love you so much and I hardly even know you yet. I don't drink coffee, by the way. It's evil. Now I want to hear more about the *Sapphire*. I know what Sally's job was. Tell me all about yours."

#

It was past seven in the evening by the time we finally went back to Sal's office to do the DNA test.

"Witnesses to history," Jenn pronounced, taking photos to mark the occasion as we did the cheek swabs.

Sal then ordered fish and chips for three from the Crestone's Room Service menu, which she and Jenn washed down with a bottle of Chardonnay and I celebrated with a lovely freshly-blended melon juice cooler, made to order by an accommodating bartender. (Sal's hotel is, in fact, now one of the few places in London which offers my favourite drink from the TopDeck Lounge on board the *Sapphire*.)

The dried swabs were packaged up. We each placed our hands on the little parcel, wishing it *Bon Voyage*. Sal popped it into the hotel's outgoing mailbox…and then we exchanged heartfelt goodnights and went our separate ways.

#

I was on top of the world. It's a real emotion, something that you can't actually describe unless you've been there yourself. All of the stress and the worry that I'd been pushing to the back of my mind was gone. I'd finally met my daughter. We'd connected—literally—and now I was looking forward to seeing her again. We had each others' mobile numbers and email addresses. And she was going to come to my flat on Tuesday to capture my essence and record it for all time.

I grew up in the glare of publicity. My parents did their best to shield us from the excesses of the press, but there were still plenty of times when photographers were invited into our home to illustrate features about Figgis Green.

My entire childhood was immortalized by a never-ending parade of professional snappers who rounded Angie and me up and posed us with our toys or made us stand unnaturally beside mum and dad and, occasionally, sat us on their laps.

I look back at those photos and I remember how annoyed we were by those interruptions to our playtime and how bored we were with the entire exercise.

I've had a few PR pictures of my own done since, but that's different. That's me posing with my guitars. Professional me, Jason Davey. I'd never actually sat for a proper session as Jason Figgis, all grown up, ruggedly handsome with my David Hemmings *Blow Up* haircut, striking blue eyes and a day's worth of stubble. I was quite looking forward to it.

I suppose I was unduly distracted. I suppose I'd allowed my imagination to wander. I suppose that because I'd forgotten about Holly, I also let my guard down.

I was making my way towards Green Park, thinking I'd take the tube up to Angel and then walk home. I don't remember much about what happened next because I was shoved to the ground and when I fell, my head crashed into the pavement.

I saw explosions of stars and a man was shouting at me as he landed a kick in my back. "Didn't anybody warn you about interfering with other peoples' property?"

And then he kicked me again.

And I blacked out.

#

I came to slowly. Like you do when you're waking up from day surgery, lying on a wheeled bed in a recovery room in a hospital, with a nurse checking your pulse and asking if you'd like some apple juice and a biscuit. Except I very definitely wasn't in a hospital, let alone a bed, and there wasn't a nurse in sight. I wished there had been, because the kind of pain I was in was something I'd never before experienced. I'd been kicked and punched and I knew where the boots and fists had landed, but everything else hurt as well. Including my head.

I was standing upright, although standing may be a bit of a misnomer. I was actually hanging by my arms, which were stretched straight up over my head. There were ropes or cords or something wrapped around my wrists and as I wrenched my head back I could see the cord was looped over a wooden rafter in the ceiling and then tied onto something behind me. My head flopped down again. The toes of my trainers were just barely touching the floor, which was concrete. I was minus my winter coat and wearing just my shirt and jeans. I couldn't feel my hands.

I guessed I was in something like a warehouse. The light wasn't very good but I could see there were brick walls and dirty windows. I could barely breathe, and each time I tried to take air in, everything hurt, including my shoulders, which felt like they were on the point of dislocation. I was incredibly cold.

"Oy," said a voice somewhere in the darkness in front of me— male. "He's awake."

I saw a pair of brown leather shoes—expensive ones, polished, clean, new—and I dragged my head up again to see who they belonged to. A man. Wearing black trousers and a white dress shirt. A short leather jacket that matched his shoes.

"Radu Melnic," he said.

"I'm off your sister's case," I said. Talking was excruciating. "I don't care what she's does with her life."

Melnic chuckled.

"I don't really care either, to be perfectly honest."

His English was immaculate. Just like Holly's. With just the slightest hint of an accent.

"What I do care about is you preventing me from earning an income. I invest a lot of time and money in my acquisitions. I'm a specialist in my field. I cater to a discerning clientele. And you have taken it upon yourself to interfere with my profits."

"I was only talking to Gracie," I whispered. It was all I could manage.

"I know what you were doing. I'm not stupid. I employ minders. Do you really think I'd let a little prize like that wander around Soho on her own? You were trying to steal my property."

I didn't say anything. It was better not to. I was in serious trouble.

"I could kill you," Melnic said. "But I don't do things like that. I'm not a murderer. I like to have a clear conscience."

He was walking around me. He disappeared out of my view. I let my head flop down again.

"So I'm going to teach you a lesson. I hope you'll learn something from it. And next time, mind your own business."

Something hit me. My back. It felt solid and pliable like a length of rubber hose. It drove the breath straight out of my body and it hurt like hell. And again. I gasped, trying to get air into my lungs, trying to keep my toes on the concrete, trying not to yell, but I knew I was going to lose that battle. The third blow burned across my back and then he started on my legs.

When he hit my calves I lost my balance. I was swinging by my wrists. I couldn't stop myself from screaming but the agony was mixed with rage. I hated him for what he'd done to Gracie. And for what he was now doing to me.

They still had corporal punishment when I was at school. I was only caned once, on the palms of my hands, but I remembered it all and I remembered the anger I felt then and it was all coming back to me now. I'd forgotten to do some maths homework the night before. Outright forgotten. And then the next day it transpired a couple of other kids had forgotten too. So the teacher asked for a show of hands. Six kids confessed. I didn't. I don't know why—I guess I was petrified of being found out and thought I could fake my way through it. Except that everyone had to pass their work forward for marking by the kid ahead, and the teacher was asking for answers out loud, and he asked the boy sitting in front of me what the answer was to the next problem, and the boy sitting in front of me—who was quite smart and could have provided the answer off the top of his head—replied, "Jason hasn't done his homework, sir." instead.

And that's how I was caught out. And sent to see the headmaster with the other six kids. And we all got caned. Not, the headmaster took great pains to explain (after consulting with my teacher) because I'd neglected to do my homework. No. In my case, it was because I'd lied about it, by not admitting to it when I had the chance. Damned if you do, damned if you don't.

Damned, anyway. My pride hurt more than my hands.

Melnic wasn't letting up hitting me. It was agony but I wasn't going to let him win. The same way I wasn't going to let my teacher and the headmaster win. I closed my eyes and thought about a song. When the cane whipped into my hands, I sang the song—to myself. I wasn't defiant enough back then to sing it out loud.

I remembered which song it was, too. It was "House of the Rising Sun", by the Animals.

I began to sing it now, line by line…barely a whisper…I was Eric Burdon and I could hear Hilton Valentine's A minor chord *arpeggio* and I was going to sing that fucking song all the way through to Alan Price's pulsating Vox Continental crescendo.

It was just about when I got to Price's organ solo bridge that I heard the gunshots. Two of them. Like firecrackers. Quick and short and distinct. Right behind me. No mistaking that sound.

The rope around my wrists was loosed and I collapsed onto the hard, cold concrete floor. I lay there, frozen, petrified, not sure what was going to happen next. I could see two motionless bodies beside me. One of them was Radu Melnic. His head was lying in a spreading pool of blood. He was still holding what he'd been hitting me with: a piece of thick black electrical cord. The kind you plug in to amps.

Whoever had shot him was untying my wrists and helping me to my feet.

A tall man. In a black overcoat. With silver-grey hair. Grandad.

"Mr. Braskey can't stand child molesters," he said. "Scum of the earth. Good riddance."

"Thank you," I whispered.

"Mr. Braskey would like a word with you."

"I think I need to go to the hospital."

"Mr. Braskey doesn't like to be kept waiting, Mr. Figgis."

He had a firm hold of my arm.

"OK," I said. "OK."

"You didn't see any of this."

"Any of what?"

"Excellent, Mr. Figgis. Let me help you on with your coat."

CHAPTER TWENTY-ONE

I really did belong in the hospital. Or at least under a doctor's care. My shoulders were barely in their sockets. My back and my legs felt like they were on fire. And the feeling was coming back into my hands. I could hardly move my fingers and they were starting to swell. The pain was indescribable.

When I'd rescued Ben Quigley in northern Canada I'd got frostbite. I didn't have the right mitts for -40°C weather. My fingers went numb and then they began to feel warm…and they stayed that way until I got inside again and started to thaw out. But it was all an illusion. As the feeling came back into my fingers, they screamed in anguish.

It was that kind of pain.

I'd caught a glimpse of the other guy as I'd limped out of the warehouse with Braskey's driver. I don't want to think about what I saw. Most of his face wasn't there anymore.

Slumped in the rear passenger seat of Braskey's blue Mercedes, I pulled up the leg of my jeans and had a look at the damage. The skin wasn't broken, but my calf was criss-crossed with red welts that were well on their way to becoming nasty, angry bruises. I imagined my back was in the same sort of shape. I was halfway sitting up, but every time Grandad accelerated through some signals I was thrown back against the leather seat and the pain was unbearable.

I wasn't paying attention to where we were going. It was dark outside and even with the streetlights I didn't recognize any of the buildings or roads. I wasn't even sure if we were still in London.

Where we ended up was another old, cold, empty brick building—I swear there must be an Airbnb arrangement in the UK involving derelict warehouses and London's criminal underworld.

I was assisted out of the car—again, the firm hand on my upper arm, precluding any thoughts I might have had of legging it out of there (not bloody likely). I was taken inside by way of a creaking door and led to a spot some feet away where there were some overhead electric lights, a couple of wooden chairs (the kind you'd find in a dusty attic, leftovers from an old dining set, literally on their last legs), a small blaze crackling nicely in a perforated steel drum, and Arthur Braskey himself, impeccably dressed in his camel overcoat and scarf.

It was freezing. I was glad Grandad had the sense to collect my coat. And that Braskey had the foresight to arrange for some primitive warmth. A picket line fireplace was better than nothing.

"Good evening, Mr. Figgis. I trust you're well?"

"Not really," I said.

"Please, sit."

He indicated one of the wooden chairs. I thought it best to comply.

Grandad was beside me as soon as I sat down. He pulled my arms behind me and had my wrists cuffed to the back support with plastic zap straps before I knew what was happening. My shoulders and back strongly protested. I strongly protested too, and so did the chair.

And then he cuffed each of my ankles to a wooden leg in front, using the zap straps to further secure those fasteners to the supporting crossbar.

Out of the frying pan, into the fire.

I was not having a good Sunday.

Braskey was standing in front of me. "I trust you've discovered the significance of the necklace?"

"Wedding gift," I said. "You and Holly were married. And six months ago, the marriage fell apart."

"Bravo, Mr. Figgis. Correct. Miss Medford began her career as a common prostitute, working her way around the cruise ship circuit. And then she progressed to dancing in gentlemen's clubs. We met at Cha-Cha's three years ago. I knew what she was and what she was after but I allowed myself the indulgence. We tied the knot in the Seychelles two months after that. Her choice. Private chalet on a pristine white sand beach. Exclusive complimentary couples spa massage. Miss Medford believed she'd hit the jackpot. Such an accomplishment for someone who'd grown up in, shall we say, less-than-advantaged circumstances. She was able to give up dancing and enjoy the trappings of a privileged country life. It didn't last, of course. The marriage became untenable. There's a bracelet that goes with the jade necklace, by the way, and a pair of earrings. It's known in jewellery circles as the Gladstone Collection. Do you know how much the Gladstone Collection is worth, Mr. Figgis?"

"I don't."

"Nineteen million pounds, Mr. Figgis. I didn't pay that much for it, of course. A mere £10 million when it became available through Sotheby's twenty-five years ago. But still…a not inconsiderable amount. When the divorce was finalized, Miss Medford left me the earrings and the bracelet, but she took the necklace. Needless to say, it was not included in the settlement. And as I'm sure you can understand, I wish to have the necklace back. Along with the cash she removed from a joint bank account which I'd foolishly arranged to open in both of our names when we were married."

"Not a gambling debt, then," I guessed.

"Of course it was a gambling debt, Mr. Figgis. The woman suffers from an addiction. I covered what she owed at first however after the divorce I saw no reason to continue."

"Did she leave you? Or was it the other way round?"

Braskey laughed. "What do you think?"

"I've no idea."

"Miss Medford had got as much as she believed she could from the marriage and felt it best to leave before I ordered her out. It was only a matter of time. Of course, she found it necessary to go back to work. Which she did."

"And the money that was stolen from her locker?"

Braskey laughed again. "Do you really believe that story?"

"I did. I guess I'm a bit naive that way. I tend to take people at face value because I'm an honest person myself. I don't believe her story anymore, though. I think she was looking for somewhere to hide out, preferably at no cost to herself, and she'd probably outstayed her welcome at other hotels around London. And then she remembered someone she'd met aboard a cruise ship when she was in the Med. That someone happened to be in management at the Crestone. I think she came up with the story that her money was stolen to get some sympathy and a free room for a few more days.

And a bonus—a place where her boyfriend could scan the hotel guests' credit cards and make a few bob on the side."

"Bravo, Mr. Figgis. You are wise to her ways. The return of the money is obviously important to me, but I'm prepared to let that go. She's likely gambled it away and is as poor as a church mouse. But I really would like my necklace back."

"What if she's sold it?" I said.

"She cannot sell it. Like a priceless work of art, it's too well-known in the jewellery world. And unlike misappropriated gold or silver, it can't be melted down or taken apart and sold in pieces. The beads by themselves are pretty, but the true value of the necklace is in the whole, not its parts."

I was about to reply when I heard my mobile ringing. It was in the pocket of my jacket.

Grandad reached into my pocket and removed it and gave it to Braskey, who placed it on one of the other chairs, where it continued to ring until my voice messaging cut in.

"I've shared some useful information with you, Mr. Figgis. I'm optimistic this will convince you of my higher intentions. I simply wish my Gladstone Collection to be restored to its previous intact state. And I believe you are still in a position to assist me in that endeavour."

"I don't think I am," I said.

"No?"

"I've dropped the investigation. I'm not sure what the official term is. Resigned the account? Recused myself...?"

Braskey smiled. He gave a slight nod of his head, and Grandad dragged me and my chair over to the nearest wall. Turning me around, he tipped me backwards, so that the chair back was balanced precariously against the bricks and the chair's front legs—and my feet—were hanging in midair.

And then he removed my trainers and socks.

Braskey got a pair of long barbecue tongs from behind the steel drum and poked them into the barrel and lifted out a red-hot piece of something that looked like a gigantic bolt.

"There are three ways of transmitting heat, Mr. Figgis. Conduction, convection and radiation. Conduction is the process involved in firewalking. Coals and woodchips are made up almost entirely of carbon, and carbon is an exceptionally poor conductor of heat. Which is, of course, the science behind the success of the exercise."

He carried the glowing red bolt across to the wall where I was immobilized.

"Most metals, on the other hand, are far more efficient at transferring heat."

He held the bolt very close to the sole of my left foot. It was searingly hot.

"If you would oblige me, Mr. Figgis. I'm aware that Miss Medford is no longer a guest of the Crestone Hotel. Where is she staying now?"

"I don't know," I said, panicking. I could hear my mobile ringing again. Fuck. "Truly, honestly. She was at the Asher the other day but she's not there anymore. I went looking for her. She's not there. Please believe me."

He didn't.

I screamed as he laid the red-hot bolt flat against the bottom of my left foot, just below my toes. I could smell my flesh burning. *Fuckfuckfuckfuck.*

"I'm telling you the truth!" I yelled. "You deranged fuckwit!"

Arthur Braskey pressed the red-hot bolt against the ball of my right foot. I screamed again, kicking against the plastic cuffs that were holding my ankles to the chair legs.

"That's for insulting me," he said.

"I don't know where the fuck she is! I wish I'd never fucking met her!"

"We have that in common, Mr. Figgis." He flipped the bolt back into the burning barrel and tossed the tongs after it. He nodded once more to Grandad, who disappeared into the darkness and returned moments later carrying two large tin buckets. He placed these on the floor in front of me, then tipped my chair forward so that its legs— and my feet—landed inside them. They each contained about two inches of freezing cold water.

Braskey picked up my mobile and looked at it.

"You have two missed calls from Trevor," he said, placing it back on the chair. "Goodbye, Mr. Figgis. I hope the next time we meet it will be under more favourable circumstances."

And then he left. With Grandad.

I sat for a few moments, waiting for my heart to recover and my adrenaline to stop screeching through my body and for the searing pain in my feet to diminish, which, of course, it didn't. The cold water helped. A little.

My chair wasn't long for this world. I could feel it wobbling and hear it creaking, all of its joints precariously held together with ancient carpentry and hundred-year-old glue.

The brick wall was about a foot behind me. Perhaps a bit more. Far enough away that I could get some momentum going. I dug into the bottoms of the tin pails with my heels and launched myself backwards with as much strength as I could muster.

The water and the buckets and my feet went up into the air as the chair's back collided with the bricks. I had the good sense to duck my head forward at the moment of impact. I heard something splinter but it wasn't enough to free me. The two buckets dropped off, clattering to the floor. The chair righted itself, intact.

I tried again. This time my feet were flat on the freezing concrete. I kicked backwards and slammed the chair into the wall. Something gave way and I crashed to the floor, the plastic fasteners still holding me fast. But a piece of the chair's back had fallen out and my left hand was free. I dragged myself—and the chair—across to where my mobile was and woke it up.

I was debating which to call first—an ambulance or Allan Pappas—when Trev rang a third time.

"Where the hell have you been?" he said. "Mark Williamson wants a meeting."

"Who?" I said.

"Mark Williamson. Knave Records. I sent him the demo on Friday. He's very keen, Jason. I promise I didn't mention your parents. Wednesday at two. I'll round up the others and meet you there."

"OK," I said. "OK." My brain wasn't cooperating. "Can you help me, Trev?"

"Sure. What's up?"

"Do you think you could come and collect me? And take me to a hospital?"

Trevor's voice immediately switched from pounding excitement to concern. "What's wrong? Are you at home?"

"Not at home," I said. "I'm in trouble, Trev."

"Where do I need to be?"

"I don't know."

"Switch on your map," he suggested, after a moment.

I should have thought of that myself. But my head was exploding and I think my brain was beginning to shut down. The concussion from when I'd crashed to the pavement after Radu Melnic had hit me had finally caught up.

The pulsating blue dot on the map on my phone indicated I was somewhere in Poplar, E14. Next to the Limehouse Cut. I conveyed that to Trev. I also had the presence of mind to describe my immediate surroundings and what I was seeing on both the satellite view and the map.

And then everything went black.

CHAPTER TWENTY-TWO

It was very late Sunday night by the time Trev found me. I was lying where I'd collapsed, still attached to the broken chair, still clutching my phone, though it had shut itself off because the battery—unlike me—had died.

It had taken Trev a good half hour to actually locate me once he'd parked his car in a derelict patch of wasteland outside the abandoned factory.

I was drifting in and out of consciousness. I remember him asking what the hell had happened and then after I'd told him, Trev being slightly paranoid that whoever had done this to me could still be lurking in the shadows, waiting to ambush him as well.

"All gone," I assured him. "Won't be back."

"Who's 'they'?" Trev said. "Or shouldn't I ask?"

"Best not," I said.

Fortunately he had one of those devices in his pocket that does 6,000 useful things, and one of its pull-outs was a little knife that he used to slice through the plastic zap straps.

I couldn't walk. I could barely stand up. He had to half-carry, half-drag me back out to his Audi. He eased me into the passenger seat and buckled me up and then momentarily debated whether he ought to call an ambulance to take me to the hospital.

"Quicker to drive me yourself," I said. "Please."

I don't know whether that was the wisest decision, considering I could have expired on the spot from whatever it is that kills you when your brain's been battered. But Trev's one of those guys who thinks efficiently under pressure. He took a minute to locate the nearest A&E and then we were on our way.

Once we were there, I was taken straight in. They don't mess about with head injuries. I remember someone helping me get my clothes off and someone else gently lying me down and hooking me up to a machine that monitored my blood pressure and O_2 levels and heartbeat and four or five other things I had no idea they could keep track of.

I remember a doctor and a nurse examining me all over and asking me questions to find out how cognizant I was.

And then discussing my injuries in medical terms and asking me more questions about how I came to be in such a state, which I'm not sure I answered to their total satisfaction. I recall telling them on a scale of 1 to 10 that my pain level was about 25. And that resulted in some paracetamol being administered, which wasn't very effective, but I suppose under the circumstances they didn't want to risk anything stronger in case my head injury got worse.

They tidied up my feet, washing off the dirt and mud and then bandaging them with gauze. They tutted over the welts and bruises on my back and legs and allowed me to stay lying on my tummy while they got an impossible urine sample out of me, and then they wheeled me off for an x-ray to make sure my kidneys weren't damaged. And when I was wheeled back into the cubicle I found Trev still sitting patiently in a chair, checking his messages.

It must have been about three in the morning on Monday by then. I really just wanted to go to sleep. And I suppose I must have dropped off because the next thing I remember I was being offered breakfast and Trev was coming back from the loo and the doctor was telling me they were discharging me and was there anyone who could keep an eye on me for the next twenty-four hours?

I assured them there was, and I was released into Trev's custody, along with instructions to keep off my feet and, if necessary, to use the crutches that were being sent home with me (and if I wouldn't mind returning them when they were no longer needed it would be greatly appreciated). I was given some stronger painkillers to be used with caution.

I couldn't quite manage the crutches. You need sturdy shoulders and hands and armpits and none of mine wanted to cooperate. Fortunately Trev was able to locate an unoccupied wheelchair in an empty corridor. He appropriated it and rally-ran me and the crutches out to his car. And then he drove me back to my flat.

#

Some old converted terraces have had lifts retrofitted around the back of the property in order to create ease of access for those who are less-than-able-bodied and those who are simply not inclined to tackle stairs.

My building is not one of them.

With Trev on one side of me and the banister on the other, I managed to hobble up to the first floor. I got my door unlocked and collapsed onto my bed while Trev made us mugs of strong tea in the kitchen.

I rang Katey.

"What's up?" she said. She was at work: I could hear one of her colleagues in the background, talking on the phone to a corporate client about airfares to New York and whether or not the hotel he'd chosen allowed early arrivals and late checkouts.

"Any chance you can come over and be my guardian angel for the next day or so?" I asked.

"Not a chance in hell until half past five," she said. "But I'm all yours after that. Shall I bring my usual wings or the special occasion ones that come with the lopsided and slightly tarnished halo? And why do you need a guardian angel?"

"Bring your entire celestial wardrobe," I said, "and I promise I'll explain more when you get here."

Trev delivered my tea and a delicious Marmite-and-butter sandwich and I told him about Katey.

"If I allow time for her to pop home and pick up some things, she won't likely be here until after seven tonight."

"I'm not absolutely certain I can stay until then," Trev said, doubtfully. "The studio's booked solid…and I've promised I'll be in by noon."

He really wanted to leave. I'm positive he'd convinced himself that bad men with even badder intentions were lurking on the stairs, waiting for the optimal moment to batter down the door and assassinate both of us.

"I'll be ok," I said.

"You sure?"

"I'm sure," I said.

#

I ended up falling back asleep and I stayed that way until Katey arrived, bang on time, bearing wine and a real pair of feathery angel wings which shared a shopping bag with some sexy new knickers and a lacy bra from our favourite lingerie shop down the road from the travel agency.

I only wish I'd been physically able to fully appreciate them.

Katey took one look at me and stowed the shopping bag in the cupboard.

"What on earth have you been up to?" she asked, with a tender kiss, as she knelt on the floor beside my bed.

#

I guess my mind and my body had simply had enough. With Katey there I was secure and safe, the way you remember feeling when you're a kid and you're home from school and sick and shivering under the blankets and your mum's making sure you have a hot water bottle and mugs of lovely warm milk with sugar and the undoubting reassurance that whatever's wrong with you, it will be all better in the morning.

I went to sleep and stayed asleep for about twelve hours.

I was jangled awake by my phone.

I reached across to the bedside table to pick it up, my back and shoulders letting me know on no uncertain terms what a bad idea that was.

"It's me," said the female voice on the other end. "Jenn. I'm about ten minutes away. I'm on a bus."

Bugger.

I'd completely forgotten about Jenn coming to take pictures of me.

"It's Tuesday, isn't it," I said.

Jenn laughed. "Yes, it is. Where have you been?"

"You don't want to know."

I checked beside me. Katey wasn't there. I was fairly certain she'd spent the night, though I had no memory of it. I caught the time on the little alarm clock I keep beside my phone. Half past ten.

"Just press the intercom button at the front door when you get here," I said. "I'll let you in. I'm on the first floor."

"Upstairs?" she checked. "The one above street level?"

"That's it."

"Thanks. I'm always a little confused by British floor numbers. See you in ten minutes."

There was a note on the pillow beside me. From Katey. Apologizing for having to go into work. Telling me about the tea she'd left me in the pot in the kitchen and the scrambled eggs and toast in the fridge. And a promise to ring me at noon to make sure I was all right.

I crawled out of bed, testing my feet. They were swollen and they hurt like hell, but if I balanced on the outside edges of my soles and my heels, I could walk. Just.

I limped into the kitchen and opened the fridge door and found my scrambled eggs and toast.

I ate them cold and then took the knitted cosy off the teapot and poured myself a cuppa that I popped into the microwave to warm up.

I swallowed one of the painkiller tablets I'd been issued at the hospital.

And then I hobbled back to the bedroom to get dressed: jeans and an old white shirt, easy to slip on with minimal effort and a compromise on the discomfort.

The downstairs intercom buzzed a few minutes after that. I let Jenn in and heard her climbing the stairs, and then, there she was.

I opened the door.

"Hi," she said, beaming.

"Hi. Come in."

She saw my very obvious limp and the gauze bandages as I took her into the living room. "Are you OK? I like the rough look—the messed-up hair and the two-day stubble—it's perfect. But what happened to your feet?"

I sat her down on my sofa, then sank into my favourite armchair and told her. Everything. Or as much as I could remember, anyway, and what I could piece together from what Trev had said.

"You have to be kidding."

"I'm not. Unfortunately."

"Wow. I'm totally blown away. You have a secret life as a private eye. Does Sally know?"

"Sal's the one who got me into this. Tea and biccies?"

"I'd love some. Don't get up—I'll help myself."

"There's cold tea on the counter," I said, over my shoulder. "You'll have to warm it up. Biscuits in the cupboard over the sink."

"I've put the kettle on to make a fresh pot," she said, coming back with a plateful of my favourite chocolate digestives, which she placed on the little coffee table.

And then she unpacked her cameras from the hard carry-cases she'd brought with her.

"Just sit there," she said. "Be yourself. The light in here's fantastic. I'm going to shoot you while we talk. You look tousled and dangerous and incredibly vulnerable."

"I am incredibly vulnerable," I said as she moved around me, her camera shutter clicking.

"Your eyes are lovely. But there's a hint of some sadness there."

"It's my tousled past," I said.

Jenn laughed and went back to the kitchen to rescue the kettle.

"By the way, I called up the Blue Devil's PR guy and I got permission to take pictures of you and your band tomorrow night at the club. He said he was OK with it if you were OK with it. I haven't got any release forms with me but I'll email them to you when I get home. It's just a formality."

"I'm OK with it," I said.

"My PR pics are legendary. You can have my services for free. My gift."

"Thank you," I said. "I'd love that."

I meant it.

One of my throwaway phones was ringing. I'd left it in the bedroom. Jenn went to fetch it for me.

It was Holly.

"What," I said, "do you want?"

"I wasn't telling you the truth."

"There's a surprise."

"I do know something about that necklace. I know a lot about it, in fact."

"Listen," I said. "It's time you stopped this bullshit. I've had another conversation with Braskey."

She didn't say anything.

"He wanted to know where you were. I told him I didn't know. Which was the truth. He decided it wasn't. I ended up in the hospital."

"I'm so sorry," Holly said.

"You can understand my reluctance to have anything more to do with you. I really don't feel like another meet-up with your ex."

"What did he tell you?"

"You owe him a lot more money than you claimed. But he doesn't care about that. What he cares about is the necklace."

"Oh yes. The precious necklace which is worth £19 million. Which he will kill me for."

"If he kills you," I said, "he won't get it back, will he? It seems a rather short-sighted decision on his part. I'm going to say goodbye now."

"Stop!" Holly said. "Don't. Please."

I waited.

"I don't know who else to trust. I do have the necklace but I've hidden it. I want you to collect it for me."

I laughed, a little ruefully. "I can barely walk. And I really don't want to give Braskey a reason to come after me again. Why can't you collect it yourself?"

"Please, Jason. I cannot go outside anymore. I know he has people looking for me. He will find me. He has too many friends."

"And what are you going to do with the necklace if I agree?"

"I want you to give it back to him. It will make him happy. He won't hurt you for that."

"No? He'll almost certainly want to know how it came into my possession. Why not just ring him up yourself and tell him where it is?"

"Because once he has it, he will find me and that will be the end of me. I want to get out now, Jason. I want to take your advice and leave England. If I give you the instructions about where to collect the necklace, and you wait a day before giving it to him…perhaps two days…then I will have time to make my escape."

I needed a smoke.

My cigarettes were on the coffee table.

I lit up, hoping Jenn wouldn't mind.

"Are you there?" Holly asked.

"I'm here," I said.

"The necklace is in Soho. With a friend who works at a walk-up on Berwick Street. Her name is Rebecca. She thinks it's just an ordinary piece of cheap jewellery. She has no idea how valuable it is."

My turn not to say anything.

"I will call her and tell her you're on your way to collect it. Her maid will let you in. Once you have it, you can ring me back at this number. And then wait until I confirm that I am safe…and you can return it to Braskey."

I still didn't say anything. I smoked my cigarette in silence as Jenn continued to snap pictures.

"Please, will you help me, Jason?"

CHAPTER TWENTY-THREE

"Listen," Jenn said, gently pulling my socks over my swollen feet. "I've been on assignment in Afghanistan. I've covered riots in the States. I don't scare easily."

"I really don't want you to be involved in this," I said. "I really don't want to be responsible if anything happens to you."

She eased on my oldest pair of battered, worn-out trainers and tied up the laces, then helped me up from the armchair.

"Don't be ridiculous," she said.

#

We went by taxi.

I recognized the Berwick Street address from my Saturday night prowl looking for Gracie. There was a peep show with a neon pink marquee advertising *Lovely Girls* and beside that an open doorway painted black, and beyond that a carmine-red vestibule with a big sign promising *Models on the 1st and 2nd Floors*, and an invitation to *Please Walk Up*.

There were, of course, stairs. Steep, narrow ones, with dodgy loose boards and no handrail. And they smelled like mildew and piss.

"Lean on me," Jenn said, offering her arm.

She was shorter than me. I tried not to put too much of my weight on her during the slow, tortuous climb. We arrived, at last, at the first-floor landing, where there was another black door and a young Asian guy in a baseball cap and a padded ski jacket who was just leaving.

"Nobody's there," he said. "Waste of time."

"The door's open downstairs," I said. "They usually shut it when they're closed for business."

"Yeah. False advertising. See ya."

The landing was set up as a kind of waiting room, with a row of mismatched chairs for punters and some discarded newspapers and magazines piled on the floor and a little reception table and chair in the corner for the maid. The walls had originally been painted off-white but had deteriorated into something resembling dirty mocha, and there was a window, though the panes were filthy and the only thing visible through the dirt was the wall of the building across the way.

From the waiting area there was another staircase leading up to the second floor, and I could see that between the two landings there was a toilet (door open) and a helpful sign: *Please only put toilet paper in the loo* and another one: *Gorgeous model on 2nd floor this way.*

Holly's instructions had specifically stated First Floor. I pressed the bell button on the wall beside the black door.

Jenn was taking pictures with her phone. "I love the atmosphere of this place," she said. "And the smell."

The smell was an attempt at something exotic, promising forbidden love and Kama Sutra enticements on a Soho budget. But tempered somewhat by the deplorable odour of old dirty bricks and old dirty toilets (undoubtedly coming from the one on the landing).

"Is that blood?" Jenn said, peering at a couple of drops of something that had dried brownish red on the wooden floor. "Fabulous."

She took some more pictures and went scouting for evidence of other leaked body fluids.

I rang the bell again. I was beginning to think the Asian guy was right and Holly's friend had taken the day off and the door downstairs had been left open for the sole benefit of the Gorgeous Model on the second floor.

Or, if Rebecca was busy with a client, at the very least her maid should have been there to tell us to wait.

I debated asking Jenn to go upstairs to ask if the Gorgeous Model had any idea where Rebecca was and, if so, when she was expected back.

Then I decided to try the handle on the black door.

It wasn't locked.

I pushed the door open a crack and peeked inside.

A single table lamp had been left on, and by its light I could see a double bed and a red sheet and red skirting around the bottom. The sheet had been pulled aside to expose the mattress. There were two pillows in matching red covers and they had been tossed across the sheet. There was a large mirror on the wall at the head-end of the bed, and a very worn patterned carpet covering the wooden floorboards. Beside the bed was the table that the lamp was on. It reminded me of a church altar, laid with a white linen cloth and holding a silver chalice, two wax candles, an incense burner (the obvious source of the Kama Sutra scent) and a CD player. On the far side of the bed was a clothes rack upon which were hanging a number of costumes, most of them sexy and skimpy, some involving feathers and black leather. Some of the costumes were on the floor, as if someone had been searching through them and didn't care if they fell off their hangers.

I pushed the door further but it wouldn't open more than halfway. Something was blocking its path.

I went inside to see what it was.

Jenn was right behind me.

"Jesus," she said.

I guessed the two females covered in blood on the floor were Rebecca and her maid. And there was no way they could still be alive. I didn't want to touch them; this was most definitely a crime scene. I didn't need my fingerprints and DNA and lint from my clothing to contaminate it—or them.

They'd been slashed with something large and sharp and wielded by someone who knew what they were doing because they'd gone for the carotid neck arteries and made doubly sure the job was done properly with some stabs to their abdomens. Their blood was everywhere: all over their bodies, pooled on the floor, splashed onto the walls.

And there was a third victim. A man with the same sort of wounds. I could see his face.

He looked familiar.

It took a second.

It was the guy who'd tried to steal my guitar out of my car.

#

I closed the bedroom door. I was trying not to panic.

I rang Allan Pappas.

"Don't touch anything," he cautioned.

"I'm well ahead of you there."

"Wait for me on the landing."

I didn't want to stick around. I wanted to be somewhere public.

"There's a coffee place around the corner," I said. "Berwick Beans. We'll wait for you there, if that's OK with you."

#

Jenn bought herself a large cup of chai tea and carried a big strong mug of coffee back to me, but I couldn't bring myself to drink it.

I'd only ever seen dead people lying at peace in open coffins.

Until Radu Melnic and his mate, that is. And they were nasty. They'd done horrible, nasty things to me. I'd been barely conscious and that had softened the shock somewhat. I hadn't really processed what I'd witnessed.

My brain was fully functional now and the two women behind the door were, as far as I knew, innocent victims. Rebecca looked in her mid-twenties, the same age as Shaniah—Cathy—the dancer I'd had breakfast with. She had long blonde hair and a sweet face and was wearing a black lacy see-through bra and matching knickers and not much else.

Her maid was much older, perhaps a former sex worker herself, just trying to earn enough money to keep food on the table and a roof over her head. She was dressed in a sort-of uniform, perhaps her idea of what a real maid would wear if she'd been inspired by *Downton Abbey* but only had a budget for cheaponlinecostumes.com: a white blouse with full sleeves and a longish black skirt, a tiny white pinafore and a little white maid's dress-up cap, which had fallen out of her hair but was still partially pinned in place.

The brutality was all too much for me.

I sat at the rough wooden table, staring at my coffee.

"I'm so sorry for involving you, Jenn."

My voice was shaking.

"It's OK." Her voice was calm and steady. "I insisted you bring me along. You don't have to apologise."

She was looking at the photos on her phone.

"I took a picture of the guy who was on his way out when we got there. I'll give it to your friend."

She showed it to me. I don't know how or when she managed to do it. But there he was, full face. Potential witness. Potential suspect. Potential innocent punter looking for a good time on a dreary Tuesday afternoon.

The police arrived fairly quickly. They were in the process of putting up their blue and white Do Not Cross tape as Allan came into Berwick Beans to collect us and take us back to the scene of the crime.

"Mind telling me what you were actually doing here?" he asked.

"Holly Medford rang me," I said. "She wanted me to pick up something she'd left with Rebecca."

"And that something was…?"

"A jade necklace. She said she'd left it with Rebecca for safekeeping. It belongs to Arthur Braskey. She wanted me to give it back to him."

"Would I be right in assuming you didn't find any jade necklaces on the premises?"

"I didn't look," I said.

Allan disappeared behind the black door and I could hear him talking to the forensics people and the pathologist and the two other police officers who were inside the room. He was gone for about fifteen minutes, and then he came out again.

"We've searched the bodies and the flat. Not a lot of places you can hide something like that. No sign of your necklace."

"I'm not surprised," I said. "Could that be why they were murdered?"

"Possibly. The killer or killers would have to have known about the necklace though. Unless they found it by accident. What's it worth?"

"Nineteen million pounds," Jenn said.

Allan whistled. "Who else did Holly tell?"

"I don't know," I said.

"Any chance someone overheard her conversation with you?"

I shook my head. "Not at my end. But I wouldn't put anything past Braskey."

"Arthur Braskey doesn't do knife killings," Allan said. "He prefers shooters. Quick and tidy."

I didn't think Radu Melnic or his friend looked particularly tidy the last time I'd seen them, but I wasn't going to mention that to Allan.

"The dead man in there," I said, instead. "I've seen him before. He tried to steal a guitar out of my car."

"Colin Cooper. One of Holly Medford's old boyfriends. She was seeing him before she married Arthur Braskey. We arrested him for theft a couple of years ago. He filed a statement saying that he'd loaned money to Holly after she'd told him her life was in danger from a loan shark. She hadn't paid it back. He'd then lost his job and was in danger of losing his house. He was given a suspended sentence and he's been living on the edge ever since."

"I left my car unlocked so I guess it was a crime of opportunity," I said. "Still. You wonder. What was he doing outside my flat?"

Allan shrugged. "Looking for digs? Work? More to the point, what was he doing here, today?"

"Unlucky customer," Jenn guessed. "Wrong time, wrong place."

"Or he knew something about the necklace," I said.

"Could be he was there for the same reason you were," Allan said. "And it could have been you dead on the floor instead of him."

The suggestion was sobering. And didn't make me feel any less shaky.

"What do you know about Stanislav Turcan?" I asked.

"Small fry. Has a habit of installing himself as a desk clerk in London hotels so he can skim customers' credit card numbers. Although his days are numbered. You can only alter your appearance and your CV so many times before the CCTV images give you away. Hotel managers talk to one another. Why?"

"He's Holly's current boyfriend. And pimp."

Allan looked surprised. "Something I didn't know. Thanks for that. Would you two mind coming back to the station with me? I'd like to take your statements."

"A return engagement," I said, unhappily.

"I promise you'll be treated with slightly more respect this time round."

CHAPTER TWENTY-FOUR

It was very late by the time we'd finished giving our separate statements and Jenn had handed over the photo of the Asian guy on her phone, as well as a few others that were deemed "of interest".

I'd finally stopped shaking. And having Allan in the interview room with me had calmed me down a little. I really was helping the police with their inquiries—and I was on the right side of the law this time. Allan was correct—I was treated with a good deal more respect this time around.

It was dark outside and Jenn and I were both exhausted—Jenn even more so because she was still dealing with jetlag and the eight-hour time difference between Vancouver and London.

"I'm just going to grab a cab back to my hotel and order some room service and crash into bed," she said. "Will you be ok getting back on your own?"

"I'll get the driver to help me up the stairs," I said. "And if he refuses I'll crawl on my hands and knees."

"You're funny. I'll come over tomorrow to pick up my cameras."

"Anytime," I said. And then I remembered the meeting at Knave Records. "But can you make it before noon?"

"I'll be there at 10.30," Jenn promised.

#

My taxi driver was obliging, especially after I offered him an additional £30 on top of the fare.

"I've got a brother with CP, mate. I'm used to this. Get your arm over my shoulder and I'll have you safely upstairs in two ticks."

He wasn't kidding.

"You should consider a second career as a caregiver for the disabled," I said. "Thank you."

"That is my second career," he said, sitting me down on my sofa. "Have a good night."

He let himself out.

I thought about getting myself some dinner. I had frozen things in packets in the freezer that I could microwave and I knew I had a new G&B Velvet Salted Caramel chocolate bar in the fridge for dessert.

And then Holly rang. Again.

"I was going to call you," I said, which was essentially true. I just hadn't yet decided what I was going to say to her. And when I was going to do it.

"Have you got the necklace?"

"There was a problem."

"What kind of problem?"

I told her.

Including the fact that the police were now involved.

"So the necklace is gone."

She sounded annoyed. Or something. What she didn't sound like was someone who particularly cared that three people had just been murdered—one of them supposedly her friend, the other a former lover—and it was very likely because she'd put them in harm's way.

"It's gone," I said.

"Braskey will hear about this."

"I'm sure he will. Which is why you should leave now. I'm giving you my best advice. Buy a ticket on Eurostar and just go."

"You won't tell the police I've been in touch with you."

"I won't tell the police," I said. "Or Braskey."

"Thank you, Mr. Private Investigator."

"Goodbye, Holly," I said.

#

I crawled into bed and slept until nine the next morning, when I woke up with throbbing feet, a stinging back and aching shoulders. It wasn't bad enough to stop me performing at the Blue Devil, though I reckoned I'd have to stay seated to get through my three sets. I use a stool on stage but I often stand up and walk around a little while I play. There was no way that was going to happen that night.

I reluctantly swallowed another painkiller—I still needed them, but I hated the idea that I might become dependent. My cigarette habit was bad enough.

At half past ten precisely, Jenn arrived to collect her cameras. I was dressed and waiting with a plate of chocolate and orange Jaffa Cakes—my standby for when I run out of digestives—and a freshly-made pot of English Breakfast.

"I've become a fan of this tea," she said. "I'm definitely switching from red rooibos when I get home."

She brought me her cameras.

"We didn't get a chance to look at the photos I took yesterday. I wanted to let you pick out your favourites."

I had to admit she was very, very good. With my white shirt rumpled and all undone and my battered and much-washed jeans, my uncombed hair and unshaved face, she'd made me look like the Blue Devil's secret swarthy rock god. She'd have given David Bailey a good run for his money in the 1960s. I made a mental note to recommend her to Mark Williamson at Knave Records for our cover art.

"I have two rolls of old-fashioned film, too," she said. "I love the graininess and the warmth. Working with digital and working with film's like comparing Spotify to old-fashioned vinyl. I'll send you a contact sheet and you can pick out what you want from those as well. And then I'll do prints. Big. Suitable for framing."

"Thank you," I said, trying to imagine how a poster-sized black and white blow-up of me, swathed in cigarette smoke and resembling something that had just rolled out of bed after a rough night on the town would look hanging on the wall above my armchair.

"And I don't think that Asian guy at the walk-up yesterday was any kind of killer," she added. "He was too nonchalant. He didn't even try to hide his face. And he wasn't in a hurry."

"He could have been a very well-trained assassin," I said. "And an equally-good actor."

"I don't think so. It's not easy to knife three people to death on your own. And those bodies looked like they'd been there a while.

The blood wasn't fresh. The killer had help."

We were interrupted by my mobile. I glanced at the screen. Dave.

"I need to take this," I said to Jenn.

"Sorry, Jason," Dave said. "I know it's early. Musicians' hours."

"I'm awake," I said. "What's up?"

"Gracie's run off again, Jason. I might not make this afternoon's meeting at Knave. We're going out to look for her again."

"What happened?"

"She locked herself in her room last night but when Helen checked on her first thing this morning, she was gone. Helen had taken her phone away but Gracie has a computer. Helen tried to see if she'd got any emails or messages but Gracie'd deleted everything. The police suggested we look for other programs. I don't know. Messenger. Facebook. Twitter. But she's got everything passworded. All we can think is that man somehow convinced her to come back to him."

"It couldn't have been him," I said. "He's dead."

There was a moment of silence on the other end.

"Are you sure?"

"Positive. They found his body on Sunday night," I said, adding, "It was on the news."

"Good riddance," Dave said. "Sorry to be uncharitable, mate. But I mean it."

"I don't disagree with you," I said. "You know Gracie's going to be harder to find this time, don't you? If she really doesn't want you coming after her."

"I know. But we have to try. You understand. You've got a kid."

"I wish I could help," I said. "But I'm not really in any kind of shape to be out walking the streets right now."

"You OK?"

"I had a run-in with a couple of gangsters."

Dave didn't say anything. For which I was grateful. I really didn't want to have to elaborate. Especially since part of the elaboration would have involved telling him more than he needed to know about Radu Melnic.

"I'll let you know what happens," he said.

"I hope you find her," I said. "Take care."

I disconnected.

"Was that about the young girl you were looking for the other night?" Jenn asked.

I nodded. "She's done another runner."

"I ran away when I was fourteen. I'd had a fight with mum and dad. About wearing makeup. Everything's so dramatic and overblown when you're that age. I climbed out of my bedroom window and got down to the ground and stormed down the street. I was furious. It was about two in the morning. I got as far as my school, and realized I had absolutely no idea where to go next and where I was going to sleep and how I was going to look after myself. Rage does weird things to your logic. And once the rage disappears, you start feeling really stupid. And then you see sense. So I walked back home and climbed back in through my bedroom window and my parents never even knew I'd been gone."

"I know what you mean about the rage," I said. "And the drama."

My other phone was ringing. The one only Holly knew about.

"Haven't you left yet?" I said, allowing my voice to convey my displeasure.

"Unfortunately not, Mr. Private Investigator. I haven't got any money."

"That's not my problem," I said. "Sorry."

"I think you will find it is your problem. Do you know this girl, Gracie Byrne? I believe her father is in your band."

A chill ran through me. I glanced at Jenn, who gave me a quizzical look back.

"What about Gracie?" I said.

"A funny thing. I was at Radu's flat in Soho. She turned up looking for him. Buzzed him on the intercom from downstairs. So I let her in. She seems to have been one of his business acquisitions. Not very streetwise. Which I suppose must be the attraction for his customers. I've no doubt he offered her virginity to discerning gentlemen many times."

"You know he's dead," I said.

"Sadly, yes. I'm sure it was Braskey."

"I'm sure you're right," I said. "He has no time for child molesters."

Holly laughed. "Braskey has pimped out more underage girls than Radu ever did. It was meant to be a message to me, of course. That I would be next. Which is why I'm calling you now, Jason. I wasn't making up stories. I need money in order to leave the country. I believe you may be able to help me."

There was a shuffling sound, and then: "Jason?"

"Gracie?"

"I'm so sorry, Jason. Please help her, ok?"

She sounded frightened.

"She won't let me leave. We're not at Radu's flat. We're in some old building in Soho. Up on the top floor."

"Is Holly alone with you?"

"No, she has a man with her. I think it's her boyfriend. I'm so scared, Jason."

Holly took her phone back.

"How much is this child's life worth to you, Mr. Private Investigator?"

"Please let her go, Holly."

"You play in a band at the Blue Devil jazz club. It must give you a nice comfortable income."

"Not as much as you might think."

"Bring me £10,000 and you can take the child home."

"I don't have that kind of cash lying around."

"But I'm sure you can get it. Grace tells me you are wealthy. Your parents made a lot of money in the music business. You can easily arrange a withdrawal of £10,000 from the bank. Bring it to me and I'll be on my way. If you refuse my boyfriend will not hesitate to push the child off the roof of this building. And it's quite a long way down."

"That won't get you my money."

"No. But it will give me some sense of satisfaction. Call it payback, perhaps? I liked you, Mr. Private Investigator, but I don't like you anymore. And I despise Braskey. So perhaps I'd be sending a message of my own. Do you understand?"

"You'll have to give me time to make the withdrawal."

"Of course. I can wait all day. Although I'd prefer you were quicker than that. And you would be wise not to involve the police this time. I will be watching from the roof, and if I see any hint that they've followed you, it will be the end of our conversation. And this child's life."

CHAPTER TWENTY-FIVE

I really didn't think I had a choice.

"Do me a favour and stay here," I said, to Jenn.

"No way," Jenn replied. "She didn't tell you to come alone. She told you not to involve the police. I'm not the police. And you still need someone to help you walk."

#

My bank's around the corner on Islington High Road, a newish place in a newish building that was put up after something old and not deemed worth saving was demolished to make way for progress. They've gone for big tinted glass windows and subtle security. Inside there's subdued lighting and comfy armchairs where you can wait for your appointment, and they have customer reps with degrees in finance who can speak four languages and still know how to do a manual deposit—which is how I like to deal with cheques and occasional wads of actual money.

It took me an hour to get in to see Craig, the manager, and to convince him to let me take £10,000 out of one of my accounts. He was genuinely unsure whether they had that much cash on hand.

He sent one of his multilingual customer reps to have a look in the vault.

"Also, I'm supposed to query all large withdrawals," he said, somewhat apologetically. "We've had too many demented grandmothers falling prey to offshore scammers."

"I don't have dementia," I assured him. "And I'm not going to buy 1,000 iTunes cards or send any MoneyGram transfers to Nigeria. It's for Jennifer."

Jenn, who was sitting in the chair beside me, smiled and raised her hand in a small wave.

"My daughter," I added. It still felt weird saying it.

"I didn't know you had a daughter," Craig said. I could tell his mind was whirring. Would I want to consider some different investment strategies? Perhaps open a new account? Make a change to my beneficiaries?

"Neither did I. I was eighteen when she was born and her mother decided not to tell me about it until last week."

Craig looked a little uncomfortable. Unexpected news of teenaged fatherhood can have that effect on a person. I made a mental note to look into my beneficiaries.

"We're doing the legal DNA stuff," Jenn added. "In case you're worried."

"I'm not worried," Craig assured her, which of course meant it was the first thing that had crossed his mind. "But can I ask what you're going to use the money for?"

"I'm a professional photographer. Jason's helping me set up a special project. Soho Street Life. The things you see. The things you don't see. I'm going to have an exhibition and then publish the pictures in a limited-edition book. I'll send you an invitation to my opening."

She handed him one of her business cards, which he propped on his keyboard.

I thanked her with my eyes. I hadn't even thought to prepare a backstory to account for my sudden need for so much cash.

"I'll trust your judgement when it comes to due diligence," Craig said, to me, as the customer service rep arrived with my money, all neatly counted into convenient bundles. "Have you got something to put this in? A briefcase…?"

"This," Jenn said, helpfully, pulling a little packet out of her shoulder bag. She unzipped it to reveal a roomy nylon carry-all decorated with pink and blue cartoon animals. "Never without it when I travel. So handy."

"Well," said Craig, "thank you for the invitation and good luck with the photos. I'll definitely make a point of coming to see your exhibition. You're lucky to have someone like Jason on board. He's one of my nicest—and most talented—clients."

#

The address Holly had given me belonged to a narrow, empty road with a functional five-storey building on the corner that had definitely seen much better days. I wasn't sure if it was slated to be completely torn down, or gutted and made over into tiny trendy lofts for wealthy millennials who had no furniture and ate all their meals in cafes and coffee shops.

There was a sign outside indicating it was For Sale, anyway. Most of its upper windows were broken and the bottom ones had been boarded up. The bricks were black with grime, reminding me of the London of my childhood, when you could still see soot coating the buildings that had survived the fires that had raged during The Blitz.

The front door had once been painted British Racing Green, but that paint was now faded and blistered and peeling. It had been left slightly open but I couldn't see much inside, as there were no lights on and the corridor behind it had no windows.

I limped back across the road so I could get a good look at the roof, five floors up.

I saw Holly standing near the edge, looking down at me.

She rang me on my mobile.

"Hello, Mr. Private Investigator," she said. "I hope you haven't brought the police with you."

"I haven't brought the police," I replied. "This is my daughter. Jennifer. She was with me when you called. She has your money."

Jenn held up the pink and blue nylon carry-all so that Holly could see it.

"I'd like to make sure Gracie's OK," I said.

Holly disappeared for a moment, then came back with Gracie.

"So you see. She is still safe."

"Can you and Gracie come down here so we can do the exchange?"

"I don't believe that would be wise, do you? I would prefer to have the advantage. You and your daughter may bring the money up to me. The stairs are just inside the door."

"Fuck," I said, under my breath.

"I'll help you," Jenn said.

We crossed back over the road. I opened the door wide and took a deep breath then grabbed the carry-all and started up the stairs. I used my free hand to grasp a rattly railing that was originally attached to the wall by a series of brackets, but which was now only held in place by a couple of screws and about a century of dirt.

I got to the first landing and stopped for a minute to rest my legs and my feet.

Then I started up the next flight.

Five or six steps along, I had to stop again.

Jenn, meaning well, placed both of her hands in the middle of my back and pushed. Hard.

"Fuck," I said, falling forward. She'd hit the spot where Radu Melnic's electrical cord had done the most damage. I was in serious pain.

"Oh God, I'm so sorry, Jason. I forgot."

"It's OK," I said, getting my breath. "I'm OK. More or less."

On the second-floor landing, where the stairs turned, I shouted up towards the roof.

"Sorry for being so slow, Holly! Your brother had a habit of teaching harsh lessons to people he believed were interfering with his business!"

Holly appeared three floors up, peering over the railing and looking down the stairwell at me.

"Too bad you didn't learn your lesson earlier," she said. "Perhaps we wouldn't have to be meeting like this. I am waiting."

It took about ten minutes, but Jenn and I finally got to the top, where there was a second door which Holly had left open. I could feel the cold winter air blowing in from the roof outside.

Holly was waiting just beyond the door, wearing her stylish winter coat, which was unbuttoned, and her fox fur hat and her high-heeled leather boots. She'd left off the sunglasses. A man in a blue padded parka, who I assumed was Stanislav Turcan, was standing over by the edge of the roof, and he had Gracie, who at least had a warm jacket on this time. But her hands were bound together in front of her with what looked like silver duct tape. And she also had a short length of it covering her mouth. She turned her head to look at me as Jenn and I emerged from the doorway. I could see the terror in her eyes.

"That's as far as you go," Turcan said. "Show us the money."

I put the bag down and Jenn lifted out all of the bundles of cash and placed them beside one another on the tarred surface.

"You two come over here now."

Jenn got up and, as we walked towards the roof's low brick perimeter wall, Turcan dragged Gracie over to where Holly was stuffing the bundles of money back into the bag.

"Give me your phones," he said, shoving Gracie down onto her knees.

Jenn relinquished hers, reluctantly.

I gave him my two disposables.

"He's got another," Holly said.

Turcan stuck out his hand.

I obliged.

And then they were gone, racing down the stairs with my £10,000.

I ran to Gracie and gently pulled the silver tape off her face and hands. I would never block someone's mouth like that. What if they got a runny nose and their sinuses swelled and they couldn't breathe? They'd suffocate and die, horribly.

Gracie burst into tears.

"I so sorry, Jason. I was so stupid. I'm so sorry."

"Shh," I said, holding her. "You're safe now. It's OK."

I pulled my original mobile out of my pocket and gave it to Jenn. Old Faithful. The one I'd handed over to Turcan was the spare that I'd used for interviewing.

"Call the police."

"Is it 911?"

"999," I said, and then I changed my mind. "Ring Allan Pappas first. His number's in the call history."

I wrapped my arms around Gracie's thin shoulders, sheltering her, comforting her. She was shivering. I knew it was more than the cold.

And then we heard screaming. Jenn turned around, startled. Gracie froze.

The screams were literally blood-curdling. And female. And they'd come from five floors below, down on the road.

Jenn, on the phone with Allan, ran to the edge of the roof and looked over.

"Oh fuck, Jason!"

Gracie and I were right behind her. Jenn tried to stop Gracie from seeing. But it was too late.

Holly was lying on her back in a pool of blood on the pavement.

Blood gushed out of a vicious slash that ran from one side of her neck to the other. More blood was seeping through cuts in her white blouse. Her eyes were open and so was her mouth and blood was trickling from that too. Her hand trembled a little, and one of her legs. And then there was no more movement.

Our phones were scattered on the pavement beside her. Jenn's pink and blue nylon carry-bag was nowhere in sight.

Someone was running away. But it wasn't Stanislav Turcan. It was another woman—and she was already halfway down the block.

#

The empty Soho corner was suddenly swarming with police cars and officers, an ambulance and a lot of bystanders who seemed to have seeped out of the surrounding buildings and were now standing on the pavement, like spectators at a parade, filming everything on their phones and sharing it with Instagram and Twitter.

Allan arrived as we were making our way back downstairs.

"I gave your description of the other woman to the officers," he said, to Jenn. "They haven't located her." He looked at me. "Do you have anything to add to what Jennifer said?"

"It happened too quickly," I said. "I only got a quick look at her before she disappeared."

"How about you?" Allan said to Gracie.

Gracie shook her head.

"We'll need a full witness statement from all three of you. OK?"

Gracie nodded. Jenn and I already knew the procedure.

"Including what the hell you think you were doing up there on the roof," Allan said, to me. "I'm all ears."

#

The paramedics did their best but I knew they'd got there too late. The knife wounds, like those which had been inflicted on Rebecca, her maid and the unfortunate Colin Cooper, were vicious and swift and had extinguished Holly's life almost immediately.

Allan drove us back to the police station. Helen arrived and went into an interview room with Gracie. Allan took Jenn into a second room. I waited outside on an excruciatingly uncomfortable wooden bench until they'd both finished.

And then it was my turn. Again.

I had no idea what Gracie or Jenn had said, but that was part of the process. Independent witness statements were meant to be just that, conducted separately, with no chance of contamination or undue influence. And Allan, as I already knew, was a fairly skilled interviewer when it came to ferreting out details. There would be no leading questions. No assumptions, no suggestions.

"Let's start at the beginning. I understand you received a call on your mobile."

"It was Holly," I said. "She wanted £10,000. She and her boyfriend had Gracie and they were threatening to kill her if I didn't give them the money. She wanted the cash so she could leave the UK."

"And then what happened?"

"I agreed. Jenn and I went to see my bank manager. I withdrew the money and we took a taxi to the address she gave me. She was on the roof with Gracie and her boyfriend. I think it was Stanislav Turcan."

"Did you recognize him?"

"I've never seen him before. Sorry. It was just an assumption on my part."

"And you went up to the roof?"

"Yes. Jenn and me. With the money."

"What happened when you got to the roof?"

"I handed over the bag with the cash in it. Holly and Turcan left with our phones. They went downstairs. Gracie was really traumatized. I was trying to comfort her while Jenn rang you. And then we heard the screaming."

"When you heard the screaming, what did you do?"

"Jenn got to the roof's edge first and looked down at the road. Gracie and I got there at almost the same time. I saw Holly lying on the pavement, bleeding badly from knife wounds. I think she was still alive at that point. I also saw a second woman, running down the road."

Allan looked at me.

"Was the woman you saw lying on the pavement the same woman you'd given the money to?"

"Yes," I said.

"You're certain?"

"Yes. Holly Medford. Tatiana Melnic. Why?"

Allan shook his head.

"That's not Holly Medford."

He showed me two photos. One was obviously a police mugshot, an unhappy-looking woman with blonde hair glaring defiantly at the camera. The other was on his phone, a picture that had been screen capped from the Moonlight Desires website. It was the same woman, this time with inviting eyes and a suggestive smile. She was wearing lacy white knickers and a lacy white bra and white stockings and suspenders.

She was completely unfamiliar to me.

"That's Holly Medford."

"Are you sure?" I said, stunned.

"Positive. I told you before—she's well known to us."

I didn't know what to say.

Allan did.

"Sorry, Jason. I think you've been had."

CHAPTER TWENTY-SIX

To say I was speechless would have been a serious understatement.

I was absolutely furious.

I went back out to the corridor where Jenn was waiting for me on the uncomfortable wooden bench.

"She's Romanian," I said. "Her real name's Sofia Popa. Her passport was in her handbag."

"Why was she pretending to be Holly Medford?"

"Fuck if I know."

I got out my mobile and rang Sal.

"Are you absolutely positive the woman you disembarked from the *Amethyst* all those years ago was Holly Medford?"

"Yes, of course," Sal said. "Her ID matched all of her documents. Otherwise ship's security would have flagged it. Why?"

"And she's the same woman who approached you and asked you for help last week?"

"Yes. Absolutely the same woman. Why?"

"Can you describe her?"

"You know what she looks like," Sal said, not understanding.

"Just tell me."

"About Jennifer's height. Quite thin. Mid-twenties."

"What about her hair?"

"Blonde. Shoulder-length, straight."

"I'm going to text you a photo."

"OK."

I sent her the picture from Moonlight Desires that Allan had shared with me and waited.

"Yes, that's her," Sal confirmed.

"And you met her in person and got her a room at the Crestone."

"I did, absolutely. I took her up in the lift and made sure she was comfortable. I sat down and chatted with her, we had tea, she told me about her money being stolen…"

"And that was when you decided to ask me for help?"

"Yes. She was a little hesitant at first but then she agreed."

"A little hesitant, or a lot?"

"I wouldn't say a lot, but she definitely wasn't keen to involve you. I think I convinced her when I told her you were just a friend who was good at solving things, not a professional."

"Did you see her at all after that?"

Sal was thinking. "Actually, no, I didn't. We only talked on the phone."

"Thanks, Sal."

"What's happened?"

"I'll tell you later. I need to sort something out."

I disconnected.

"Holly Medford definitely checked into the Crestone," I said to Jenn. "The real Holly Medford. Not Sofia."

"What happened to Holly? Did Sofia murder her? Steal her identity?"

I shook my head. "I've no idea."

My mobile was ringing. It was Trev.

"You ok, Jason? We're at Knave Records."

I looked at the time. I'd completely forgotten about the meeting at two. It was now twenty to three.

"Oh fuck, Trev. I'm sorry. Can you apologise to everyone? I'll be there in fifteen minutes."

#

Outside the police station, I lit up a desperate cigarette while I waited for a taxi.

"You left your cameras at my flat," I said, to Jenn. "I'll bring them to the club tonight. Just ask at the door to be let in. I'll take care of it."

"Thank you," she said, with a kiss. "Good luck."

The taxi took me over to Denmark Street, which was only about ten minutes from the police station if I'd had the energy and the ability to walk.

Knave Records was on the second floor of a Grade II listed building that had started life as a yellow brick terraced house in the late 17th century. In the early 1800s it had been converted into a shop. I remembered going there with my dad when I was a kid to look for new guitars. The doorway was painted bright blue and it still had the same signage outside. It probably still had the same owners.

Just to the left of the bright blue door was a second open doorway which led to a staircase with an elaborate iron balustrade. The staircase went up to the second floor, where there was a door with a frosted glass window and a painted sign:

KNAVE RECORDS
PLEASE COME IN

Trev, Rudy and Ken were sitting at a boardroom-style table in a room just off the main reception area. The guy we were supposed to see, Mark Williamson, was standing beside the receptionist, checking his phone messages. I knew what Mark looked like: I'd checked him out on LinkedIn and also on Knave's website, where he'd helpfully posted his headshot.

He was tall and bald—too young for it all to be natural—and he was wearing new jeans and a crisp red and black plaid shirt. I wondered if he was one of those guys who went to toney salons to have his entire body waxed.

"I'm so sorry," I said, extending my hand. "Jason Davey. I was talking to the police. Someone was killed and I had to give a statement."

"Mark Williamson," he replied, grimly amused. "They didn't suspect you of doing it, did they?"

"Witness," I said. "From a distance. And not a very helpful one, unfortunately."

"Come inside." He led me into the meeting room. "Can I get you a coffee? Tea? Juice?"

"Tea would be very welcome," I said, sitting down between Rudy and Ken. "Did Dave call?"

"Dave did call," Trev confirmed. "He sends his regrets. But he didn't elaborate. I'll fill him in."

Mark gave my tea request to the receptionist, who went into a tiny adjacent kitchen and popped a teabag into a mug and plugged in an electric kettle.

"Let me begin by telling you how impressed I was with what I heard on your demo," Mark said, sitting down at the head of the table without closing the door. "I like your sound. Of the three pieces you sent, I was particularly impressed with 'Smoke Drifts'. Well done."

"Thank you," I said. "Trev gets most of the credit for making it sound good."

"I'll get right to the point. Knave Records has a male/female vocal duo who've been under contract with us for quite a while. Ayres & White. Ryan and Elise. You've heard of them, I know."

"I have," I said. "Easy listening."

"Music for the middle of your mind," Ken replied. I'm sure he didn't intend it to sound quite so condescending.

If Rudy and Trev felt the same way as Ken, they weren't letting on.

"Ryan and Elise have recently decided to change direction, upping their sound, aiming for a younger demographic. Less Soft Adult Contemporary, more Hot Uptempo AC. They're going into the studio to cut a new album and then they're going out on tour. And they're looking for a new backing band."

I glanced at Trev.

"I played your demo for Ryan and Elise and they love your sound. The tour's being put together for this fall. It'll take in England and Ireland, of course, then venues in Germany, France and the Netherlands, then up into Scandinavia. And after Christmas, major cities in North America—New York and LA, Chicago and a couple of other TBA's...up into Canada—Toronto and Montreal, possibly Vancouver. After that we're still negotiating, but Japan looks good and maybe Australia and New Zealand if we get positive advance ticket sales. What do you say?"

My heart was sinking. I think Rudy, Ken and Trev's hearts had plummeted to rock bottom a few seconds before mine.

"How long would we be touring?" Rudy asked. I knew he was going through the motions to be polite. Drummers are like that. Mediators. Peace-makers. Open to all options. To a point.

"Six weeks before Christmas, and another eight weeks afterwards, if Australia and New Zealand pan out."

"And we'd be the backing band," Ken checked.

"Correct."

"We're headliners at the Blue Devil."

Mark smiled. "You're secondary headliners. Not the main act. And you're upstairs. Not in the main lounge."

"So a recording contract isn't on the cards," Trev said, also getting to the point.

"If you were a big name, like Ayres & White, I might consider it. But nobody beyond the Blue Devil knows who you are."

"Our audiences know," I said.

"Nobody beyond the Blue Devil," Mark repeated. "I wouldn't say it's never going to happen. But the big money's in touring and merchandise, not recordings. You have to know that. With downloads and streaming services we make fractions on the penny. I'm in the business of generating a reasonable profit from our acts. I'm offering you a chance to be a part of that with Ryan and Elise."

I didn't say anything. I glanced again at Rudy and Ken. Trev was looking at me.

I swore I would never do it. Ever.

But.

"If," I said, carefully, "we threw the name Figgis Green into the mix…"

"Your parents' band," Mark said.

I must have looked surprised.

"I like to be prepared when I meet artists for the first time. There's no mention in the bio material you have online, of course…but our receptionist loves digging and she's the one who discovered the Figgis Green fan chats when she googled Jason Davey. You're apparently a very hot topic."

I didn't say anything. I was aware of some peripheral interest in my life. I'd had no idea I was that popular.

"Anyway," Mark said. "Fan chats aside, today's music buyers are too young to care much about Figgis Green. There might be some curiosity, some nostalgia from their parents, maybe some genuine interest from the die-hards, but not enough to warrant a standalone deal for you and your band. When was the last time Figgis Green charted? 1990?"

"1991."

"Family connections are useful but these days having a famous dad rarely results in similar success stories."

"Julian Lennon," Rudy agreed. "Stella McCartney."

"Rarely," Mark repeated. "I don't need a decision today. Go home and sleep on it. Give me a call tomorrow."

#

We didn't go home. And sleep was the last thing on our minds.

We walked 'round to the Sheep and Shears, an old pub dating from the 1890s, a hundred years before Figgis Green's last big hit and still as popular with today's young audiences and their nostalgic parents as it was back in the day.

It has red leather seats and polished wooden tables, a bar surrounded by beautifully-preserved dark wood, and a red-painted plaster ceiling that still boasts its original Victorian light fixtures. It has an amazing tile floor and huge mirrors on its walls, advertising old-fashioned mineral waters and long-extinguished cigarettes.

And it was packed.

At the back, a party of four was just leaving. We appropriated their table before anyone else could spot the impending vacancy.

"Your usual?" Trev checked. "Perrier? Pellegrino?"

"I'm feeling dangerous," I said. "Make it a Coke."

That made him smile. He went to the bar and came back to the table with our drinks: pints for Rudy, Ken and himself and a very large Coke for me.

He sat down.

"I gather," he said, "that, collectively, we're less than enthusiastic about the offer."

"Collectively," Ken replied, "we'd be twenty feet from stardom on the back of a tour where the audience can't tell the difference between Miles Davis and Thelonious Monk."

"Collectively," Rudy said, "I doubt that Ryan and Elise's audience would even know who Miles Davis and Thelonious Monk are."

"Or care," I added.

"Sorry, Jason," Trev said. "I know this has been your dream for a long time."

"Decades," I said, trying not to let my unhappiness show.

"I'll say it," said Rudy. "I'm not keen on touring. I don't feel like being on the road more than I'm off it, and I know Dave would never agree to it. Not now, with Gracie."

"Not to mention what would happen to our gig at the Blue

Devil," Ken added. "I quite like having a regular job. As far as regular jobs go in this business."

"I've got a studio to run and songs to produce," Trev said. "And bookings well into next year. Jason?"

"I agree with Rudy," I said. "I don't want to tour. I might have considered it when I was younger and just starting out. Not now. I remember how much it took out of my mum and dad. No thanks."

"Then I think," Rudy said, "we're all pretty much in agreement that Ryan and Elise fucking Arsewipe can stuff their Hot Uptempo Adult Contemporary World Tour right up Mark Williamson's bottom."

CHAPTER TWENTY-SEVEN

I went home to change and to have something to eat—though I wasn't very hungry—and to collect Jenn's cameras.

Wednesday nights at the club are usually busy, but there's always an extra table or two for special guests. I made sure our Security guy at the front door knew Jenn was coming, and that, upstairs, she'd have a good seat with an unobstructed view of the stage and an open tab at the bar and the kitchen.

We had a good first set. I positioned my stool so that I could just see Jenn, off to my left, without the lights completely blinding me. She'd attached a telephoto lens to one of her cameras and was shooting closeups. I purposely avoided looking directly at her. I always think pictures of performers are so much better if the photographer's managed to capture them unaware, just being themselves, without worrying about what they look like or whether or not they have to strike some kind of artificial pose.

Just before the break, I took over the mic.

"This one's for my daughter, Jennifer, who's in the audience tonight."

There was a small amount of appreciative applause, and Jenn put her camera down to acknowledge it—and me—with the most beautiful smile I've ever seen.

My heart soared.

We played "Here to Stay", another of my favourites by Pat Metheny, and then Ken, Rudy and Dave left the stage and I went to sit with Jenn at her table.

"I like your music," Jenn said, before I could ask. "I've never really thought about listening to any kind of jazz before. I'm more a fan of ancient rock bands. You know. Mick Jagger wearing tight trousers. Freddy Mercury wearing hardly anything at all."

"Jason Davey wearing joggers and old man plaid slippers," I said.

"You're not old," she said, fondly. "And I can't even begin to imagine you wearing plaid slippers. Big grey woolly ski socks though, yes, very definitely."

Kieran, who was working as a waiter at the club to pay his fees at drama school, brought me a Pellegrino and a Caesar for Jenn, garnished with a pickled bean and a lemon slice.

"I'm so impressed that they actually know how to make a Caesar here," she said. "And that they actually have the right ingredients."

"That's down to me," I said. "You can't sail in and out of Vancouver once a week for a couple of years without picking up some decent Canadian cocktail knowledge. It's my contribution to the Blue Devil's international appeal."

Kieran was coming back to our table.

"Sorry, Jason," he said. "There's a woman at the bar who needs to speak to you. She says her name's Holly and it's quite urgent. I showed her where you were sitting but she wanted to stay there."

Jenn and I both looked.

It was most definitely the blonde from Moonlight Desires.

She was wearing jeans and leather boots, and a padded winter jacket, which was unzipped to show off a white angora sweater.

"Stay here," I said, to Jenn, and then I followed Kieran back to the counter.

"Holly Medford," she said, immediately. "Tatiana Melnic, as you may know me. Is there somewhere more private where we can talk?"

She looked frightened and I had a pretty good idea why.

"This way," I said, taking her back to our dressing room, where Ken and Rudy were drinking coffee and checking their emails and Dave was on the phone to Helen.

"Apologies, guys," I said.

"It's not necessary for them to leave," Holly said. "In fact, I prefer them to stay. There is safety in numbers."

She made sure the door was shut securely.

"No lock," she said.

"Sorry."

"Braskey will most definitely be in the club by now. I already recognized two of his men sitting at the tables. There will be more outside. I don't know how they found me. Please, I need your help."

Her English was impeccable, just like Sofia's. And her slight Eastern European accent was almost identical.

"He will kill me."

"I don't doubt it," I said. "Would you mind telling me what the fuck's been going on?"

"I married Braskey. The marriage ended. I took what I felt I was owed. I went into hiding."

"The jade necklace," I said.

"For what I put up with while I was married to him, I consider the necklace a non-returnable investment. It is mine. He gave it to me."

"Where's the necklace now?"

Holly unzipped one of her jacket pockets and showed me what was inside. There it was. A string of perfectly round green beads. The source of so much deception, so much violence, so many lies.

"What about the £10,000 you claimed was stolen from your locker?"

"I made it up. When a person is afraid, they can make wrong decisions. They can panic. I only wanted somewhere safe to stay for a few days. I thought it might help when I asked Sally for a room. I always remember her kindness aboard the cruise ship. I didn't know she would ask you to become involved. And I didn't know who to trust. I asked my friend Sofia to stand in so that no one—you included—would be able to describe me."

"No one except Sal," I said.

"I'm very sorry for all of the trouble I've caused."

She looked nervously at the door.

"I have a ticket on a plane to Larnica at 7.15 a.m.," she said. "I will be safe there—a friend is waiting for me. He works aboard the cruise ships. But I must first get to Heathrow. Will you help me?"

Something told me if I didn't, I'd regret it for the rest of my life. I had no wish to throw her back to Braskey. And I wanted—needed—explanations.

I slipped outside and went back along the corridor and stood where I knew I couldn't be seen, checking out who was in the audience. I spotted Grandad occupying a table close to the main exit. If there was anyone else from Braskey's stable in the audience I didn't recognize them. And there was Braskey himself, just arriving, bribing one of the hostesses to get him a table close to the stage where I couldn't avoid seeing him while I played.

I went back to the dressing room.

"Dave," I said. "Can you go out and fetch Jenn? Don't make a big scene. Just have a quiet word. Tell her Braskey's watching. She should bring all her things. Cameras. She'll understand."

He went.

I knew Rudy rode his motorbike into London every night for our gig. Bikers don't have to pay the Congestion Charge and it costs him nothing to leave it one of the dedicated spots in the big multi-level parkade a couple of roads over. His helmet was sitting on the counter in front of the mirrors.

"Have you got a spare one of those?" I asked

"In the bag on my bike. Why?"

I removed a wad of money from my wallet. "Mind taking a cab home tonight?"

Rudy thought for a moment, then accepted the cash. "You don't have a motorcycle license, do you?"

"I'll risk it," I said.

"Have you ever actually driven one?"

"Twice," I said. "My sister's husband has a Triumph Rocket III."

Rudy whistled his appreciation. "Good luck."

He removed the keys from his collection and handed them over as Dave came back with Jenn.

"Braskey saw me leave," she said.

"It's OK. He doesn't know who you are."

"You sure about that? He knows everything else about you."

"Not what's coming next. I need your jacket. Have you got your chit?"

"Yes, sure." She produced the little paper ticket from the coat check.

I rang the club's front office.

"Jeremy," I said. "Can you possibly pop up to our dressing room?"

He was there in less than a minute.

I gave him Jenn's coat check.

"Don't draw attention to yourself. Just collect her jacket and take it down to the office. Then bring it back up to me—use the old stairs."

Safety regulations dictate that there have to be multiple ways in and out of the club's two public floors. Our audiences only know about the ones that are posted with lit signs. They have no idea there's an old, original staircase dating from when the building was first built. It's too rickety and narrow to qualify as a fire escape and it has never, as far as any of us know, been renovated or upgraded. But it's useful for secret liaisons, quick smokes when it's raining outside, and dodgy getaways.

"I also need your boots," I said, to Jenn, after Jeremy had gone. "Please."

I handed them to Holly, who took her own off and zipped Jenn's on over the legs of her skinny jeans. She also remembered to extract the jade necklace from the pocket of her jacket before exchanging it for Jenn's. She put the necklace into her bag—the sum total of everything she was worth crammed into a black Polo Ralph Lauren tote.

Jenn manoeuvred her feet into Holly's ankle boots. "Nice," she said.

"Rag & Bone," Holly replied, a little sadly. "My favourites."

"I'll look after them," Jenn promised.

"Ken," I said. "Is Patrick working tonight?"

"Yes, his usual shift."

"I need a huge favour. I'm not even sure if it's possible. Can you reach him?"

My absence from the stage caused a bit of a commotion. It was meant to. First, there was the delay. The audience was beginning to get restless. It was ten minutes past the time we were supposed to start our second set and the house lights were still up. Our bartender had no idea what was going on. Kieran and the other serving staff were none the wiser.

At last, Jeremy made an announcement, using one of our mics on the stage.

"Good evening, ladies and gentlemen. The band wishes to apologise, however their lead guitarist has unfortunately been taken ill. He was involved in an accident earlier in the week and his injuries have proven to be somewhat more serious than initially believed. An ambulance has just arrived and the management would greatly appreciate it if everyone would please stay seated until the paramedics have gone."

Patrick and his colleague carried a sitting stretcher up to the dressing room, strapped me in and wheeled me through the club to the main exit. I did my best to look anguished and in serious pain. It wasn't difficult.

Jenn walked beside me with all of her camera gear and Holly's winter coat. She's quite a good actress. She was close to tears. She had me convinced.

"Are they buying it?" I whispered, on the stairs.

"Absolutely," Jenn replied.

I was bundled into the back of the ambulance and Jenn climbed in after me, along with Patrick.

Lights flashed and sirens wailed as we pulled away from the Blue Devil's front entrance.

"Where to?" Patrick inquired.

"Dean Street Car Park," I said.

Patrick conveyed the directions to his colleague.

We were there in two minutes.

"Thank you," I said. "I hope you won't get into any trouble."

"We were on a break," Patrick said, unbuckling me. "It's been a quiet night in London town. We won't say anything if you don't."

Jenn clambered out of the ambulance after me.

"I'll see you tomorrow," I promised. "I'll fill you in about Knave Records."

"Stay safe," she said, with a kiss.

I walked across to the dedicated motorcycle bay inside the multi-level parkade. Holly was already there. She'd left before me, going down the rear stairs and slipping out of the Blue Devil's back door. She'd taken the narrow paved lane behind the club and gone right past one of Braskey's men, who'd been stationed on the corner but wasn't looking for someone wearing Jenn's down-filled blue winter parka and knee-high brown leather boots and, for added safety, Rudy's bike helmet.

Rudy had a black and silver Triumph Bonneville T120. A classic, styled after a 1959 original. The spare helmet—a flashy Union Jack open-face with an attached visor—was in the sidebag. I popped it on and fastened the chin strap.

"Which terminal?" I checked, making sure Holly was securely installed behind me before I started the engine.

"Five," she replied.

"Hold on tight," I said. "I'll have you there in forty-five minutes."

I was being optimistic. Google Maps was telling me I could do it in less time than that. Google Maps didn't know I'd forgotten more about driving a motorbike than I could actually remember.

I started the engine and took a moment to reacquaint myself with the machinery. And then I roared out of the Dean Street Car Park and shot up the narrow road and around Soho Square Gardens, past St. Patrick's Church, where Tommy Steele married a dancer from the Windmill Theatre in 1960 and nearly caused a riot, then down the equally narrow Greek Street all the way to Shaftesbury Avenue, otherwise known as the A401.

It was, by then, nearly 1 a.m. I love being wide awake when most people are fast asleep. I sped past Soho's lights and taxis and cafes and clubs and its late-night pedestrians, feeling like I owned the city, driven by adrenaline and the certain knowledge that I was besting Arthur Braskey, the bastard.

I soared down Shaftesbury Avenue, past *Les Mis*, and cut around the back of Piccadilly Circus by way of Great Windmill Street, thoroughly enjoying the freedom Rudy's bike was giving us, wistfully wishing that I wasn't obligated to wear the helmet.

We were on Coventry Street and then Haymarket, the cozy social grazing of Soho giving way to Pret A Manger and Planet Hollywood and the grand architectural commerce of the Theatre Royal and the back side of Trafalgar Square.

A quick turn west and we were on the A4—Pall Mall—with its gleaming white gentlemen's clubs and private residences and then Google sent me north up St. James's Street to Piccadilly and we were roaring past The Ritz. It suddenly occurred to me that our circuitous tour of central London had probably taken in parts of the city that Holly knew very intimately—along with the gentlemen who frequented them. But her arms around my waist had never tightened or loosened and, if she was feeling anything other than tense caution, she wasn't letting it show.

We were in the tunnel under Hyde Park and then we were out again and roaring through Knightsbridge—Patsy and Edina territory—Harvey Nicks and then Harrod's, and as we sped past the V&A and the Natural History Museum I finally felt that we were out of Braskey's reach. My sense of relief was palpable. I relaxed. And as we negotiated the Hammersmith Flyover and, a few minutes later, the lane change onto the M4, I was at last confident we were safely on our way to the airport.

#

We were there in less than half an hour. I know traffic to Heathrow can be a bugger at times, but in the middle of the night, it's a doddle. I've been out that way before, usually sitting in the back of a taxi and not really paying attention to the road. And especially not paying attention to the signs directing me to Terminal 5 and all of the choices for drop-offs and parking and ways to get completely and utterly lost.

I paid attention this time, and after a couple of wrong lanes and some quick corrections (and even quicker curses), I managed to find the place where you could park a motorbike. At that hour it was mostly empty.

It felt good to get the helmet off, although the smell of jet fuel instead of fresh country air left a lot to be desired.

"You OK?" I checked, helping Holly off the bike.

She removed her helmet as well. "OK," she said. "Thank you. I owe you more than I can ever explain."

"Let's get you safely inside," I said. "Your flight's not 'til seven. We've a few hours to kill yet."

"You don't have to stay."

"Yes," I said. "I do."

CHAPTER TWENTY-EIGHT

Airports at two in the morning are amazing places. I used to enjoy being wide awake aboard the *Sapphire* at that hour, wandering through the deserted passenger areas, seeing the cleaners and the tidy-uppers, the night crew, the odd lost souls who'd drunk too much and become disconnected from their companions, the insomniacs and the diehards who were there to party and sleep be damned.

Airport terminals are much the same. During the day they're packed to the rafters with stressed-out travellers and lineups, comings and goings, goodbyes and greetings, everybody looking for something or someone or someplace.

Late at night, after the planes stop, airports go into a sort of hibernation. The lights are all still on, but they seem somehow less glaring. The noise level drops to a whisper. The check-in counters are empty, the shops are shuttered, the Arrivals and Departures screens stay fixed on the last planes in and the first ones out.

Terminal 5's like a giant aircraft hangar, all swooping clean lines and glass window-walls. I knew there was a coffee place on the Arrivals level; I was praying it was open, because I really needed something to eat and something else to keep me awake.

My faith was rewarded. Like the Windmill Theatre, they never closed. I bought two toasted tea cakes with plenty of butter and two strong mocha lattes, served in thick china cups, and we sat in comfy armchairs on opposite sides of a little round table.

"So just to be perfectly clear," I said. "You really did marry

Arthur Braskey…"

"Yes, I really did marry Arthur Braskey. It lasted for three years and then he demanded a divorce."

"He says you wanted to divorce him."

"He would. He's never the person who is in the wrong. Always the one who has had wrongs done to him."

"Why did you marry him?"

Holly smiled. The same attractive smile I'd seen in the photo from Moonlight Desires.

"He's a very rich and powerful man. I was flattered by his attention. Wouldn't you, given the choice?"

"Not necessarily."

"You haven't come from the same world as me. But he is like an evil octopus—he has arms and fingers into everything. He knows everything. He knows everyone. He is vain and he is controlling and he is cruel."

"You won't get any arguments from me about that," I said. "So you took the necklace and talked Sal into giving you a free room at the Crestone, and then when Sal asked me for help, you decided to switch places with Sofia."

"I told you, yes. For my own safety. I didn't anticipate Sally would contact you. You became an unintended complication. And once you'd become involved, Sofia and I had no choice but to go along with you. To have done otherwise would have raised too many suspicions."

"How did you know Sofia?" I asked. I was beginning to crave a cigarette. But I wanted to get the whole story. And I wasn't entirely convinced that if I disappeared for twenty minutes, she wouldn't do the same and I'd never have another opportunity.

"We met aboard the cruise ships. And then she was a dancer at Cha-Cha's and she got me a job there. Someone from a similar background as my own who was only too happy to make a little bit of extra money on the side, pretending to be me for a few days. She worked as an escort as well. Though not at Moonlight Desires. Freelance."

"So that's how she knew all the details about you and the money you had stolen four months ago?"

"It was Sofia who did the stealing. But I didn't know that until recently. If I had, I would never have asked for her help."

That did surprise me. "What about the threatening note?"

"She annoyed some girls from Estonia. They sent her a letter, warning her to stop."

"It wasn't sent to you?"

"No, not at all."

"Once you and Sofia had made the switch at the hotel, weren't you afraid Sal might notice?"

"Sofia was always careful never to see her in person."

"Sal took me up to your room in the lift. She was going to join me when I first met you—Sofia. She would have seen then that Sofia wasn't you."

"But she had to leave," Holly said, with a small, knowing smile. "Because of a disturbance at the front desk."

I looked at her.

I remembered the catering arrangements in her hotel room, the pastries and the cups and saucers for two. Not three.

And the message that Sal took on her mobile, requesting her urgent presence downstairs.

"Close call," Holly added, biting into her tea biscuit.

I spread some lovely soft cultured butter onto my own warm, toasted slice.

"So what was the plan, exactly? How long did you think you could get away with it?"

"It was only meant to be until I had time to arrange to sell the necklace to a private collector from Hong Kong. But he was concluding some business in Los Angeles and couldn't come to London immediately."

"And after you'd sold the necklace?"

"Sofia and I agreed we would part ways and I would disappear and no one would be any the wiser. But there were…unfortunate developments."

"No kidding," I said.

"I took the necklace to my friend Rebecca for safekeeping. But Sofia knew of this, and she was greedy. I trusted her and she betrayed me. When I went to collect the necklace, I found Sofia and Turcan had been there before me. I know it must have been Turcan who killed my friend and her maid and poor Colin who was also in the room. Turcan is a criminal. Always in the gym, making muscles. Taking pills. They make him vicious."

"Poor Colin was once your lover," I said, "and you owed him rather a lot of money."

"I regret that," Holly said. "I will always regret it."

She paused.

"Perhaps he was there, trying to find me."

I wanted to believe her.

"Sofia left it to you to discover the murders. I'm sure she must have thought if you believed the necklace had disappeared, Braskey would too. But she became even greedier when your friend's daughter went to Radu's flat. It has one of those keypad locks on the door. Radu must have given Turcan the code. They knew one another from the gym."

"Why was Sofia at Radu's flat?"

"Who knows?" Holly shrugged. "They knew he was dead. Perhaps they thought they could steal his things."

"And how," I said, "do you happen to know about all of this—about everything that's gone on over the past week?"

Holly smiled again.

"Your friend Sally is not the only person to have thought of hiring a private investigator," she said.

"I need a ciggie," I said, standing up. "Will you be here when I get back?"

"Of course. Where else?"

There were a couple of designated smoking areas outside the terminal, near where the buses stopped. I lit up and took my time, half-expecting the table to be empty when I returned. It wasn't. Holly was still there, drinking another mocha latte, eating another toasted tea biscuit, this time with orange marmalade.

"Who killed Sofia?" I said, sitting down again.

"Turcan."

"You know that for a fact?"

"I was there. I saw him do it."

"Why were you there?"

"I wanted my necklace back."

"How did you know where she would be?"

"I told you. I hired a private investigator."

I truly, honestly, didn't know if what she was telling me was the truth. But, in all honesty, it truly no longer mattered.

"Was that you I saw running away?"

She nodded.

"And you're sure it wasn't you who killed her?"

"I'm not a monster. Not like her."

"Why did Turcan kill her?"

"He is as greedy as she was. They discovered they couldn't sell the necklace on the open market. And they didn't know the name of my private collector. Turcan cared only about the ransom money for the girl. He took it. He left the necklace."

"Which you removed as she lay dying in the road."

"I had very little time. But yes."

"What will you do with it now?"

"I intend to carry through with the private sale. The only difference is a change in venue. I will meet my collector in Cyprus instead of London."

She finished her coffee.

"Do you have any money on you now?" I asked.

"Not much," she said. "Enough for a chocolate bar on the other side of Security, perhaps. And a bottle of water."

I slipped £50 out of my wallet and gave it to her.

She looked surprised. "That isn't necessary. I'm being met in Larnica."

"I would feel better if you took it," I said. "Please."

"Thank you." She put the bills into a little leather change purse inside her bag. "I owe you a very great debt. If it weren't for you, I have no doubt Braskey and his men would have taken me and I would now be dead."

She stood up.

"And now I think it is time for me to disappear. This is the last you will hear about Holly Medford or Tatiana Melnic, I promise."

She leaned down, and kissed me. On the lips. Not seductively. Not enticingly. As a friend would.

"Goodbye, Jason."

She left the black motorcycle helmet on the floor beside her chair.

I stayed where I was, watching her walk away in the direction of the ladies' loo.

After about ten minutes, I too got to my feet, collected both helmets, and went back outside to the little parking area where I'd left Rudy's bike.

#

I rode the motorcycle back to Rudy's house and parked it in his drive. I posted his keys back to him through the slot in his front door and left him a phone message just to be sure. I walked to the nearest tube station—Putney Bridge—and found a taxi driver willing to take me home to Pentonville Road. It was, by then, about 5 a.m.

"For what it's worth," Jenn said, later, after I'd slept and woken up and rung her to make sure she'd got back to her hotel OK, "I think you made the right decision about the Knave Records deal. I think you're a great private eye. And I know you love your club gig with a passion. I can hear it when you play and I can see it in your eyes and on your face. I'll send you a couple of the photos I shot last night."

She'd taken them with the big lens. Close-ups of me during our first set, lost in Charlie Byrd's "Scherzo For An Old Shoe", which we'd arranged for guitar, drums, keyboards and sax.

"You're there" she said, "but you're in another world. I think you'd have lost that if you'd gone on the road with Bryan and Louise."

"Ryan," I said.

"Whatever their names are. You don't belong in a backing band, Jason. You thrive on being the guy in the spotlight. You're the main act."

#

I didn't think I'd heard the last of Arthur Braskey. And I wasn't wrong.

Two nights later, I was leaving the club after our show. We'd stayed for a couple of drinks. It was very late. The lights were off and the bartender had gone home.

As I waited on the pavement for my cab, I spotted a familiar blue Mercedes turn the corner at the end of the block.

I spun around and bolted back towards the main door.

It was locked.

The Mercedes stopped at the curb.

"Mr. Figgis."

I froze.

"Mr. Figgis," Braskey said. "I have no intention of causing you further harm. I have something for you."

I turned to face him. There was no fucking way I was going anywhere near the open door of that car.

With a weary sigh, Braskey climbed out and walked across to where I was standing and handed me Jenn's pink and blue nylon carry-bag.

"I've kept £2,000 for out-of-pocket expenses and ancillary costs," he said, "but I think you'll discover the balance of your £10,000 intact."

I took the bag.

I didn't dare breathe.

"The unfortunate Mr. Turcan will not be engaging in any further criminal activity."

I didn't dare speak.

"I rang 'round to all of the hospitals. None of them had any record of you being admitted on Wednesday night."

"I don't know where Holly went," I said, before he could ask.

"I believe you, Mr. Figgis. Your role was to engineer a clever distraction. It worked. I applaud you."

He walked back to his car and climbed into the rear passenger seat.

"Next time you undertake a private investigation, Mr. Figgis, make very sure you know who you're dealing with. Good night."

He shut the door, and the Mercedes motored quietly away into the dark, wet Soho night.

ABOUT THE AUTHOR

Winona Kent was born in London, England. She immigrated to Canada with her parents at age three, and grew up in Regina, Saskatchewan, where she received her BA in English from the University of Regina. After settling in Vancouver, she graduated from UBC with an MFA in Creative Writing. More recently, she received her diploma in Writing for Screen and TV from Vancouver Film School.

Winona has been a temporary secretary, a travel agent, the Managing Editor of a literary magazine and, most recently, a Program Assistant at the School of Population and Public Health at UBC. Her writing breakthrough came many years ago when she won First Prize in the Flare Magazine Fiction Contest with her short story about an all-night radio newsman, *Tower of Power*. More short stories followed, and then novels: *Skywatcher, The Cilla Rose Affair, Cold Play, Persistence of Memory, In Loving Memory* and *Marianne's Memory*, as well as a novella, *Disturbing the Peace*.

Winona lives in New Westminster, British Columbia and is an active member of the Crime Writers of Canada and Sisters in Crime.

Please visit her website at www.winonakent.com for more information.

67758162R00133

Made in the USA
Columbia, SC
31 July 2019